Worth Waiting For

Book One (The O'Connors)

Jax Burrows

Jax Burrows / Manchester UK

Jax Burrows
P O Box 599
Manchester
M12 0DY
United Kingdom
https://www.jburrowsauthor.com

Publisher's Note: This is a work of fiction. Names, characters, places, and incidents are a product of the author's imagination. Locales and public names are sometimes used for atmospheric purposes. Any resemblance to actual people, living or dead, or to businesses, companies, events, institutions, or locales is completely coincidental.

Cover design by James T Egan, http://bookflydesign.com/
Book Design © 2019 BookDesignTemplates.com
Formatting by Polgarus Studio

Worth Waiting For/ Jax Burrows — 1st ed.
Print Edition ISBN 9781081648992

This book is dedicated to my Auntie Sheelagh who died recently.
A lovely lady who will be sadly missed.

Contents

Chapter One

'Clear!'

The crash team shocked the patient and moved away from the bed. Staff Nurse Lexi Grainger stepped forward and started CPR straight away, increasing the chances of the defibrillation technique working. But it was hard going. Soon her arms started aching and she was panting with the exertion. Another member of staff would soon take over, and continue the rotation process, but she had to keep up the rhythm until then.

An elderly man brought into A&E a couple of hours before with bruises, lacerations and a periorbital haematoma, from being catapulted over the handlebars of his bicycle, was fighting for his life. He hadn't seen the debris that was scattered across the road after the high winds the previous night and ended up in Resus. One minute he was chatting happily to Lexi as she gently wiped the blood off his face, the next she was shouting for the Medical Emergency Team. He had an IV inserted, had been intubated and was receiving oxygen but his heart was stubbornly refusing to start again.

That was A&E. You never knew what was going to happen next.

'Right, we'll shock him again.' Lexi kept up the chest compressions until given the word by the doctor. While she worked, she thought over the "Chain of Survival"; the sequence of steps that maximized the patient's chance of living. The first was recognizing the cardiac arrest and starting resuscitation immediately. Tick. The second was prompt initiation of CPR. Tick. The third was performing defibrillation as soon as possible. Tick. The fourth was post resuscitation care. That would be provided as soon as they could bring him back.

'Clear!'

They all stepped away while the patient was shocked again, his body jerking with the current passing through it.

'Okay, continue,' said the team leader, and Lexi was just about to start compressions again, when someone beat her to it. Large, male hands had already started pumping the patient's chest and Lexi felt intense relief. Someone had taken over and she could have a rest. Something about those hands looked familiar. Short, perfectly manicured nails, strong fingers with black hairs near the knuckles. Her heart started racing again, for a completely different reason.

Her gaze moved upwards to the man's face. He had his

head bent over the patient's chest and she couldn't see him properly. But she didn't need to. She knew who he was.

The shock must have shown on her face, as the team leader chuckled and said, 'This is Dr Casey O'Connor, our new trauma consultant; he's joining us from a large teaching hospital in London and we're lucky to have him.'

'Oh.' He glanced up briefly before looking down again at the patient. But that brief glimpse had been enough to transport her back four years.

Casey O'Connor. So, that was his name. She'd tried many different names for her man of mystery when she daydreamed about him. Then at night, when the sexual fantasies had left her tense and frustrated with longing, she tossed and turned, eventually getting out of bed to gaze at the moon from her bedroom window. The moon was shining that night, too. The full moon of summer solstice that had shone just for them, during the best twelve hours of her life.

'Clear!'

They all moved away again, and she stared into his eyes across the bed, a mesmerizing green with a dark black ring around the irises. He was staring back at her, and not in a particularly friendly way. Was it the tension of trying to save a man's life, she wondered, or because she'd left the following morning without even saying goodbye?

'We've got him back,' said the team leader. Lexi nearly collapsed with relief. The man had been in her care when he arrested, and she felt personally responsible for his welfare.

'Thank you everybody.'

They all went about the business of attending to the patient's after-care, calmly and professionally. Lexi, however, felt too emotional to do anything useful, so turned to move away from the cubicle.

'Just a sec.'

Lexi froze at the sound of that voice. She turned around slowly and came face-to-face with the man of her dreams. Seeing him now, without the drama of the last half hour, she thought he was even more gorgeous than she remembered. His dark blue scrubs made the green of his eyes even deeper. He was tanned and fit, and Lexi's heart was beating so fast, she thought she was going to pass out and join the patient on the bed.

'Yes?' She waited for him to speak. He glanced at her name badge then looked back at her face.

'We meet again. Lexi Grainger.'

If ever there was a time to try to deny it, it was now, but Lexi couldn't speak. She was struck dumb by the suddenness of his appearance in her life again. She had assumed that he was back in London, forging his brilliant career, whatever that was. They had deliberately not disclosed personal details. She had been sure their paths would never cross again. What was he doing in Leytonsfield?

'Yes. I'm surprised you remember.' She attempted to smile and act as if it had all been a long time ago and of no consequence, but she wasn't the fantasy woman she had pretended to be then, acting a part. She stood before him now as the real Lexi. No more pretence. Her priorities in life had changed completely since that night.

He took a step closer and lowered his voice so that only she could hear. She stared into the depth of his green eyes and shivered.

'Oh, I remember, Lexi Grainger. I remember everything about that night. Against my better judgement and despite four years of trying, I haven't been able to forget you. Even though you obviously never gave me a second thought after you crept out of my flat the following morning.'

Heat rose to her cheeks at his closeness, caused by desire, and the depth of the guilty feelings that had been impossible to shake. At the time she believed there'd been no choice about leaving the way she did, but the accusation that she hadn't thought about him stung.

'Why obviously?'

'Why didn't you stay long enough to say goodbye? Wouldn't that have been the polite thing to do?' He clenched his fists and then relaxed them again, the frown lines deepening.

'I don't think either of us were concerned with etiquette that night, were we?'

Lexi was conscious of the Resus team quietly working all around them preventing them from talking freely, but she didn't want to talk to him at all. She wanted to get away to think and work out what she was going to say to him. In a moment of madness, she thought about not telling him, but that was crazy. They were going to be working together, and he had already said that he remembered everything. But she wanted to tell him in her own way. Prepare him first.

Then his bleep went off, and he cursed under his breath. 'I need to get this. We'll talk later.' He strode off to find a phone and she made her escape out of Resus and towards the reception area and the staff room. She was due a break anyway and desperately needed a strong coffee.

*

Theresa, another staff nurse, was already in the kitchen making herself a drink. She turned when she heard Lexi come in and gestured to the kettle. 'Want a brew?'

'Coffee please. Strong with sugar. Are there any biscuits left?' Lexi collapsed into an armchair and breathed out slowly, trying to calm her nerves.

Theresa made the coffee and searched the cupboards for the biscuit box. The doctors were always putting it back in the wrong place.

'How about the new consultant then? What a hottie! Have you met him yet?'

Theresa put the mugs on the table with the Tupperware box containing the biscuits.

'Thanks. Yes, I just did.' Lexi selected a custard cream and bit into it.

'And? What did you think?' Theresa was watching her. She was single and on the lookout for a husband. Single doctors of senior registrar grade and above were scrutinized and judged according to Theresa's list of essential requirements. Her standards were incredibly high, which was why she was still single.

'He seems very nice.

'Very *nice*! Are you mad? The guy's as hot as freshly roasted chestnuts. He's gorgeous! Very *nice* indeed.'

'Okay, so he's good looking and knows it. He came across as a bit arrogant, in my opinion.'

Theresa stared into space whilst munching on a biscuit. 'I bet he's really assertive in the bedroom. You know, the type that just takes charge and sends you into orbit in three seconds flat.'

Lexi felt heat spread up into her neck. The memories of Casey O'Connor's expertise in the bedroom flooded into her mind and she nearly choked on her custard cream. Theresa wasn't far wrong in her assessment. What she wouldn't give for a repeat performance. As if that's ever going to happen. When the good doctor found out the truth, he'd be the one going into orbit. He'd go ballistic. She shivered at the thought of the confrontation to come.

Theresa was watching her.

'What?' she asked.

'I worry about you sometimes.'

'What do you mean?' Lexi frowned at her and took another biscuit. Her diet was far from healthy when she was on duty in A&E. Any break she took was a chance to ingest as much sugar as she could to keep her energy up until she got home and could eat lots of fruit and vegetables.

Theresa spoke with her mouth full of biscuit. 'You're twenty-nine years old, a single mother, you work all the hours you can to make ends meet, you never go out and haven't had nooky for four years. And then sex-on-legs turns up on our doorstep and you're finding fault with him. You should think about dating again.'

Lexi was tempted to tell her friend to mind her own business, but Theresa was only looking out for her.

'I'm fine as I am. Jade and I are fine. It's because I have a three-year-old daughter that I'm careful who I see. She's my priority. Has been since the day she was born – and always will be.'

Theresa's voice softened. 'I understand that, honey, and I think you're doing a great job. I'm not sure I could manage as well as you do. But...' Theresa looked watchful as if she wasn't sure if she should say the next part.

'Go on.'

'Well, don't you ever get lonely? Don't you think about a man's strong arms around you?'

The only man she dreamt about had just barged back into her life and she didn't know how she felt about it. It was one thing using the memories of a hot night of sex to fuel her sexual fantasies; whenever she day-dreamed about being one of the heroines in the romance novels she loved, or when she read a chapter or two before sleeping, the hero always morphed into her mystery man whose identity she now knew. It was *his* strong arms that held her, his mouth that crushed hers and dark green tantalizing eyes that gazed at her in adoration. But it was quite another issue to be faced with the reality of an angry, hurt man who she had to work with every day.

This man was Jade's father. He was no longer a man of

mystery who she could fantasize about. He was flesh and blood, moods, personality, intellect and genes. She often wondered, as she watched Jade speak her first words, smile, frown, throw tantrums and laugh – did she take after her mother or her father?

'And there's another thing.' Theresa hadn't finished.

'What?' Lexi didn't want to ask but knew that her friend was going to tell her anyway.

'One day, you're going to have to find a father for that little girl. It's not fair otherwise. If she can't have her real daddy, she'll need a step-daddy.'

'She's got me, she doesn't need anyone else.' It was time to get back to work. She didn't want to have this conversation. Theresa didn't know what she was talking about.

'You have to admit, children do better with two parents, don't they?'

Lexi got up. 'I wouldn't know, I'm afraid. I was abandoned as a baby, I didn't have either parent growing up. I was brought up by the state. Thanks for the coffee, Theresa.'

Lexi swept from the room, leaving Theresa staring after her open mouthed.

What was wrong with her? She never talked about her childhood to anyone. Jess was the only one who knew the truth. The appearance of Dr Casey O'Connor was already affecting her. He could potentially turn her life upside down, and she liked her life exactly the way it was. Well, she wouldn't let him. She'd be on her guard and make sure she didn't let her mouth run away with her again.

Chapter Two

Casey finished his conversation with the on-call registrar in Cardiology and put the phone down. The patient may need stenting, so before the specialists could review him, he would stay in Resus for monitoring, then be sent to the Cardiac Unit to be stabilized before surgery. Casey's older brother, Riordan, was Lead Consultant in Cardiology and his patient would be in good hands.

Resus was filling up, most of the bays had patients being treated, waiting to be scanned or sent to a ward or ICU. It was busy, but nothing like the frenetic, out-of-control atmosphere of the London teaching hospital he had just left behind. He'd been getting close to burn-out there and had needed to make a major decision about his future.

Like a homing pigeon he had landed back in Leytonsfield, to talk it through with the people who loved him and knew him the best. The welcome he'd received had been warm. From his family, the few old school friends he was still in touch with and the staff of the A&E department which would become his new home.

What he hadn't expected to find was the woman who, four years ago, shared with him the best sex he had ever experienced, and then vanished like morning mist.

He still wasn't sure how he felt about Lexi Grainger. She'd captivated him the first time he'd seen her sitting alone while her friends were on the dancefloor. Her ash blonde hair was soft and hung down her back like a fragrant waterfall. Her pale grey sleeveless dress moulded to her body like a second skin. She wore little make-up but didn't need it. Her complexion was a natural peaches and cream; the colour even the most expensive products never achieved.

He'd asked her to dance, and instead of saying yes immediately as he'd expected, she looked him up and down with a half-smile.

He'd tried for light-hearted and said, 'Most women I ask to dance don't have to think about it for this long.'

'I've always believed that if something's worth having, it's worth waiting for.'

'And you, I would guess, are definitely worth having?'

She got up slowly and sashayed towards him. 'Oh yes,' she said, 'I'm definitely worth waiting for.'

She was gorgeous, and he suspected she had wanted him as much as he wanted her. It was lust that had pounded his heart and caused adrenaline to surge around his system. He'd felt the same way about another woman once, but he'd let his feelings for Helen develop into more than lust and he'd paid the price. She'd broken his heart and he was not about to let another woman close enough to so much as touch it. It was under lock and key to everyone except family and close friends. People he could trust.

It was easy to make such promises from a distance. Now, the lady who had shared his bed one summer solstice four years ago was no longer a fantasy figure. She was real and working alongside him as an A&E staff nurse. His body told him the sexual attraction was still there and as strong as ever. He still wanted her. What he didn't want was any emotional entanglement. He'd been there, done that and got burned for his trouble. He wasn't going back down that road, not even for a beautiful blonde with china blue eyes and a mouth tasting of ripe strawberries that could perform miracles on his aching flesh.

Even more reason to stay away from her. A night of hot sex was one thing but falling for someone was something else entirely. Something he was determined he would never do again.

*

As Lexi strode towards the exit, eager to get out of the hospital, she bumped into Theresa.

'Oh Lexi, I'm glad I've caught you before you left. I just wanted to apologise for my faux pas before. I had no idea you'd been in care. I'm such an idiot - an idiot with a big mouth. Please forgive me.'

'Of course, there's nothing to forgive.' They hugged, and Theresa kissed her on the cheek.

When they broke the embrace, Lexi noticed Casey watching them as he bought a bar of chocolate from the vending machine. She tried to ignore him, but knew from the way Theresa started preening, that he was coming over.

'Afternoon ladies.' He was all charm now, smiling widely.

'Casey. How're you getting on – first day nerves settled yet?' Theresa turned on her charm too. Attractive, with short blonde highlighted hair and big cherry brown eyes, she was never short of admirers. It looked to Lexi that she had Dr Casey O'Connor in her sights.

Casey flirted back with Theresa and Lexi wished that she could just walk away. She was late anyway and had better things to do than play gooseberry to these two.

'Right. Bye then.' She tried to escape but Casey stopped her by putting his hand on her arm.

'Not going, are you? I thought we could have a chat. Have a coffee and catch up?'

Lexi could feel Theresa's gaze burn into her. She was going to be annoyed now she'd found out that Lexi had known Casey all along, but she had other things on her mind as the touch of his hand burned her skin with memories of other touches, other caresses and she shivered.

'I can't I'm afraid, I'm meeting someone. I need to go. Maybe another time.'

Casey looked disappointed and dropped his hand from her arm. 'Okay. Another time.'

She hurried through the automatic doors that formed the entrance to the Accident and Emergency Department and was relieved when she saw three figures sitting in a row on a bench a few feet away.

'Mummy!' Jade got up, and ran to her, flinging herself into her arms.

She hugged her daughter. As she held her close, her body relaxed, and her heart rate returned to normal. Just to hold the little girl felt so right, so perfect, that whatever else was wrong in her world, in that moment, Jade made it right.

'Hi, hon. Heavy day?'

Jess and Craig had appeared next to them and she was grateful for Jess's perception. Her friend worked in a cake shop and regaled her with amusing stories of the customers and the antics of the staff, but she always understood when Lexi was feeling stressed and needed a listening ear.

Her son, Craig, who was eight and obsessed with games, had his head bent over some device or other. He could have been on the moon for all the notice he took of his surroundings.

'You could say that,' she replied to Jess. 'How about we treat ourselves tonight and have a take-away?'

Jess frowned. 'But it's not Friday.' They shared a cottage, so they could help each other with finances and childcare and encouraged each other to keep to a strict budget.

'Well it's either that or a bottle of Pinot Grigio. I need something.' She acted out gasping and staggering like a parched man in a desert. The kids laughed, then Lexi heard someone clear their throat from the direction of the entrance.

'Who's he?' Jess whispered.

Lexi glanced over to see Casey watching them with a frown that was getting deeper with every minute that went by. 'He's one of the new consultants.'

He walked slowly over to them and stood still as a statue. No one spoke. They were all holding their breath as they looked from Casey to Jade. The little girl looked like her mother, with ash blonde hair and a heart-shaped face. But her eyes gave her away. Emerald green with a black ring around the irises. Eyes that looked out at the world in wonder and joy. Eyes the same shade as her father's. The man who was staring at her as if he had just seen a ghost, whose whole body was vibrating with tension and, Lexi suspected, anger.

He turned to face her at last and his voice was deceptively quiet. 'Aren't you going to introduce me to your daughter?'

*

Rage simmered below the surface of his studied calm. He tried not to show it in front of the children. His anger was directed at one person only. The lady who was staring at him with wide blue eyes, looking like a rabbit caught in the head-lights. A guilty rabbit.

'Yes, of course,' she said. 'This is Jade. Jade, this is Doctor O'Connor.'

Casey knelt so he was at eye level with Jade. She smiled at him, so he smiled back.

'Hi, Jade.'

'Hi. Do you work with my mummy?'

'I do, darling, yes. But I've just started working here so I don't know many people yet.'

'Mummy'll be your friend, won't you mummy?' She turned her face up to Lexi who had the grace to look embarrassed.

'Uh… yes, of course.'

'Good. I need all the friends I can get. Now, do you mind if mummy and I have a quiet word before you all go home? Could you stay with…' He looked up expectantly at the woman who was hovering close to the children, listening to every word.

'Jess.' She stepped forward with her hand out to shake. 'Lexi and I share a cottage. We're both single mums, you see, and we help each other.' He stood up and shook it. 'And this is my son, Craig, but you won't get much response from him, he never looks up unless there's food on offer.'

'Hi, Craig.'

'Hi,' said the boy who glanced up and back down to his tablet in a flash.

'No problem; I'll look after the kids.' Jess beamed at him and he liked her immediately. She had tattoos and piercings, short dyed black hair and the most amazing grey eyes he had seen on a woman. He decided that what you saw was what you got with Jess. Which made a refreshing change after all the devious women he'd known in his lifetime.

One of whom was looking at him in alarm. 'I don't think… we don't really have the time… can we talk tomorrow?'

'No, now.' He was brusque with her but was on an extremely short fuse.

'We need to get the kids home and fed, so I really do think we should leave this until tomorrow, Casey.' Her eyes flashed fire at him, but what had she got to be annoyed about? He was the one who had been lied to. Again.

'Look, here's the deal. Either you and I have a very short conversation now in which I ask you a straightforward question and you do me the courtesy of giving me an honest answer, or I'll call round to your place this evening and we can talk all night if that's what it takes.'

Lexi looked furious and lifted her chin to look him in the eyes. He stared back, unblinking. She seemed to deflate suddenly and closed her eyes as if she was in pain. He felt a stab of guilt, but it was fleeting as his anger was the dominant emotion and swamped any other feelings he might have had for the lady.

'Okay,' she said. She looked over at Jess who nodded. Casey wondered how much Jess knew about his night of passion with her bestie, but then he wondered a lot of things. His mind was whirring, and he couldn't focus on anything but the one question he needed an answer to. All the rest could wait until later.

'Right. We'll go over there, just out of earshot. I need to be close to the department in case they need me.'

They moved away from Jess and the children, but in sight of the front entrance. He felt bad about leaving his post in Resus, but this wouldn't take long.

'I have one question, Lexi, and I think you know what it is.' When she didn't answer, he continued. 'Jade is about, what? Three?' Lexi nodded but still didn't speak. 'I'll bet she was born in March, nine months after the Summer Ball. Am I right?' She nodded again.

The tension between them was electric. He hated the way he was treating her, but she had lied to him. She was the second woman who had decided not to tell him she was carrying his child. At least this time she had gone ahead with the pregnancy, but didn't she think, while she was busy making plans for the rest of her life, that the father should be somewhere in the equation? But no, she hadn't even bothered to try to find him. He wasn't even given a say. In any of it.

Casey felt the rage building inside him and took two deep breaths to try to control it. Losing his temper would get them nowhere.

'Is Jade my daughter?'

'I -' Lexi began.

'And before you lie to me, just remember that I'm not stupid. And I *will* demand a DNA test if I have to.'

The silence stretched on and Casey's nerves stretched with it.

'That won't be necessary. She is your daughter.'

Suddenly all his anger melted like snow in the hot sun, to be replaced by a feeling he had never experienced before. A mixture of joy, fear and overwhelming, heart-stopping love. He looked over at his child, holding Jess's hands and swinging around, her head back, blonde hair loose and flowing.

'She's mine.' It was said almost with wonder as if he couldn't quite believe it. He was a father. It was almost too much to take in. 'Why didn't you try to find me?' He was close to tears but had so many questions that he needed answers to before he could fully let go of his resentment towards Lexi. He'd missed out on three years of his child's life and he needed to know why.

'I did.' Lexi looked and sounded sincere, but he had been hurt before by a woman's evasiveness.

'Well, you didn't try very hard.'

Lexi let out an exasperated sigh. 'You have no idea how hard it is to find someone who is determined not to be found. I didn't even know your name, I didn't know where you worked. I asked around with just your description to go on and no one could help. I tried, Casey, you have no idea how hard I tried.'

'For how long?' He was being unreasonable, he knew it. For he had tried to find her with the same lack of success. He had tried everything but hire a private detective and the only reason he hadn't done that was because he had no information to give to one. "*She's gorgeous, blonde hair, blue eyes and dynamite in bed.*" He would have been laughed out of the man's office.

'For a long while. Eventually, when I had no luck, I decided that the baby was my priority.'

'My daughter.'

'Our daughter.' It sounded strange to him as it must to her. But the truth was that Jade was his and he needed to start being a father to that little girl.

'Will you tell her tonight?'

'What?' Lexi looked panicked and shook her head.

'Do you want me to be there when you tell her?'

'No!' It was almost a shout and Casey felt his heart harden against her.

'Why not? She's mine, you've just admitted it. Don't I have the right to be there?'

'You need to leave this up to me, Casey; you don't know her like I do. I'll tell her when the time's right. On my own.'

'The time is right now, Lexi. I've missed out on three years of my child's life. Three years of milestones, magic moments, birthdays and Christmas; times that I can never get back. You've had all those things. Are you going to deny me any more time with Jade?'

Lexi's shoulders slumped as she faced the full blast of his pain and anguish, but her chin was raised in the next moment and she stared back at him defiantly.

'I need to prepare her, I can't just blurt it out.'

'What have you told her about me?' Lexi couldn't meet his eyes and a cold feeling crept into his stomach. 'For pity's sake, please don't tell me she thinks I'm dead!'

'No, of course not!' Lexi looked irritated with him. He knew very little about the mother of his child. They had been intimate with each other but had never had a real conversation. He knew nothing about her past, her dreams and fears. He wanted to know everything.

'What then?'

'I told her you couldn't stay and had to go away for work.'

'So, you told her a pack of lies?'

'She's too young to be told the truth.'

'Well, I'm back now and I have no intention of ever leaving her again. Tell her that, when you tell her who I am. I intend to be very much a part of my daughter's life.'

Pete, the Charge Nurse, ran through the automatic doors and looked frantically around. When he spotted him, he dashed over.

'It's a Code Red, Casey, guy with an arterial bleed, they'll be here in eight minutes.'

'Right. Let's go.' Casey turned away without a backward glance, and they both ran back towards the entrance to A&E leaving Lexi staring after them.

Chapter Three

After the usual evening ritual when the kids had been fed, bathed and had listened to a bedtime story before being tucked up for the night, the two women curled up on the sofa together, sharing a bottle of white wine.

'So, this doctor is your one-night stand then?' asked Jess. Lexi had told her that Jade was the result of a night of hot passionate sex with a man she would never see again. Jess, being the sensitive friend that she was, had never questioned her. But now she wanted all the details.

'Where did you meet him?'

'At the Summer Solstice Ball arranged by the registrars at the hospital I worked at in London. I didn't really want to go, to be honest, as my boyfriend had just dumped me, and I wasn't feeling very sociable. My friends said I should get back out there and bought me a ticket. I didn't know who

Casey was and had never seen him before that night.'

'What happened?'

'He asked me to dance. And we did.' She stopped as the memory of being held in his arms and nearly drowning in his intense green eyes, took her back to that night. She could hear the music and feel the heat between them. 'We went back to his place and, well … made love. All night.' She wished she could find the words to express how wonderful it had been. Every cliché that came into her head was inadequate. To be wanted so much by such a gorgeous man had been beyond her wildest dreams. Jess picked up on her mood anyway.

'And I'm guessing by your expression it wasn't so shabby?'

Lexi sighed. 'Shabby? It was the most amazing night of my life. And I conceived Jade. She was an accident but still, the most precious gift I've ever been given.'

'Why didn't the two of you see each other again?'

Lexi poured more wine before she answered. 'At the time we just wanted a one-night stand. It was a kind of madness us getting together, a mid-summer madness. Ironically, we both tried to find the other afterwards, but without even a name to go on, it was impossible.'

'How do you feel about him now? Seeing him turn up like that must have been a shock.' Jess fixed her with a penetrating look as she took the glass of wine Lexi offered her. The two women had been friends for many years and very little got passed Jess.

She wasn't sure how to answer. How did she feel? 'I don't

want things to change. I'm happy being a single mother. Jade's happy and we've got you and Craig, but I can't ignore the fact that he's Jade's father and wants to be part of her life.'

'You'll have to let him see her.'

'Of course.'

*

Lexi had hoped for a quiet day, maybe in the Minor Injuries Unit, where she could treat cut fingers and sprained ankles at her own pace. Her head and heart could have coped with that. She wouldn't have minded listening to the patients talking about their woes, it would have saved her from having to think about her own. Even the "revolving-door" patients; the ones who came to A&E on a regular basis for comfort and company, mainly people with mental health problems and those who just couldn't cope with life, would have been a pleasant change from the life and death dramas of Resus.

It wasn't to be, of course. She was back in her role as trauma nurse in Resus and the team leader for the day was none other than Dr Casey O'Connor.

He was the first person she noticed when she walked into the department and, as usual, the sight of him took her breath away. He wore burgundy scrubs, his cheeks were smooth as if he had just shaved, and his short hair was brushed back from his face. Some of the nurses were looking at him as if they could eat him up on the spot and Lexi felt a flash of irritation. Or was it jealousy? She wished her body wouldn't betray her like this every time she was in the same room with him, it was going to make working together that day, and all subsequent days, uncomfortable and filled with tension.

'Good morning.' He spotted her and came straight over.

'Good morning. How are you?' Now he was close to her, she could see the bags under his eyes, so maybe he had also found it difficult to sleep the previous night.

'Good. Well, not so good actually.'

'Oh?' She hoped he wasn't going to accuse her of all manner of things as he had the previous evening.

'Listen. I need to apologise to you for my behaviour. I was angry yesterday and should never have spoken to you the way I did. It was a shock, finding out I was a father. And on top of seeing you again, well, it was one shock too many. I shouldn't have taken it out on you. I'm sorry.'

Lexi watched his eyes as he spoke and saw sincerity there. Standing so close to him, breathing in his unique scent and hearing his deep, rich voice, slightly husky now as he spoke softly so people couldn't overhear, reminded her of their night together and she wanted him all over again. The feeling was almost as intense.

She was conscious of the staff, moving quietly but efficiently around Resus. Theresa kept throwing glances their way. She hadn't spoken to her that morning. Another joy in store; apologising for her white lie.

Casey must have been thinking of their colleagues, too, as he stepped back but spoke without raising his voice. 'We need to talk.'

'I know, and we will, I promise.'

'Will you have dinner with me? Tonight? We're on the

same shift, and I'll try to get away in time. I can pick you up at seven.'

'You want to take me out to dinner?' She hadn't expected that. She had wondered the previous day about Casey's love-life. He obviously wasn't married as he didn't wear a ring, but he must have a partner, or at least a girlfriend.

'Yes, if that's okay with you. There's so much I want to ask you and we can't really talk with Jade there. And Jess and Craig. In a restaurant, surrounded by people, we can be civil to each other.' He smiled. How could she say no? But she needed to know in what capacity he was asking her.

'Is this a *date*?'

He seemed amused by her question as his mouth twitched and his green eyes danced with mirth. 'It can be a date if you want it to be, Lexi.'

'No, I don't! Of course I don't. It's simply the opportunity to talk about Jade and arrangements for you to see her. That's all it is.'

He nodded but was still laughing at her. 'Yes, of course, I concur.'

The red phone rang and all the staff in the immediate vicinity turned towards Pete, the Charge Nurse who answered. The man was busy scribbling something down on a notepad that was kept next to the phone. He then moved to the intercom and spoke, 'Code red, adult trauma, ETA ten minutes.'

'Here we go,' said Casey, his body tensing and his whole demeanour changing from the teasing, sexy guy of a minute ago to a competent, alert team leader. 'Right everyone, get ready, you all know what to do.' He walked over to the charge nurse and they stood talking together.

Lexi felt the familiar thrill of excitement and slight sickness as the adrenaline started to flow. Code red meant that the paramedics had evidence that the patient was in danger of bleeding to death. What happened in the first hour of the patient being treated could make a huge difference. If the staff got it wrong, or missed something, a person's life could easily be cut short. It wasn't called the "golden hour" for nothing.

*

'This is Alice, thirty years old, she was T-boned by another car. Had to be cut from her car.' Casey listened intently as the paramedic gave the report on the patient who had just been brought in. She was in a bad way and, as he listened, his mind was already busy with the order of emergency treatment she would need.

'Top to toe, GCS of 13, blood pressure ninety-five over sixty, no head injury, bruising from seat belt, closed tib and fib injury on left, haematoma left forearm, pelvis asymmetrical, receiving oxygen.'

'Okay, thanks Mike.' The paramedics left, satisfied they had given the trauma team all the information they could. Casey watched as one of the doctors checked her over, calling out his findings. Casey made a decision based on the information he was rapidly processing. He was most concerned about her low blood pressure. 'Right, pelvic scan to be done, stat. She has a weak radial pulse and I suspect she's bleeding into her pelvis. Can we have one unit of blood, please and then we'll continue resuscitation in the scanning department. We need to know now what's going on with this lady's pelvic injuries. If the pelvic fracture has caused lacerations, she could have extensive internal bleeding.'

The blood transfusion was an attempt to stop her going into cardiac arrest. The layman would worry about the blood loss they see externally, but Casey knew that most people who bled to death did so inside their own body cavities.

The team worked quickly to hook up the bag of blood and get a line inserted for fluids and medications and to draw blood for testing. When she was ready, they moved off as one towards the lifts to take them to the scanning department.

As team leader, Casey's policy was never to tell his staff what to do, but to let them get on with the work they were trained for and be there when he was needed. Ultimately, the buck stopped with him, but he was happy with that when he had a good team around him.

Casey watched Lexi as she worked quickly. She was focused and didn't even look up; she kept her attention on her patient. She was a good nurse and his admiration for the lady was growing steadily. He tried not to think about Jade as every time he thought about the little girl, his emotions went into melt-down. He needed to be focused now and concentrate solely on the patient in his care.

Alice's scan showed that her pelvic fracture had lacerated surrounding tissues and stopping the internal bleeding was their main concern. Apart from the tibia and fibula injury to her lower leg, she had no other major injuries. She needed surgery, so she stayed in Resus until a theatre was available for her.

'Right guys,' Casey said when he had returned to Resus, 'let's clean this place up.' Five minutes later, the red phone rang again. 'Leytonsfield A&E.' He wrote down the details of another adult trauma that was on its way. This time a builder had fallen off a roof. Casey sighed. It was going to be a busy day.

Chapter Four

'You're not going to wear that, surely?' Lexi was getting ready for her dinner with Casey when Jess came into her bedroom carrying a pile of freshly ironed clothes.

'What's wrong with it?' She studied herself in the full-length mirror, frowning at the frumpy woman who glared back at her.

'Nothing, if you were going for a job interview, but a black skirt and white blouse doesn't exactly scream "sexy". And put your hair down, it looks lovely flowing over your shoulders. You can't go on a date looking like that.'

'It's not a *date*. Dr O'Connor and I are merely going to discuss arrangements for him to see Jade.'

'In an Italian restaurant, on a school night?'

'How do you know it's going to be Italian?'

'It's that new place that's opened in the Precinct, I bet.

Everyone's raving about it. Dead expensive.'

'Well wherever he's taking me, it isn't a *date*.' Maybe if she said it often enough, she would start believing it herself. Part of her wished they were going on a date. To be wined, dined and pampered by an attractive man would be a rare treat, but tonight, they would have a quick meal and then he'd bring her home. She couldn't afford to let her guard down with Casey. She didn't know him well enough. In fact, she hardly knew him at all.

Jade came running into the bedroom, closely followed by Craig.

'Right you two, help me find something pretty for Jade's mummy to wear tonight. A nice dress and some killer heels.'

She went over to the wardrobe and started rummaging around. Jade followed her, whilst Craig sat cross-legged on the floor staring at his phone and humming quietly to himself.

'I don't think your son is interested in my attire,' said Lexi.

'Well, I bet the gorgeous doctor will be. How about this?' She pulled a dress out of the wardrobe and waggled it in front of Lexi. It was one of her favourites; a dark blue wrap-around with three quarter sleeves and a low neckline. She had a lovely silver pendant that was just the right length, falling neatly into her cleavage. She could wear that and her blue court shoes. The dress came to just above her knees and clung to her figure, accentuating all her good features, such as her bum. She had always liked her bum, though would never admit that to anyone.

'Maybe. It's got possibilities.' Who was she kidding? It

wasn't as if she had a whole wardrobe to choose from. She only had a handful of dresses.

'Try it on. Turn your back, Craig.' He did as he was told while Lexi took off her blouse and skirt and pulled the dress over her head.

'There you go, it looks lovely. What do you think, Jade?'

'You look bootiful, mummy.'

'Oh, thank you, angel.' She kissed her daughter and stroked her silky blonde hair. 'You'll be okay with Jess and Craig tonight, won't you sweetie?'

'Yeah, we're having popcorn.'

'I thought we could watch *"Frozen"* as a treat before bed.'

'Again,' muttered Craig from the floor.

'Well, next time, you can choose, okay? Now, let's go and start the popcorn and leave Lexi to get ready.'

The three of them made their way down the narrow stairs to the ground floor with a great deal of excited chatter from Jade.

Lexi and Jess had rented a stone cottage with three bed-rooms and a bathroom upstairs, a kitchen and open-plan living-room with a massive old stone fireplace downstairs. It was centrally heated, but Lexi sometimes lit the fire as it created a welcoming ambience. The September evenings were already getting chilly.

Jess and the kids would spend the evening in front of the TV eating popcorn and drinking juice, whilst she would be in a fancy restaurant with the most gorgeous man she had ever met, trying to be knowledgeable and sophisticated and not drop food down her dress.

What would they talk about apart from Jade? Did she have enough interesting conversation to last three courses? Or would he talk, and she listen? The image of a pair of green eyes gazing intently at her suddenly made her nervous. He had only seen her socially on one occasion, and then she had been acting a part. Pretending to be a sexy siren to give her courage. She was hopeless in social situations and being dumped by her boyfriend had drained her of the little self-confidence she'd had.

Tonight, he would see her as she really was. What would he think of the real Lexi? Did it matter? He wasn't interested in her anyway, just his daughter.

She got dressed quickly and pulled her hair away from her face to apply her make-up. A light foundation, minimal eye shadow, but a dark blue liner and mascara to accentuate her eyes. A pink lip gloss and light blusher and she was done. There, that would have to do.

She stood in front of the mirror and fastened the silver pendant, then stepped back to admire her reflection. It was a Yin Yang design, the two pieces fitting perfectly together.

She slipped into her shoes and brushed her hair. After selecting a jacket from the wardrobe and opening the bedroom door, she heard the doorbell chime.

'I'll get it,' Jess shouted.

She listened to the sound of the front door opening and Jess politely saying "Hello". When she heard the reply, his voice sent tingles through her entire body. Even at this distance, his presence had the power to turn her to jelly. She would walk sedately down the stairs, hopefully without tripping in these heels, then greet him as any sane woman would greet her dinner companion for the night.

Taking a deep breath, she made her way downstairs, but when she caught sight of Dr Casey O'Connor, dressed for a night out, her knees nearly buckled beneath her. He had looked hot at the Summer Ball in his tuxedo, but he looked equally spectacular now. He wore black trousers and a white shirt open at the neck, with a black leather jacket. He looked positively edible.

'These are for the ladies,' he said, handing herself and Jess a huge bunch of flowers each. 'And these are for you two.' He gave Craig a game for his Xbox and Jade a doll. It was a ragdoll with a blue dress and blonde pigtails. Jade said thanks in a shy voice.

'Oh, how thoughtful, you didn't have to go to all this trouble,' Lexi said, trying to be polite, but the look that Casey gave her stopped her from saying anything more.

'It's no trouble,' he replied. Of course, it wouldn't be. Jade was his daughter and showering her with presents could be one way he made up for the lost years. She would have to put him straight. Spoiling her wasn't the right way to go about getting to know her. They had a lot to talk about at this meal.

'Say "thank you" Craig,' said Jess.

'Thanks, that's really cool,' said Craig before retreating to his place on the sofa.

'Thanks for these. Nobody ever gives me flowers.' Jess seemed overwhelmed as she stroked the petals of the exotic blooms. Brownie points to the doctor. 'In fact, I'll just put them in water. Where are you going? Just out of interest,' Jess asked as she moved towards the kitchen.

Casey looked at Lexi. 'I thought we could go to *Rocco's* in the Precinct, if that's okay. I've heard good things about it.'

Jess raised her eyebrows at her with a barely suppressed grin but said nothing.

'Yes, that sounds perfect. Shall we go?'

'Right.' He opened the front door and waved goodbye to them all.

'Bye everyone.' She kissed and hugged Jade, then walked out of the cottage and saw the silver BMW outside. Could this date get any better? Then she remembered that it wasn't a date. Well, not officially, but it was the closest she'd come to one for a long time.

As Casey held the passenger door open for her, he whispered, 'You look beautiful.'

'Thanks,' she whispered back. It was going to be an interesting evening.

Chapter Five

Most of the Italian restaurants Lexi had frequented were noisy, exuberant places with badly drawn murals of Tuscany on the walls, cheap wine and red and white check plastic tablecloths. She usually ordered pizza and ice-cream. However, as soon as she stepped over the threshold of *Rocco's*, as Casey held the door open for her, Lexi entered another world. It was the height of sophistication with a décor of dark wood, soft lighting and silver candelabra on the tables. A spiral staircase linked two floors and, by the murmur of voices and clinking of cutlery on plates, there were more tables for diners upstairs.

A waiter, dressed all in black, showed them to a table for two, tucked away in the corner. 'Is this okay for you, sir?' he asked Casey.

'Perfect. Thank you.'

The waiter held their chairs for them as they sat, then Lexi picked up a menu to give her time to get her breath back and her heart rate under control, but when she saw the prices, her heart rate threatened to shoot through the roof. It hadn't occurred to her, when Casey asked her to dinner, to check that he would be paying for it. Or would they pay for their own meal? If that was the case, she would only have a starter.

The wine waiter left them the wine list and Casey picked it up and scanned it. 'What would you like, Lexi? Do you have any preference?'

'I'm happy to leave it up to you.' She wasn't used to dining out and didn't want to order the wrong thing. Casey took the hint and ordered a bottle of Lambrusco Rosso Amabile with the meal and a French Martini as an aperitif.

When the wine waiter had gone, Casey smiled at her. 'Do you want to order now, Lexi, or do you need more time to think?'

Lexi's head was spinning. She just wanted time to stand still, so she didn't have to think. She wanted to drink in the sight of the gorgeous doctor, hear his sexy voice and admire the way he was in complete control, but he was watching her, those penetrating green eyes fixed on her face, and waiting for her reply.

'Um…, I think I'll go for the lemon and saffron marinated chicken breast, and the calamari as a starter.'

'I'm going to start with calamari too, then have the fillet steak with *cavolo nero*, roast garlic and a pine nut polenta. I'll think about dessert later.' He closed the menu and put it on the table. 'That's settled then.'

Almost straight away the waiter came over to take their order and another waiter brought their French Martini.

Lexi took a sip and groaned in ecstasy. Vodka, raspberry liqueur, pineapple juice with a twist of lemon. It tasted scrumptious and she wished she could have more than one, but it was an *aperitif* and they had the wine to drink yet. She didn't want to get drunk in front of Casey. That would be the ultimate humiliation. She needed him to know she was a good mother to Jade. Good mothers didn't get drunk.

'You're not as I remember from that night.' She looked up to find Casey watching her with narrowed eyes.

'I'm not? In what way?' Then she was acting a role, now she was being herself. She had changed in other ways over the last four years. She was a mother now and Jade was her reason for living. Her life had purpose whereas before, it had none.

'I don't know…' he said, 'you're more serious, not quite as… well, "out there".'

She wanted to giggle. Out there? What was that supposed to mean anyway?

'I suppose we're both different to the way we were that night. Neither of us were looking for anything but a good time for a few hours.' *"Good time"* was an understatement. It was the second-best night of her life. The first being the night she gave birth to Jade.

Casey was quiet for a long time. 'Why did you leave like that? Why didn't you stay and say goodbye? I woke up and you'd gone.' He didn't sound accusing, just sad.

'I just thought it was for the best under the circumstances.'

'And those circumstances being…?'

'That it was a one-night stand, nothing more. I was trying to save us both embarrassment.'

'And it didn't occur to you that maybe that one-night stand could have turned into something more?'

She was saved from answering as the waiter served the first course. She was relieved but puzzled. Had Casey wanted to see her again? Is that what he was trying to say? That was hard to believe.

It wasn't until she started eating that Lexi realized how hungry she was. The calamari were delicious; cooked in batter with a dipping sauce. She glanced at Casey who was eating his meal with relish. He was obviously a man who enjoyed his food. What other appetites did he have, apart from the obvious one? She nearly choked on her squid as a vision of Casey making love to her with passionate abandon entered her mind, unbidden.

'Are you okay?' Casey asked in concern.

'Yes fine,' she croaked, 'went down the wrong way.' She sipped her martini and tried to control her rampaging thoughts.

Casey finished his starter first and sat back in his chair. Lexi was aware of him watching her, and she took a deep breath, not wanting to choke again. She tried to think of something to ask him. They knew so little about each other.

'Were you working in London four years ago?'

'Yes, I was a registrar then, but needed a change, so, when

my brother told me about the consultant post at Leytonsfield General A&E I applied.'

'Your brother? I had no idea your brother worked at the hospital.'

'Riordan's Lead Consultant in Cardiology.'

'Are you from Leytonsfield?'

'Yep, born and raised. There are four of us; Riordan, me, then the twins – Josie and Jay. Josie's a midwife and Jay is a paramedic. My father's a GP and my mother used to be a mid-wife, but she stopped work when she had us.'

'Are you close?'

'Yes, very. They are the reason I came back here, because I missed my family. No matter how far we travel with our careers we all end up back home eventually. Josie's in Aus-tralia at present and Jay's in America, but they'll be back for Christmas.'

Listening to Casey talk about his family was painful for Lexi. She had longed to be part of a big family like that. Peo-ple who were close and looked out for each other. The closest she had to family was Jess and Craig. She and Jess had been brought up in the same children's home and they were as close as sisters.

Casey leant forward on the table and looked her in the eye. 'So, you see, Lexi, Jade has a big family waiting to meet her and fall in love with her. Riordan is a single dad and his son, Tom, is six years old. I bet they'll be great friends.'

'Have you told your family about Jade?' The calamari turned to ash in her mouth. Jade didn't know about her father yet; surely, he hadn't told this huge family of his? What would they think of her? They'll hate her on sight when they find out that they have had a granddaughter for three years and didn't even know.

'No. I want Jade to know first. Then I'll introduce them, but she needs to be told soon. I wanted to make a fuss of her tonight when I collected you, but I couldn't, I had to act as if I was a stranger to her. Do you have any idea how that makes me feel? She's mine, Lexi, as well as yours.'

The truth of that statement hit Lexi like a punch to the stomach. Jade had always been her daughter, only hers, but from now on she would have to share her with this man – this stranger – and his extensive family. Irrationally, she visualised Jade slipping away from her.

'Yes, I know. Please be patient, Casey, I will tell her soon.'

They fell silent as the waiter brought the main course and poured the wine. Lexi picked up the glass and took a sip. Casey had started his steak already and finished before Lexi was halfway through her chicken. She wanted to tell him it wasn't a race. She had always eaten slowly, savouring her food. With Casey, it didn't seem to touch the sides.

Again, she had to suffer him watching her as she ate. This time, he asked the questions.

'So, what about you? Where are you from?'

'London. Born and bred. I trained as a nurse in St Mary's, then got a job in a hospital on the outskirts of London.'

'And your family?'

This was the question she'd been dreading. Although she

should be used to telling people she was an orphan by now, it was different where Casey was concerned. He'd just been regaling her with details of his family life as if his circumstances were completely normal. He probably thought everyone had family like that. The reaction she usually got was pity and she didn't want this man's pity, but she wasn't going to lie.

'I don't have family. I'm an orphan.'

She couldn't look up. She didn't want to see the look in his eyes. She heard him whisper, 'I'm sorry,' and his voice sounded startled as if it was the last thing he expected her to say.

'Don't be, I'm fine. Jade and I are fine. What you've never had, you don't miss. Isn't that what they say?'

'They? Whoever "they" are tend to talk a load of rubbish. It can sometimes be the thing you've never had that you yearn for the most.'

Casey's words nearly proved to be her undoing. He had inadvertently hit the nail on the head. For she wanted what he had so much. She had lain in bed, as a child, dreaming up an imaginary family. She used to talk to them and pretend that they answered her. Then, when she grew up and started reading romance novels, she always chose the ones with babies and families. She used to pretend she was the heroine of the novel and relived their happy-ever-after over and over in her mind.

She put her knife and fork down, as she couldn't eat another mouthful. She kept her head down as tears burned the back of her eyes.

'If you'll excuse me, I'll be back in a minute.' He headed off in the direction of the toilets and Lexi was grateful for his thoughtfulness. He was giving her time to get herself together. She shook herself mentally and wiped her eyes.

When he returned, he said, 'I've decided, I'm going to have the tiramisu.'

She managed to smile and say, 'Sounds good, I'll join you.'

'How about a coffee? I'm just going to have an espresso as I'm driving but why don't you have a liquor coffee?'

'Okay, I'll have mine with Tia Maria.'

'Good.' He summoned the waiter and gave their order.

*

Casey was shocked. She had no family. At all. He really hadn't expected that. Thank goodness for Jess and Craig, at least she had their support with Jade. A single mother completely alone must struggle in so many ways, yet she insisted she was okay and managing fine. She was a proud lady, as well as a beautiful one.

He watched her as she ate her dessert, each mouthful being savoured and enjoyed. Lexi probably didn't get the opportunity to dine out often. Well that would change now. In fact, he was determined that a lot of things were going to change from now on.

He ate too fast; all his family told him so, especially his mother who warned him every time they had a family meal that he would be prone to indigestion if he wasn't careful. As a doctor, he was used to eating on the run and found it hard to break the habit, even when he had hours to enjoy a meal.

The other reason he finished his meal quickly was because he was desperate to ask Lexi more questions about Jade but didn't want to do so until they had finished eating. When she was enjoying her coffee, he would question her.

He had hoped the martini and wine would relax her a bit, but she still seemed tense. He needed to earn her trust, especially as they would be spending a great deal of time together, the three of them. Provided he got his way, of course.

The coffees arrived, and the empty plates were cleared. He decided to be proactive and dive in straight away.

'Can I ask about the birth? Was it natural?'

Lexi looked up and smiled. 'Yes, but she was a week late.'

'First babies often are. How much did she weigh?'

'She weighed seven pounds four ounces. She was perfect.' Lexi stared off into the middle distance and he felt his heart constrict. How he would have loved to have been there the moment his daughter made her appearance. Then something occurred to him.

'Were you alone? I mean apart from the nursing staff, of course.'

'Jess was my birth partner. She came to stay in London for a couple of weeks to help out. She was the one who suggested I come back with her to Leytonsfield. I couldn't afford to stay in London so, when Jade was a month old, I moved up here.'

'Do you like it here?'

'Yes, Leytonsfield suits me. It's a quieter pace of life. The people are nice, and the Cheshire countryside is pretty.'

He nodded. They sipped their coffees as Lexi gazed around the restaurant at the other diners.

'And um... what kind of things does Jade like doing?' He was racking his brains to come up with questions while Lexi seemed in a mellow mood, but the thought of everything he had missed out on was like someone raining blows down on his head. She was his child, he shouldn't have to ask anything. He should know all about his little girl already. He hated the thought that he was a stranger to her and was desperate to remedy the situation.

'She's an ordinary three-year-old. Well, three and a half. She has lots of friends at nursery, is popular, polite, a bit cheeky. She plays with dolls but can be a tough little thing. She's not a girly girl but she's not a tomboy either. She's just... well, Jade.'

He couldn't help smiling at the picture Lexi was painting of his daughter.

'I'll be a good dad to Jade, I promise. I'll look after her. I'll look after both of you.'

There was a flare of anger in Lexi's eyes, 'I don't need looking after, I've been looking after my daughter since she was born. I don't need your help.'

She drank the rest of her coffee then pushed the mug away from her and folded her arms.

'I'm not criticizing the way you've looked after her; you've done a great job, anyone can see that. But I'm here now, and I'm not going away. I fully intend to be a proper father to her. I want to be involved in every aspect of her life.'

Lexi was quiet, but he could see by the tension in her face that she wasn't happy about something. Maybe he should back off, give her some more time to get used to the idea of him being part of Jade's life. But so much time had gone by already. He wasn't a patient man and didn't know how much longer he could wait.

He remembered something she had said to him the night of the Summer Solstice Ball; *"If something is worth having, it's worth waiting for."*

They were silent until the coffees arrived. 'I thought about you, you know, after that night,' he said.

'Did you? I bet you didn't try to find me though, did you?' Her eyes were huge, and she looked at him hopefully.

'That's where you're wrong, I tried very hard. But like you, I didn't have enough information to go on. If I'd known you were pregnant, I would never have given up. I'm sorry you had to go through it all on your own.'

They both fell silent again and Casey knew the evening had come to an end. He paid for the meal and drove her back to the cottage.

She looked beautiful, bathed in autumn moonlight, as she stood on the doorstep, with her front door key in her hand. He wanted to kiss her but wasn't sure how that would be received, so he took her hands in his, 'I've really enjoyed tonight, Lexi, thank you. Would you like to do it again sometime?'

She smiled and nodded so he kissed her knuckles gently. She didn't pull back, so he leant forward and kissed her on the lips. She felt warm and soft and tasted of coffee.

'Good night, Casey, and thanks for a lovely evening.'

He saw her into the house and heard her bolt the door on the inside, only then did he walk back down the path to his car.

Chapter Six

As soon as Lexi walked through the automatic doors into the A&E department, she noticed the smell. It was citrus; fresh and clean, instead of the usual antiseptic with undertones of blood that pervaded the whole department. Maybe the receptionists had brought in an air freshener.

The smell was everywhere; in Minors, in the waiting area and even in Resus. What was going on?

'Isn't it beautiful?' said Theresa as they waited with the others who had just started their shift to hear the reports of the patients already in Resus. 'It's your Dr O'Connors idea. Essential oils diffused into the atmosphere will decrease stress and make everyone calmer, apparently.'

'Uh, that'll be the day,' said one of the porters who had overheard their conversation.

'Well, it's worth a try. He's left questionnaires for everyone. After a week, he wants us all to fill in the answers on how stressed we feel; before the oils and after.'

The porter walked off chuckling to himself and shaking his head.

'I love this one, it's called "Wild Orange." How cool is that?'

'Very cool,' said Lexi.

'So, are you two an item now? I know you've got history. Is history repeating itself?'

'No, it is not. And we don't have history, we only met the once.'

Theresa looked at her sharply. 'If you say so.'

Luckily there was no time to say any more as the sister in charge of the nursing staff that day told her team where she wanted them to work.

Lexi was assigned to a young woman called Shelley who had been brought to A&E having been found on the street, unconscious. She'd taken a mixture of drugs and alcohol, but it wasn't certain if her overdose had been accidental, as she had tried to take her own life before. She was unhappy about being in hospital and was threatening to discharge herself. She had been medically treated and was still vomiting, but they were waiting for the Mental Health Team to assess her and decide on further treatment.

Lexi's heart sank. Her job was to try to persuade the patient to stay as she needed to be looked after. Shelley was a regular; another "revolving door" patient and was aggressive when she didn't get her own way. She drank too much and swore like a trooper. All of which Lexi was used to from the patients, many of whom had issues that she couldn't imagine having to deal with.

Lexi wasn't good with that side of nursing. She liked the excitement and drama of trauma nursing but wasn't especially happy with the mental health side. She had no confidence in her ability to talk to people and knew that nothing she could say to Shelley would make any difference if the woman had made her mind up to go.

Having spent most of the morning with her patient, getting nowhere, Lexi was relieved when Casey stuck his head around the side of the cubicle curtain.

'Hi, how are you doing?'

'Who're you?' Shelley asked.

'Dr Casey O'Connor, I'm one of the consultants here.'

Shelley looked him up and down. 'Casey; that's a strange name for a man.'

'It's Irish and it means alert and watchful. You know Ben Affleck, the actor?'

Shelley nodded and looked slightly less suspicious.

'He has a brother called Casey.'

'And are you?' Shelley asked.

'Am I what, Shelley?'

'Alert and watchful.'

Casey laughed, and Lexi felt the familiar tingles up and down her spine whenever she heard that sound. He was being his most charming and Lexi remembered how it felt to be on the receiving end of Casey's charisma.

'I do my best.' His voice was deep and resonant, and Lexi

shivered. Shelley was smiling now, and Lexi was relieved at the transformation. Casey had got through to her after five minutes whereas she had failed after trying for a couple of hours. She needed to leave them alone, so Casey could work his magic.

'Shall I get you some tea?' She spoke to Casey who answered for them both.

'That would be lovely, wouldn't it Shelley?' He pulled up a chair to the side of Shelley's bed. 'Milk and two sugars, please.'

'Right.' She left the cubicle with a sigh and went to make them tea. She could have got it from the vending machine in a paper cup but decided that this occasion called for special treatment. Shelley needed to know she was cared for and a mug with properly made tea would give her that message. Sometimes it was the small things that mattered to a person, especially when they were feeling vulnerable.

She inhaled the aroma of orange and smiled. Casey was such an enigma. As trauma team leader he was assertive, unemotional and efficient. Yet he cared about the well-being of his staff and their patients, and was sitting talking to a frightened, introverted young girl as if he had all the time in the world.

She hoped that Jade would grow up to be as caring as her father.

The thought of Jade made her think about the difficult task ahead of her. She couldn't put it off any longer. She needed to tell her daughter that Casey was her father. How would

Jade react? Kids could be so unpredictable.

When she went back to the cubicle with the tea, Casey and Shelley were talking quietly together. Her patient looked more relaxed, and even thanked her. She slipped out of the cubicle and left them to it.

As she was nearing the end of her shift, Casey strolled towards her. He was straight and to the point.

'Have you told Jade yet?'

'I'm going to do it today. I'm off duty now, so I'll pick the kids up as Jess will still be at work. I'll tell her when we get home.'

'Really?' Casey beamed, and Lexi felt a stab of guilt that she had left it so long. It meant so much to him.

'In fact, would you like to join us for tea tonight? We won't have anything fancy, probably just fish fingers.'

'I love fish fingers. Thanks, Lexi. What time?'

'About six.'

'Great. See you later.' She watched him stroll off and could have sworn he had more of a bounce in his step.

*

Once Craig was ensconced in front of the TV with a bowl of grapes with banana and apple slices, watching his favourite children's TV programme, Lexi took Jade into the kitchen and sat her down at the kitchen table. She put a bowl of fruit and a glass of milk in front of her. The doll that Casey had brought her was sitting on her knee and Jade pretended to feed her fruit before putting it in her own mouth.

'I need to tell you something, sweetie.' Jade watched her

with eyes so much like her father's that she sighed. 'You remember I told you that your daddy had to go away for work?'

'Yeah.' Jade put a grape in her mouth and chewed.

'Well, he's come back now and wants to get to know you.' She waited anxiously for Jade's reaction.

'Where is he?'

'Remember when I went out to dinner with a man, a doctor?'

'The man that gave me Bluebell?' She picked her doll up and put her on the kitchen table.

'Yes, his name is Casey O'Connor and he's your daddy.'

'Oh.' Jade thought for a moment and then said. 'Is he going to live with us?'

'No, darling, he has his own home, but he is going to have tea with us tonight. Is that okay with you?'

'Will he bring me another present?'

'He might, but you mustn't expect him to buy you something every time he sees you. Daddies aren't just about presents, they're about…' She had to stop and think. She had never known her father and the men in the foster families she had briefly stayed with had never felt like real family to her. What were daddies about? She didn't know, but Jade was waiting expectantly for her to finish her sentence. 'Well, he'll be your friend and want to talk to you and take you out to nice places.'

'Will he play with me? Craig never plays with me much.'

'Yes, your daddy will definitely want to play with you.'

'Mummy? Is Daddy going to go away again?'

She would give him the benefit of the doubt. 'No darling, Daddy won't go away again. He is going to stay here, in Leytonsfield.'

'With us?'

'Well, like I say, he'll have his own home, but we'll see him a lot.' This wasn't the time to tell her about her extended family. One shock at a time. She didn't look shocked, in fact, she looked completely unconcerned. Maybe she needed to let the news sink in, and questions would follow later.

'What are we having for tea?'

'Fish fingers.'

'Yay! My favourite. Can I go and watch TV now please?'

'Of course you can, Jade, but can I have a hug first?'

Her daughter ran to her and hugged her. She kissed the top of her head, thankful that what she thought would be an onerous task had turned out to be relatively easy. This was only the beginning. Meeting Casey's family would be a lot hard.

Chapter Seven

The doorbell rang on the dot of six.

'I'll get it,' shouted Lexi as she hurried to the front door. Jade followed her, clutching Bluebell tightly.

Casey stood on the doorstep holding an enormous white box. She was glad to see that he had dressed down in blue jeans and a black T-shirt, but still managed to look smoking hot. She wore jeans too but had put on one of her prettiest blouses with cap sleeves and lace around the neck.

'Hi, come in.'

'Hi. Have you told her?'

'Hi Daddy!' said Jade, peeping out from behind Lexi's legs.

Casey's face changed from anxious concern to a huge grin and Lexi thought she detected a sheen over those beautiful green eyes. All designed to increase her feelings of guilt at not telling Jade sooner. The job was done now and the two of them could get to know each other. One hurdle down, another to go. She wasn't going to think about meeting the O'Connors yet. That was for another day.

'This is for all of you,' said Casey handing the box to Jess who took it into the kitchen to open it.

Casey knelt in front of Jade. 'Hi, Baby, can your Daddy have a hug?'

Jade looked at Lexi who nodded. She held out her doll.

'Bluebell needs one too.'

'Bluebell, that's a beautiful name.'

'It's 'cos of her blue dress.'

'Wow, what a clever girl to think up such a good name.'

'Mummy helped too. A bit.' Jade was obviously enjoying the attentions of her daddy. And who could blame her? Lexi knew exactly how enticing Casey's attention could be.

'Well, let me hug you both together.' He gently enfolded Jade and Bluebell in his big, strong arms and Lexi felt a pang of longing. It was an irresistible combination in a man; a mixture of gentleness and strength. The promise of protection and tender, loving care. Suddenly she was overwhelmed with gratitude that Jade had her father in her life. Casey would always be there to look after her.

Following closely on the heels of gratitude, however, came the shadow of fear. What if Jade came to love Casey more than she loved her? That was stupid. She was her mother. Jade would always love her. Love wasn't rationed; there was enough to go around.

'Wow! Look at the size of this…' Jess's voice from the

kitchen made them all turn in that direction.

Casey stood up and laughed. 'I wasn't sure what to bring, but I saw that in the window and couldn't resist.'

'This certainly didn't come from the shop I work in,' Jess said.

'No. I was in Knutsford today and went to an exclusive cake shop there.'

'I've seen some big cakes, but this is massive. Black Forest Gateau guys. Come and look.'

The cake was in three layers with cream and cherries in the middle and chocolate icing.

'Does it have alcohol?' Lexi knew the children shouldn't eat it if it did, but they had already seen it and denying them a piece now would be a disaster. The evening was starting out so well, too.

'No, luckily it's a non-alcoholic version.'

'Good man,' said Jess and put the cake in a safe place.

'Do you want to see our bedroom?' Jade obviously wanted to get her daddy's attention back where it belonged.

'I'd love to, sweetie.' Jade took Casey's large hand in her tiny one and led him towards the stairs.

'Come on then. You have to be careful on the stairs as they're steep.'

Lexi watched them climb the wooden stairs ever so carefully, still holding hands, Jade chattering happily all the way up.

Jess was watching her with a smile on her face. 'Going well so far.'

'Yes. Long may it last.' She felt relief but couldn't shake off a slight feeling of unease. She didn't know Casey well and he was now alone in the bedroom Jade shared with Craig. She was sure it would all be fine. Father and daughter would soon be inseparable. Casey was kind, gentle and loving to Jade. It had been obvious, too, by the reaction of the little girl, that she was impressed with her new daddy.

So, what was bothering her? She was feeling left out. Surplus to requirements. It had just been the two of them for so long. They were a team, and now there was a man in the mix. That was crazy. She had to shake this feeling. Jade needed to have a relationship with her father, and she needed to get out of the way and let it happen. She and Jade were rock-solid. Nothing would ever come between them. Not even a gorgeous hunk like Dr Casey O'Connor.

'Craig! Please set the table for me, pet.' Jess called to her son who was in his default position, in front of the TV.

'Why me?'

'Two reasons: one I'm asking you to and two, you won't get a piece of that delicious cake if you don't.'

Craig heaved a sigh and hauled himself upright. 'Oh, alright then.' He lumbered into the kitchen to collect the cutlery and a tablecloth. They didn't usually bother with a cloth, but today they had a special guest.

'I'll help you,' said Lexi. After all, she had nothing else to do at that moment. She wished she could be a fly on the wall to hear what Casey and Jade were talking about.

*

'I wish I had my own bedroom, I hate sharing with a boy.'

'But you like Craig?' Casey sat on the edge of the bottom

bunk, being careful not to bump his head on the top bunk. Their sleeping arrangements weren't ideal. Craig was eight already, and he remembered himself at that age. He'd had his own bedroom and would have hated having to share, especially with a girl.

Craig seemed an amiable enough kid, absorbed in his own world of computer games, but what would happen in a year or so? Jade would need her own bedroom.

'My best friends are Matilda and Jasmine. Matilda's got a new daddy and he's going to be living with them.'

'Oh. That's nice. What happened to Matilda's old daddy?'

'He left. Her mummy didn't like him anymore.'

'Oh.' Casey was at a loss how to respond but Jade didn't seem to notice, she chattered away, seemingly delighted to have a captive audience. And such an attentive one at that. She showed him her toys, her clothes, the pictures she'd drawn at nursery, and then came to sit next to him on the bunk.

'Do you like mummy?'

'Oh yes, very much.' At least he could answer that question.

'Does Mummy like you?'

'Ah …Yes, I think so.'

'Good, 'cos I don't want you to go away again like Matilda's old daddy did.'

'Oh, darling.' He picked her up and put her on his knee, holding her tight and relishing the feel of her softness and her sweet scent. 'I am never going to go away, I promise. I'll always be here for you, whenever you want me. Okay?'

She nodded, and he hugged her tighter.

*

'Do you like fish fingers, Daddy?' Jade asked him. She was sitting next to him at the table on a chair with two cushions.

'I love fish fingers.' He wasn't used to being called "Daddy". It would take a while to adapt to his new role. He was determined that he was going to be the best father a kid ever had. Jade was a delight, with a quick mind and the sign already of a cheeky side to her nature. She giggled a lot, especially when she was stretching the truth about how accomplished she was at everything.

He remembered his nephew, Tom, being the same at three years old. Eager to tell everyone that "I can do this" and "I can do that". It was a natural stage in a child's life.

Jade looked like her mother but had bags more confidence than Lexi seemed to have.

'So, Craig, do you like sport?' He was determined not to leave the other child out this evening, but Craig was non-committal and seemed to want to be left out of the conversation.

'Not much.'

'So, what do you like?'

'Computer games and watching TV.'

'What about you?' Jess interrupted, maybe trying to protect her son from further questioning. 'What were you good at when you were a kid?'

'Swimming. I swam for my school and won a few medals.'

'I can swim,' said Jade. He looked at Lexi who was

grinning and shaking her head.

'No, she can't,' Lexi mouthed silently.

'How about you two?' he asked Jess and Craig.

Craig shook his head and looked down at his plate.

'I can doggie paddle,' Jess said. 'It wasn't something the children's home thought was an important skill.'

Casey took two pieces of bread and butter and carefully put two fish fingers in between with a squirt of tomato sauce to make a sandwich. He was so engrossed in what he was doing and thinking about a plan that he was sketching in his mind, that he hadn't realized everyone had stopped eating and was watching him.

'Am I breaking a rule of etiquette? Is this not allowed?' He was conscious of being in Lexi and Jess's home, and in the company of their children. Maybe they had rules he didn't know about.

Jess started laughing and Craig grabbed two pieces of bread and copied him.

'We always make fish finger sandwiches,' said Lexi, 'but didn't know whether it was the "done thing", she sketched quote marks around the words in the air with her fingers, 'so we told the kids not to do it today.'

'Oh, I would say it's definitely the "done thing". The four of us always did it when we were kids.'

'It's the best way to eat them,' Jess said as she followed the others.

'As long as the kids eat the peas as well.' Lexi replied.

Casey was enjoying himself with this little family but was

determined that he would enforce a few rules of his own where his daughter was concerned.

'I think Jade should learn to swim,' he said in between bites of his sandwich, 'the children's home are wrong, it's an essential skill. In fact, I think all of you should have swimming lessons and I can arrange that with the leisure centre I belong to.'

'Oh, I don't think…' Lexi began.

'Cool!' Craig said, showing more animation than he had all evening.

'I'd love to learn to swim, I've always wanted to.' Jess looked across at Lexi. 'If you're sure.'

'Right, that's settled then. If you're not doing anything on Saturday how about coming to the Family Fun Day there and we can book you in for lessons? Riordan's taking Tom, so he can book Jess and Craig in as guests and I'll book you and Jade. I'm going to upgrade my membership to a Family and Friends one anyway as they have plenty of events I'd love to take Jade to.'

'What Daddy?' Jade was jumping up and down on her seat with excitement.

'Oh, there's lots of things for kids. Zumba, street dance, football…'

Everyone looked happy except Lexi who was glaring at him.

'Jade's too young for all that, Casey, she's only three, and I don't need lessons.'

'I'm three and a half,' said Jade with a mouth full of peas.

'I started swimming as a toddler. The younger they start,

the better. Trust me, Lexi, it'll be alright. She'll be perfectly safe. In fact, on Saturday, I'll take her in the pool with me and introduce her to the water gently.'

'Let me think about it.'

Chapter Eight

Jess and the kids relaxed in front of the TV while Casey helped Lexi wash up. They didn't have a dishwasher, so Lexi washed, and Casey dried. She was aware of him as they stood side-by-side in the tiny kitchen. He was so tall and male, he seemed to fill the small space with his physical presence.

He must have noticed her animosity as she was still smarting from his high jacking of their Saturday. How did he know they hadn't already made plans? They hadn't, of course, but that wasn't the point. He was right, of course, Jade did need to learn to swim and she couldn't teach her. Casey had won medals for swimming so who better than her Daddy? But she'd be watching from the sidelines; in fact, she wasn't going to take her eyes off her daughter on Saturday.

She glanced at Casey. He had his head down, drying a plate thoroughly, with a half-smile on his lips. The lips that had touched every inch of her that special night that Jade was conceived. She wondered what he was thinking about. Despite her overwhelming attraction to this man, she had to see him as Jade's father and nothing else. And they needed to be civil to each other for their daughter's sake.

'I haven't asked you how Shelley is. Did she open up to you at all?'

'Eventually. We ended up having quite a chat. It's the usual story. She's eighteen and living with a group of people who are highly dependent on drugs. Parents disowned her when she became pregnant-'

'I didn't know she was a mother.'

'She isn't. She had a miscarriage. Boyfriend dumped her. And even after the hell she went through, her parents didn't want her back. So, she drifted to the centre of town and lives in a squat.'

'Poor kid. As if life isn't hard enough.' Lexi's heart went out to the frightened young woman. 'No wonder she doesn't trust people.'

'Exactly. Anyway, I made her promise to cut down on the drink and drugs and eat properly.'

'Do you think she will?'

'Your guess is as good as mine. All we can do, as health professionals, is warn her of the danger if she doesn't look after herself and be there to pick up the pieces.'

'What about the suicide attempts?'

'I think they're just a cry for help. We need to keep an eye on her though. I doubt it's the last we've seen of her.'

Lexi put the last plate on the draining board. 'Would you like tea or coffee?'

'Tea please.'

Lexi filled the kettle and wondered what else to say. Work seemed to be a safe topic. Better stay with that. 'So, how's the essential oil experiment going?'

Casey laughed, and Lexi had a feeling a déjà vu. The first time she had heard that amazing sound was the night of the Summer Solstice Ball. She had never heard anyone laugh like he did. A deep rumbling like a bass drum that vibrated through her body liquidizing her insides. It made her want to throw herself at him and kiss him senseless. To stop herself doing anything so reckless, she moved away from him and collected the mugs, pouring milk for Craig and Jade.

'It's going amazingly well. I've had some positive feed-back already but can't wait to see what people say when they fill in the questionnaires. They're anonymous so staff can be as rude as they like.'

'What made you think of it?'

'I want to get the Complementary Therapy Team involved in our patients' care. There's so much they can offer people who are frightened and in pain. It's something I've been thinking of doing for years.'

'You surprise me,' Lexi said as she poured the tea into white mugs and added milk and sugar, 'I had you down for the no-nonsense fix-'em-up and move-'em-out kind of trauma consult-ant. Oils and massages don't really fit that image.'

Casey leant back against the counter and crossed his arms.

'When I was a young doctor – junior house-officer to be precise – I did my first stint in A&E, which is when I knew that was where I wanted to work.' Lexi handed him a mug and sat at the kitchen table, sipping her tea and listening. She could never grow tired of hearing him talk. He spoke quietly but eloquently, and it wasn't long before she was spell-bound.

'The consultant-in-charge that day told me to go and sit with a lady who was deteriorating rapidly with chronic heart failure and wasn't going to make it. We were just keeping her comfortable as there was nothing we could do for her. I was horrified. I was there to save lives, or so I thought. I wanted to be in the thick of it like on the movies, people pulled back from the brink – that kind of thing.'

Lexi nodded. She, too, had harboured dreams of being a hero before she discovered the reality of A&E.

'The last thing I wanted to do was to waste the morning with a patient I couldn't help and who was ninety if she was a day. Her husband had died, they'd never had children and she was alone, having outlived the few relatives she'd had. The nurses were too busy to stay with her apparently. You can imagine how resentful I felt?'

Lexi nodded. She could picture the angry, restless young man he must have been at that age.

'Anyway, I went into the cubicle and she smiled at me. She had a lovely smile. She reminded me a bit of my Gran.' Casey stared off into space, remembering. 'I asked her if there was something I could do for her and she pointed to a bottle of hand-cream on the cabinet next to the bed. So, I put some in the palm of my hands and started to gently rub it into her hands. Her skin was like paper and I was terrified I'd tear it or hurt her in some way. But she whispered that it felt lovely, so, I just kept doing it. I did it properly, massaging it into her fingers and wrists. She talked to me about her home, her husband and their life together, all the people she'd loved and lost. Then she stopped talking, closed her eyes and just lay there with a beautiful smile on her face.

'So, I kept rubbing in the hand-cream. On her forearms, her feet, her legs. Over and over. Her body gradually relaxed and I wasn't even aware that she had died until I realized how cold she had become.'

Lexi couldn't speak, so let the tears fall down her cheek. Casey didn't notice, however; he was back there in that hospital with the old lady, reliving the memories.

'I learnt two things that day; one, that patients deserve a good death as much as they do a good life and two, the power of human touch. So, you see, Lexi, essential oils, massage, visualization and relaxation techniques are as much a part of treating our patients as medication and surgery.'

Lexi was wiping her face and blowing her nose when Casey walked over and kissed her on the top of the head. 'Sorry, didn't mean to upset you, I get carried away sometimes.'

The feel of his hands on her face suddenly and his mouth moving towards hers made her forget where she was until a little voice said, 'Daddy? Are you kissing Mummy?'

They both jumped as Jade came into the kitchen for her milk, but Casey recovered well and said, 'Yes, that's okay, isn't it?'

'You must kiss me too. And Bluebell.'

'Okeydokey. If you two ladies would like to step this way…' Jade dissolved into fits of giggles as Casey puckered up and scooped her up in his arms.

*

To be able to tuck Jade up in her bed and read her a bedtime story was something Casey had yearned to do ever since he had found out that she was his daughter. He read to Tom on occasion; stories out of the Marvel Universe, Doctor Who and Harry Potter. Three-year-old girls were different. Or so he had thought. Judging by the books that she wanted him to read, they weren't that much different at all. Caterpillars, bears and dragons seemed to feature quite heavily.

He must rid himself of his gender stereotyping and take his cue from his little girl. Maybe he should ask Lexi about it. Jade was obviously very feminine with her pretty face and long blonde hair but that didn't mean she would grow up to be a model. She could just as easily become a politician or an astronaut.

'Daddy, you're not reading.'

'Sorry chick, just drifted off for a minute.'

'Are you tired?'

'No, sweetie, just lost concentration there for a second. Now, where were we?' Jade snuggled down in the bed and hugged Bluebell to her.

It took three books; one that she wanted to hear twice, before she finally fell asleep. He kissed her gently on the forehead and crept down the stairs.

Lexi was sitting on the sofa on her own sipping a glass of wine. On the coffee table in front of her sat three large photo albums. His heart jumped when he saw them. Hopefully, these were photos of Jade as a baby. Now he could fill in the gaps and picture her first three years.

Lexi poured him a glass of wine and he took it from her, their hands just touching briefly, which sent a shiver through him. He sat close to her on the sofa.

'Thought you might like to see these. They're just happy snaps but some of them are quite good.'

'Thanks. I'd love that. I want to thank you for tonight; it's been wonderful. Jade's a beautiful little girl and you've done a great job of bringing her up.'

Lexi put her head down and blushed. 'Well, you are her father, and I feel bad about not being able to find you…'

'We're both to blame. I should have tried harder too.' When she looked up at him with her eyes the colour of Blue-bell's dress, he wanted to take her in his arms and kiss away the frown lines but that would be a bad idea. A very bad idea. They were Jade's parents, nothing more. Whatever remnants of the attraction they had felt for each other remained, it had to be squashed. It was in the past. They had been strangers then. Now, they needed to behave like responsible adults and get to know each other as friends and colleagues.

'Where's Jess?' He took a sip of his wine.

'Having a soak in the tub.'

Good. Then they wouldn't be disturbed. They could talk freely and discuss Jade's future, but first, he was longing to look at his daughter as a baby. He opened the first album and was quickly engrossed in the photos. Lexi talked him through them, explaining where they were and how old Jade was in each photo.

'Does she look like you as a baby?'

Lexi went quiet and looked down. 'I wouldn't know.'

'Don't you have any pictures of your childhood?'

'No. Some of my foster families took pictures but they kept them for themselves. The home didn't bother with things like that.'

Casey put his glass down and closed the album putting it on the coffee table to look at later. He moved closer to Lexi and placed his arm along the back of the sofa but didn't touch her.

'That must have been tough. Do you want to talk about it?' He wanted her to talk to him, but Lexi was still putting barriers up against him and he wasn't sure why. Maybe she thought he wanted to rekindle the fire they had experienced at Jade's conception and was trying to send him signals that she didn't approve. He would have to extend the hand of friendship to her and let her know that he wasn't interested in her in that way. Even though it wasn't strictly true. He still wanted her in his bed but could never trust a woman enough to let her into his heart.

'Not really. There's nothing much to say.' Her voice was sad, and he desperately wanted her to feel better about herself.

'It sometimes helps to talk. But only if you want to.'

'People always assume that others have had the same

experiences they have had. They take things for granted. Growing up without parents is isolating. You're different. You stand out from the crowd because you're not like everyone else. It's okay as an adult, but a constant source of pain as a child.'

'In what way?' He spoke quietly to encourage her to keep talking.

'In primary school, every Mother's Day and Father's Day we had to make cards for our parents and say how special they were. I remember one class where the teacher made us write a poem to our mothers telling them why we loved them. What could I say? She gave me up a few hours after I was born. When I told the teacher why I couldn't write the poem she made me tidy the classroom instead. All the kids were scribbling away busily, and I was sweeping the floor.'

Casey felt anger at the insensitive teacher who hadn't had the sense to tell Lexi to write a poem to someone else; a friend perhaps. Then she would have been doing the same as the other kids, but to a different person. Casey put his arm around Lexi's shoulder and hugged her to him in an instinctive gesture of comfort. She put her head on his shoulder and he inhaled the clean smell of her shampoo.

'Then there was Easter, Christmas, parents' evenings. I was in a nativity play once but there was no one in the audience who had come to see me, amongst all the proud parents taking videos and smiling through their tears. I'm going to make damned sure I go to everything that Jade takes part in when she starts school.'

'I'll be there too,' he said.

'Thanks. Jade will be like all the other kids then. I don't want her to feel different like I did.'

Casey felt deeply moved by her story which was the complete opposite to his childhood. 'You must have felt desperately lonely.' His voice croaked, and he surprised himself at the depth of protectiveness he felt towards her. She was his child's mother and he wanted to look after them both.

Without stopping to think, he turned her face to his and gently kissed her on the lips. At first, she didn't move but then she responded, and her mouth opened to him. He had forgotten how luscious she tasted, and his kiss grew more demanding. He held the back of her head, his fingers caressing the skin on the nape of her neck, then his hand slid down her front to stroke her breast through the fabric of her blouse.

She gasped but didn't push him away, so he undid the buttons and cupped her breast, feeling her nipple grow hard at his touch.

Their kiss grew more frantic and he felt his body react, pushing against the zip of his jeans. His breathing deepened, and she moaned softly as he caressed her.

A door opened upstairs, and Lexi put her hand on his arm to stop him.

'Jess has finished her bath. Don't worry she won't come down; she'll go straight to bed.'

The interruption had given him a chance to think. The sudden fire that had exploded in his belly had shown him that he still wanted her as much as ever. And her response proved that she felt the same way. But they couldn't. It would bring too many complications into their fledgling friendship. They had to think of Jade and keep their hands off each other. He felt ashamed of his inappropriate behavior and wanted to reassure Lexi that she could trust him.

'Things will be different for you now. You and Jade. I'll look after you both. Jade will have two loving parents to be there for her at every school event in her life. And every other time she needs us. You're not alone anymore.'

She stood up and glared at him, her hands on her hips, her blouse still undone.

'Jade and I are fine, Casey, we don't need looking after. We were fine before you turned up and we'll be fine afterwards. I will always be there for her, no matter who else she has in her life. I'm glad you want a relationship with her, but don't think anything has changed.'

Casey stood up too and held his hand out to her, but she ignored it. 'I'm sorry... I didn't mean to upset you. I was just trying to-'

'Yes, I know what you were trying to do. Take charge. But this isn't A&E and you're not in charge of us. And, while we're on the subject, I'd be grateful if you run any ideas you have by me before you get the kids all excited. We'll go to the leisure centre on Saturday, but please ask me first before you start making arrangements for Jade.'

Chastened, Casey dropped his hand and nodded. 'Right. Sorry. Got it. I'll ask you first.'

'Thanks, I'd appreciate that.'

They stood in the centre of the room, not touching, the

magic of the kiss forgotten. Time to go. Lexi saw him to the door, and he thanked her politely for the evening and told her the time he would pick them up on Saturday.

As he drove away, he couldn't help feeling admiration for Lexi. She was beautiful, soft and sweet, with a rod of iron running down her back. She had learned to look after herself and her daughter. She was a force to be reckoned with. Not the man-eater he had assumed she was when they had first met, but a strong woman who just wanted the best for her child. There was a depth to Lexi Grainger that he could only guess at.

If things had been different, and he thought he could risk his heart in the hands of another woman, she would be the one he'd choose. As it was, they could be close in different ways. Parents to their little girl, work colleagues and, hopefully, friends.

Chapter Nine

Lexi inhaled the scent of lime when she arrived in A&E to start her shift at six o'clock the following evening. It was the first night of a three-week stint and she braced herself for the usual ebb and flow of patients during a long and undoubtedly eventful stretch of night duty.

As she walked through the front doors and headed to the staff room to put her bag in her locker, she gazed at the people in the waiting area, some were in couples or on their own. Others seemed to have brought their entire family with them.

Was it her imagination, or did the patients looked slightly less stressed than usual? She wanted Casey's experiment to be successful but suspected it would have more effect on the staff than the patients themselves. But even if that were the case, it would still be worth doing.

Casey had texted her that afternoon and asked if it was

okay for him to supervise Jade's bedtime that night and read her some more stories. He had some books that used to belong to Tom that he wanted to show her. How could she refuse? Jade never stopped talking about her father and it would take some of the pressure off Jess.

After listening to the handover from the day staff, she headed to minors with Sarala who was going to be working with her.

'What do you think of my nails?' the nurse asked, stretching out her long, slender brown fingers, tipped by short nails painted in coral pink polish. Both the backs of her hands and her palms were covered with exquisite henna designs. Sarala had spent the weekend at a Hindu wedding and was still buzzing from the excitement and romance of it all. Lexi wondered if she had slept before coming on duty.

'They're absolutely gorgeous, as are the Mehndi. Will you do some for me?'

'Only when you get married, then I will.' Sarala laughed and checked the cubicle they were in to make sure it was well stocked.

'What about you? I bet you get married first.'

'Not until I find the perfect man and that could take some time.' She laughed again, the sound like wind chimes in a breeze. Lexi loved working with Sarala, she was always so upbeat.

'I'll never get married. Jade and I are fine as we are.' She refused to think about Casey, but Sarala had no such qualms.

'What about your daughter's father, the scrumptious Dr

O'Connor? I've seen the way he looks at you when you're looking away. I bet he'd marry you. After all, he's already sampled the goods so knows exactly what he'd be getting.' All her colleagues now knew about her relationship with Casey.

'Sarala! Inappropriate. Anyway, we had one night together. Neither of us had any intention of seeing the other one again. We're civil to each other now for Jade's sake.'

'Babies change everything. Ask my sister, she's pregnant with number four.'

It was time to change the subject and to start treating the patients, so Lexi gave Sarala a look which Sarala returned with a grin and a huge wink.

The first hour or so passed swiftly. She stitched the finger of an eighty-year-old man who had cut it open on a knife. She helped a little girl who was having an asthma attack and who had to be admitted for observation.

Then there was an elderly man who had fainted in the supermarket; he lived alone and hadn't eaten for two days. On further questioning, the senior registrar, the most senior doctor on duty that night, decided that the man had early-onset Alzheimer's and he was admitted to the geriatric ward.

After that, Lexi and the other nurses, including the more qualified and experienced nurse clinicians, ran Minors almost without doctors. They were needed in Majors and Resus. There's always a shortage of senior doctors in A&E, especially at night.

The waiting time for patients to be seen had been two

hours when Lexi had started her shift, but by midnight, with the arrival of drunks, drug addicts and domestic violence victims, it had increased to three. The triage nurses were busy. Ambulances arrived in steady succession bringing in more and more patients.

Lexi had been looking forward to not seeing Casey at work for a while, to get her thoughts together and to avoid the overwhelming distraction he caused when he was anywhere near her. But now, with the waiting area filling up, all the resus beds full and a constant stream of patients waiting to be seen, she longed for his familiar confidence, strength and charismatic leadership. There really was no one like Dr Casey O'Connor for making the patients and his team feel that they were in the hands of a competent leader.

And those hands! The magic they could bring about when they were engaged in more intimate activities. Lexi pushed that image out of her head and went to call the next patient.

By two o'clock in the morning, Lexi was tired and frustrated. One of the drunk patients had urinated on the floor and she decided to mop it up herself instead of waiting for the cleaner who had been called to another area.

All she wanted was a cup of tea and a sit down but knew that she wouldn't get either for several hours. She passed Sarala as they rushed down the corridor in opposite directions. Her friend raised her eyes to heaven and muttered, 'Why are we doing this to ourselves?' But they both knew the answer to that. Because they loved nursing and couldn't imagine being anywhere else.

At four o'clock, the paramedics brought in a familiar figure. It was Shelley who looked as if she had been beaten up. Her face was bruised and dirty, she had blood dripping from a scalp wound and she was either drunk or on drugs. As she had no life-threatening injuries and was fully conscious, she was put in a cubicle in Minors after being examined by the triage nurse. She needed to be monitored closely and Lexi was the only nurse available to do it.

'Hi, Shelley. Remember me? I looked after you last time you came in.'

Shelley opened one bloodshot eye and glared at her. 'Where's that doctor?'

There was no use pretending she didn't know who Shelley meant. 'Do you mean Dr O'Connor? He will be back on duty tomorrow. It's four o'clock in the morning, Shelley.'

Why do some patients think doctors should be on call twenty-four hours a day? Don't they realise that they also need to eat, sleep, live a life… Oh, what was the point? She was tired, that was all. It had been a long, stressful night and it wasn't over. She knew she wouldn't get anywhere with Shelley who was already trying to clamber off the narrow bed. She'd need to put the sides up to keep her from falling and breaking something.

'No, honey, don't do that. Get back on the bed and I'll treat that wound, it looks nasty.'

'Want that doctor. Get him. Now!' Lexi's spirits sank at the belligerent tone of voice that Shelley used. She was not going to be pacified easily. Lexi may even have to call security if she got violent.

'I tell you what, let me look at your wound and as soon as Dr O'Connor comes on duty, I'll tell him you're here. Have you eaten anything today?'

'Take your hands off me… get him now or I'm off.'

Lexi was just about ready to give up when Sarala stuck her head around the curtain. 'Ah, Shelley,' she said, 'I thought I heard your dulcet tones. Right. I'm going to clean you up and I don't want to hear any more nonsense from you. And this nurse is going to have a well-earned break. Aren't you?'

Lexi could have hugged Sarala with gratitude as she pushed her out of the cubicle with the strict instructions to go and have a cup of tea and a biscuit.

When she was in the staff room, huddled on a chair, cradling her mug of welcome tea, she wondered why she couldn't cope with patients as well as Sarala and Casey did. Was it because she'd had little experience of being the assertive one? In the children's home and foster homes, she'd been quiet and obedient, knowing that flying under the radar was the best way to survive. The more attention you drew to yourself, the more trouble was sure to follow.

Even during her nurse training, she went along with the crowd, not wanting to suggest anything in case people laughed at her or thought her stupid. But when she had Jade, the realisation that this tiny human relied on her for everything, stiffened her backbone and she started to stand up for herself. So why couldn't she ever be strong in front of the patients instead of adopting a maid-servant role?

Maybe she needed assertiveness training. It would help

her at work and where Dr Casey O'Connor was concerned too. She couldn't let him walk all over her, making plans for Jade without her input, and thinking he was running the show. She'd talk to her manager about it.

Lexi drained the last drop of her tea, rinsed and dried the mug and put it back in the cupboard. She sighed. Back to the fray.

The last two hours of her shift passed uneventfully and relatively quickly. Before she left A&E, she looked in on Shelley who was fast asleep with a blanket over her head. Lexi carefully lifted the corner of the blanket to check on her. She snored slightly with her mouth open. The bruises were livid against her pale complexion, but she was sleeping peacefully. Poor kid. She looked so young and helpless. Lexi wished there was something she could do for her. Hopefully, a social worker would speak to her before she was discharged. And she was known to the Mental Health Team. Maybe between them, they could get her some help.

She covered Shelley's face again and tiptoed out.

*

It was quiet when she let herself into the cottage. They would all still be asleep. In another hour Jess would get the kids up and make them breakfast. Lexi was too tired to even wash her face. She was going to get undressed and crawl into bed. Oblivion, that was what she craved.

When she opened her bedroom door, she looked over at her bed to see that someone had beaten her to it. A male someone by the size of the figure huddled in the centre of the queen size double, wrapped in a duvet with only the top of his head showing. He was lying in almost the same position Shelley had been, but his dark brown hair sticking out of the top of the duvet gave him away. It was Casey.

What the heck?! Why on earth was Casey in her bed? And what was she going to do about it? She should shake him awake and tell him to leave. She needed to sleep. Night duty was hard and extremely tiring. She'd worked almost eight hours straight before she'd managed to have any kind of a break and she should eat before sleeping but was just too damned tired. Sleep came first. Always.

Or, at least, it would do if she could shift her unwelcome guest who had crept, Goldilocks-style, into the bed that was just right, and fallen asleep.

She tiptoed closer and noticed the pile of clothes dropped carelessly in a heap on the floor: trousers, shirt, socks and briefs. A pair of black shoes peeped out from under the clothes. All belonging to Casey. Which meant one thing. Casey was completely naked under the duvet. Naked and curled up in the foetal position, warm and cosy and breathing deeply.

The thought made her heart race and her breath catch in her throat. The last time she had been near a naked Casey, they had been lost in a passionate embrace, his strong arms hugging her to him and his hot, tense flesh quivering at her touch. She remembered every second of that night and relived it over and over in her mind. And now, here he was, in her bed, naked and sexy.

She sat down on the edge of the bed and wondered what to do. The movement, however slight, must have been enough to wake him. He rolled over, stretched, then jumped as he caught her watching him.

'Oh. Hi.'

'Hi yourself. Comfy?'

Casey sat up, running his hands through his hair and making it stick up straight. 'Sorry, I didn't mean to stay all night, but I was so sleepy after reading Jade umpteen bedtime stories, that I thought I'd just catch forty winks.'

'Yes, that happens to me as well. Sometimes I fall asleep before she does.'

The duvet had slipped over Casey's hips as he had sat up. Lexi tried to keep her gaze from straying to his groin. She admired instead his firm chest muscles with the smattering of dark, wiry hair and his six-pack that flexed invitingly as he yawned. His body was just as delicious as she remembered it from four years ago. He kept himself in top condition. She wondered if it was down to the swimming.

'Anyway,' he said rubbing his eyes, 'you're back early, aren't you?'

'No, my shift finished half an hour ago. It's nearly seven o'clock.'

'Is it? Oh Crikey! I'm going to be late.' He made as if to push the duvet off him, then stopped and looked at her from under lowered lashes. 'Uh…'

She tried to hide a smile as Casey gazed at her in embarrassment.

'Is there a problem?'

'Well… it's just that… my clothes are on the floor and I'm… well…'

'Naked?' Lexi couldn't keep the glee out of her voice at the sight of Casey looking embarrassed. That was definitely a first for her. 'There's nothing there that I haven't seen before.' She knew she was being naughty, but it was her bed, and by rights, she should be fast asleep by now.

Casey's expression changed from shock, to confusion and finally a wicked grin spread across his face. 'Okay, since you insist.'

He pushed the duvet off himself and swung his legs over the side of the bed. He stood up slowly and faced her, his hands on his hips and his manhood on display for her perusal. The sight of Casey in all his glorious nakedness made her whimper. He was even more gorgeous than she remembered, if that were possible.

She gulped and stood up quickly with her back to him. That was far too much male beauty to be presented with before she went to sleep. Her dreams were erratic enough normally, but Heaven knows what they would be like now.

She heard him give a deep chuckle as he dressed.

'Shelley's back, by the way. She was asking for you. She had quite a bad cut on her scalp and bruises on her face.'

'Was she sober?'

'No. Far from it, in fact.'

'Damn. Okay, thanks. I'll go and see her.'

She turned to find him tucking his shirt into his trousers.

'Right. Your turn.'

'I have no intention of undressing in front of you, Casey.'

'But you made me expose myself to you. That's hardly fair, is it?'

'You were already naked, and it serves you right for sleeping in people's beds without permission.'

'So, if I ask nicely, will you let me sleep with you?' His grin was wicked, and Lexi knew she should stop whilst she was ahead. She was far too tired for sexual banter with the good doctor. Her brain was about to turn to mush if she didn't sleep soon.

'No, you cannot. Now, please go.'

Casey walked around the bed and held her face gently in his hands. She expected him to kiss her and wanted him to but dreaded it happening at the same time. If he did, they would both be back in her bed, naked, and sleep would be the last thing on their minds.

But he didn't. He kissed her softly on the forehead. She closed her eyes and listened to the sound of his rich voice, whilst trying to ignore the memory of his naked body, now thankfully, fully clothed.

'Sleep sweetly Angel. I'll pick you guys up at ten on Saturday for the Family Fun Day. Good thing you're not working Friday night. And don't worry, it *will* be fun.'

Then he was gone.

Lexi discarded her clothes and left them in a heap on the floor as Casey had done. She snuggled down under the duvet, enveloped by the scent of him that lingered on the linen, the warmth he had left behind in the bed comforting her. But the thought of his recent nudity sent erotic pictures flitting across her mind. She fell asleep with the image of a wicked smile below the most dazzling green eyes she had ever seen.

Chapter Ten

Casey woke early on Saturday morning with mixed feelings about the day ahead. He had always attended the summer Family Fun Day at the leisure centre with Riordan and Tom as he enjoyed his role of uncle and had taught his nephew to swim when the boy was still a toddler. This time, however, he would be attending the public event as a father. It would be his first time being a "Daddy" with the rest of the world watching. What if he stuffed it up? Did something wrong?

He had seen Riordan and Tom together often enough to know that the role of "daddy" wasn't the easiest one in the world to get right. Tom was a sensible little boy, willing to listen to reason, but Casey had seen his brother tearing his hair out on several occasions when Tom had wanted something he couldn't have, and Riordan had to put his foot down.

He needed to stop worrying. He'd signed up for this and

he was going to see it through to the end and make the best job of being a "daddy" that he could. He was lucky, he had his parents and siblings to lend a hand. He couldn't begin to imagine how Lexi had coped on her own for the past four years. She had no one except Jess, who was a great friend, that much was obvious, but nothing could beat the love and support of blood relatives and he couldn't wait to introduce Jade to his family.

As he drove to the cottage, he thought about Shelley. She had discharged herself before he had managed to talk to her again and he feared for the young woman's safety. She appeared to have no family in her life but, unlike Lexi, she wasn't coping and was drowning in a sea of poverty and, quite possibly, domestic abuse. He'd already spoken to the Mental Health Team to see if there was a hostel they could get her into. Provided she'd go, of course.

When he pulled up outside Lexi and Jess's home, Jade was in the window seat, kneeling up, her nose pressed to the glass. She waved when she saw him, and he felt a rush of love so strong he had to take deep breaths before he got out of the car.

The front door opened, Jade came hurtling out, and flung herself into his arms. 'Daddy, I've got my cossie on. D'you wanna see?'

When he had duly inspected her swimming costume, he'd carried her into the house to be met by three people, bags, towels and other paraphernalia, all ready for a family day out.

'Are you guys ready?' he asked trying to ignore the storm clouds that had gathered over Lexi's head. She was obviously unhappy about something. Maybe she'd relax more when they arrived at the venue.

'We've been ready for hours,' Craig said as he picked up one of the bags and carried it outside.

'Right. Let's go then.'

It took twenty minutes to get the kids in their child seats in the back and store the bags in the boot as, every time they seemed to have settled, one of them wanted to go back into the cottage for something. Jade wanted the toilet. Craig had forgotten his headphones. Finally, they were on their way.

Casey gave an exaggerated sigh and laughed. 'Is it always like this?' he asked Lexi who was sitting in the passenger seat. Jess was squashed between the kids in the back but seemed perfectly content.

'Welcome to parenthood,' Lexi said dryly. She was frowning, and Casey decided to have it out with her before they went any further. He didn't want anything to spoil their family day out.

'Are you okay? You seem tense. Is something wrong?'

She turned anxious eyes in his direction. 'It is safe, isn't it? The pool, I mean. Jade's never been in a pool before, not even a baby one. I'm just concerned, that's all.'

So that was all that was bothering her. He hastened to reassure her. 'Of course it's safe. I won't let her out of my sight. There's four of us adults to three kids. Most kids don't get that level of supervision in the pool. She'll love it and so will you. Okay?'

He put his hand over hers and gave it a quick squeeze. He

was looking forward to seeing her in her swimming costume. Did she wear a bikini? Whatever she wore, she'd look fantastic. They were going to have a great day. Their first one as a family and he couldn't wait.

He remembered her face when she had seen him naked. She had turned away in feigned disgust, but not before he had seen the flare of lust in her eyes. Maybe she wanted him still. As much as she had the first night they met. As much as he still wanted her. Not that he was going to act on it, but it was still an ego-boost to know the strong attraction he remembered wasn't just a product of his fevered imagination.

Today would be a day for showing off. They would swim together, in skimpy costumes, their bodies wet and glistening. And today was also a chance for him to show off his prowess at swimming to Lexi and his daughter. He felt quite the macho man at the thought.

Yes. It was going to be a good day.

Chapter Eleven

'Daddy! There's a bouncy castle. Can I go on it?' Jade's excitement had reached fever pitch and Lexi feared that there would be tears before bedtime unless she managed to calm her down.

Casey had turned up at the cottage that morning looking happy and hot in knee-length camouflage shorts and a black polo shirt, his long, tanned legs rippling with muscle and looking incredibly sexy. She couldn't deny her attraction to him, much as she would have liked to.

Today, he'd be wearing a swimming costume – hopefully not one of the indecently brief versions – for some of the day, which would almost be as bad. She knew exactly what lay enticingly underneath the material of his costume, and her overactive imagination was perfectly capable of filling in the details. Casey was the sexiest, most desirable man she had ever known, and she would need all her powers of concentration to look after her daughter and ignore her growing desire for Jade's father. At least she wouldn't be getting in the water with him.

'Can I have my face painted, Daddy?' Jade was already asking for everything she saw around her. The grounds of the leisure centre hummed with activity as children ran around, signing up for classes and queuing to have their faces painted, join the junior Zumba class or enter the hula-hoop competition.

Lexi spotted a few of the parents from Jade's nursery and Jess was waving madly to some of the mothers of children Craig's age. It looked exactly what it advertised – a simple fun day filled with healthy and enjoyable activities for all the family. So, why did she feel such dread at the thought of going inside? Of course, she knew the answer to that one.

Jade was still entreating Casey to let her do everything at once. Should she intervene, or step back and see how Casey coped with his daughter's excited demands? It was something he was going to have to get used to and fast.

Luckily, Jade's attention was diverted elsewhere as Casey spotted his brother and nephew.

'Hi, guys,' he yelled and a tall, slim man with glasses and dark blond hair, holding the hand of a small boy, came over to them. Lexi recognized Dr Riordan O'Connor as the consultant cardiologist who attended A&E when he was on call but hadn't realized until recently that he was Casey's older brother. He smiled at her when he recognized her.

'Hi there, you must be Lexi, and who's this little lady?'

'Jade,' said her daughter shyly.

It struck home then that this day would be an emotional one for all of them. Riordan and Tom were meeting a member of their family who they hadn't even known existed until just recently. Casey was playing the proud father for all he was worth. Jess and Craig were having a nice mother and son day out and she… how was she supposed to feel? Was the anxiety that churned inside making her feel slightly sick and hot all over, a normal reaction? It was if you suffered from a phobia.

To take her mind off her symptoms, she concentrated on Riordan and Tom, but that just brought home the guilt feelings she couldn't shake; she should have tried harder to find Casey when she had discovered she was pregnant.

By rights, the O'Connors should hate her and accuse her of selfishness at not telling Casey about Jade. But Riordan was beaming at Jade and making a fuss of her. Tom and Craig were chatting about their favourite movies in the natural way of young children who seem to be able to make friends at the drop of a hat.

Riordan smiled at her too, and she detected only sympathy and warmth in his gentle grey eyes. No condemnation at all.

So why couldn't she relax and enjoy the day as the others were doing?

That was easy to answer. It was the wretched swimming pool inside the leisure centre. She was terrified of water and would have given anything to be able to stay outside in the late summer sunshine, where she was warm, dry and safe.

Casey had swung Jade up into his arms and was making his way towards the main doors, his family and Craig following closely behind. She and Jess trailed after them, Lexi feeling heavier and more anxious with each step she took.

When they arrived at the pool, the men and boys headed to the male changing rooms, while Lexi, Jess and Jade walked towards the female ones.

'Mummy? Where's Daddy going? Can't I go too?' Jade's anxious little voice, indignant that she had been parted from her beloved father for even a second, pierced her heart. Jade was obviously besotted with Casey.

'He's gone to get changed, sweetheart. Come on, let's put your clothes in the locker and wait for him to come back, yeah?'

Wasn't this what she'd always wanted ever since Jade was born? That one day she could have two loving parents to care for her? Yes... but... when she had accepted that she had done her best to find Casey and it was a completely futile exercise, she also realised that she could provide her daughter with everything the child needed. Lots of single parents do a brilliant job of raising their children alone, giving them all the love and care they needed to thrive. Then, after a while, she realized that she liked being on her own. She loved the freedom to go where she liked, choose the best that life had to offer for herself and her daughter. Money was limited but it always had been, and they had Jess and Craig, so were never lonely.

But now, the wonderful, accomplished, Dr Casey O'Connor

was sweeping the daughter off her feet in the same way he had swept the mother. And she could only look on from the sidelines with a slight feeling of envy. Was that it? Was she jealous of Casey? What about when the novelty wore off and Jade had tantrums and was demanding and fractious and Casey had just spent a long, tiring shift in A&E? Would he still be able to keep his cool and be Jade's knight in shining armour? That remained to be seen.

Lexi sat on a bench with Jade on her knee to wait for the men. She tried to ignore everything she hated about swimming pools; the smell of the chlorine, and the way every sound echoed and the wet floor that could be so dangerous and slippery underfoot.

There was a female lifeguard on duty who was keeping her eye on the kids who splashed and shrieked in the water. But Lexi wasn't reassured, and she hugged Jade to her tightly.

Jess came and sat next to her, wearing a fetching navy one-piece bathing suit that showed off her slim figure. 'Aren't you going in?' she asked.

'No. I think I'll just sit and watch this time. I've got a cold coming on.' She didn't look at her friend who could always tell when she was lying.

'A cold? You haven't mentioned it before.'

'I just felt it this morning. A bit of a sore throat.'

'That's a shame. Thanks for this, by the way. It was kind of Casey to let me and Craig join in a family event.'

'Well, you are family – you're my family. The only one I've ever had.'

'Aww, thanks.' Jess sounded so grateful that Lexi felt her throat constrict. Luckily, at that moment, the men returned and Jess wolf-whistled cheekily at the sight of Riordan and Casey in their swimming costumes. Fortunately, they both wore respectable board shorts and had towels slung over their shoulders. Even so, they were attracting admiring glances from some of the women.

Casey came over and stood in front of Lexi. 'I thought you would be changed by now.'

'I'm not swimming today.'

'Why?' His voice was sharp, and Lexi knew that she wouldn't get away with lying to him. 'I thought you were going to help me look after the kids.'

'I can't. I'd be no good in an emergency. You'll have to look after Jade yourself. But take care of her. Please.' She hugged her daughter to her until Jade squirmed to be let go.

Casey sat on the bench next to her. Jess had walked away and was talking to Craig and Tom.

'Okay, what's going on?'

'Nothing's going on, Casey, I just don't feel like swimming that's all.'

'Oh.' Casey looked embarrassed suddenly as if something had just occurred to him. 'Is it because you've got… you know what?'

He thinks she's got her period. Why didn't she think of that? But he was looking so sheepish that she had to tell him the truth.

'No, it's not that. If you really must know, I'm terrified of the water. I hate it.'

'Really? Why didn't you say?' He sounded incredulous. A champion swimmer would never understand anyone hating the water.

'I didn't want to ruin it for everyone else.' Jade was talking to the boys and looking over at them. Lexi was aware that their conversation was holding everyone up.

'But you *can* swim, can't you? You said you didn't need lessons.'

'No, I can't swim, and I don't need lessons as I have no intention of trying.'

Casey put his head in his hands and groaned. 'I wish you'd told me all this before. You need to start confiding in me, Lexi, and you need to stop living your life on the side lines. Take part, get involved, start taking risks, – life's for living.'

With that he stood up and dived into the pool. Riordan dived straight after him and Tom laughed joyfully. 'They're having a race! Come on Dad!' he shouted.

'Come on, Casey!' shouted Jess and Craig.

'Daddy! Go faster!' Jade shouted, jumping up and down. Jess had one hand on her shoulder, but Lexi's heart was still in her mouth at the sight of the daughter so close to the edge of the pool.

Was she the only one who wasn't enjoying herself? Casey's criticism had stung. He sounded disappointed in her and had every right to be. She wasn't the confident woman he had first met. That woman would be in the thick of it, having fun and taking risks. She hated that she lived her life in fear, but her experience was that there was a lot in this world to be fearful of. Especially as a mother.

Casey had been surrounded by loving family all his life. People who would have comforted him when he had been hurt or scared. He would have been able to test his strengths and abilities and push himself to the limit, secure in the knowledge that there would always be someone there to pick up the pieces if it all went wrong.

Lexi had never had any of that. Her childhood had been spent in loneliness and fear. The bravest thing she had ever done was to pretend she was someone else, the night she had met the sexiest man in the universe. And given herself uncon- ditionally to that man. The man who was now powering up and down the pool, his limbs strong and sure and the water glistening on his golden skin. The water was his element; he looked completely at home in it.

Casey won by a wide margin and both men were laughing as they pulled themselves out of the pool next to where the children were screaming and jumping up and down with ex- citement.

'Not bad for an old man,' Casey said as he clapped his brother on the shoulder.

'You had a head start, otherwise you wouldn't have beaten me,' Riordan said laughingly.

'In your dreams.'

Jade lifted her arms up to Casey to be picked up and he scooped her up in his arms and kissed her. 'Your turn now, Princess.'

Lexi's stomach lurched at his words and a little voice in

her head repeated, *"please keep her safe, please keep her safe."*

He dressed her in a pink float vest and armbands and instructed Craig and Jess to put on armbands as well. They hurried to do as Casey bid them and Lexi wondered if Jess was exhibiting more bravado than she was feeling. But then her motto was *"fake it 'til you make it"* – she wasn't letting Casey know how nervous she was. Lexi admired her friend and wished she had her courage. They had both endured the same upbringing, but Jess faced new challenges head-on, whilst she shrunk back into the shadows, hoping nobody noticed her.

She watched enviously as Casey demonstrated how to hold the float in front of them and kick. He held Jade tightly, but Lexi still cringed every time someone splashed her, or she drifted too far away from the side. Jade, however, seemed totally unconcerned. She was hell-bent on showing her new Daddy how good she was at kicking.

At one point, she turned and shouted, 'Watch me, Mummy!' Casey looked her way too and gave her the thumbs up sign. She smiled, her emotions a jumble of pride in her daughter and admiration and desire for the sexy man who stood in the shallow end of the pool, water sparkling in his hair and his delicious muscles rippling as he carefully held on to his daughter.

Jess and Craig were clutching their floats and kicking for all they were worth. Tom was attempting to swim a length with Riordan by his side in case he flagged and needed help.

And what was she doing whilst the rest of them were having fun? Sitting on the side of the pool watching, too frightened to take part. She despised herself in that moment. What kind of example was she setting her daughter? She wished she'd brought a new costume as Jess had done, and at least showed that she was willing to try. But it was too late now. That chance had gone.

After about half an hour, Casey lifted Jade out of the water. 'Okay, sweetheart, that's enough for your first lesson. We'll have lunch and see about that face painting, shall we?'

Casey hauled himself out of the pool and stood, dripping water down his masculine body, while Jade turned and watched Craig and Tom who were jumping into the shallow end together.

'I wanna go back in,' Jade wailed.

'Not today, sweetheart – go to Mummy for a shower.'

'No.' Jade said and walked to the side of the pool as if she was about to launch herself after the boys.

Lexi was up in a flash and went to grab Jade, but Casey was there first and held his daughter easily under one arm. Lexi was too near the edge and felt herself slipping forward. She cried out and a large, strong, masculine arm encircled her waist and pulled her backwards away from the water.

'What the hell do you think you're doing? You nearly fell in.' Casey's tone was stern, but she detected a note of anxiety in his voice. All she could think of, however, was the feel of his body, wet and warm, pressed up against hers. He smelt of chlorine and the unique scent of hot male. His arm held her fast against him and he put his wet face next to hers and whispered, 'Don't scare me like that, okay?'

Riordan's voice interrupted her lustful thoughts. 'Having trouble keeping your women in check, Bro?' He was chuckling, and Lexi turned and glared at him.

'It's not funny; Jade nearly fell in.'

'Sorry,' said Riordan, looking totally unrepentant.

'Okay, guys. I think it's time we all had a shower, get changed and then have lunch.'

The boys cheered, and everyone ran to do his bidding. Dr Casey O'Connor was back in charge.

Chapter Twelve

The café in the leisure centre was full and noisy, but they managed to find a table to seat all of them, after borrowing a few of the cheap red plastic chairs from other tables. There were posters on the walls of people doing sporty things next to the menu which was basic but had meal deals for the kids and enough choice for everyone to order something they liked.

Craig and Tom sat together, chatting about what character they were going to be when they had their faces painted.

'I want to be Spiderman,' Craig said.

'I'm going to be the Hulk,' said Tom.

Riordan sat next to Tom and Jess sat next to Craig which left himself, Lexi and Jade sitting together. Lexi still had a face like thunder and Casey felt a flash of irritation. What was wrong with her? He had done his best to make this day special and everyone else seemed to be having a great time. Craig had made a new friend in Tom, Jess was eager to start their swimming lessons and Jade had taken to the water like a little mermaid. All Lexi's fears had proved to be unfounded. Everyone was safe and happy.

All except the lady herself, who seemed to become more withdrawn as the day progressed.

What else could he do? It was almost as if Lexi resented his efforts and was trying to sabotage his attempts to be a good father to Jade. Well, it wouldn't work. Being a father to that little girl was the most important role he had ever undertaken, and he was determined to succeed. He wasn't a quitter. Unlike Lexi who didn't seem to want to try anything new, never mind see it through to the end.

He remembered how she'd felt in his arms when she'd nearly flung herself into the water after Jade. She had trembled all over as he held her, and he had ached to kiss her. There was such a strong attraction between them, which grew stronger each time they were close.

After they'd ordered their meal – chicken nuggets and French Fries for the kids and pizza for the adults – Riordan smiled at Lexi. 'Sorry about earlier. I hope I didn't upset you with my thoughtless comment.'

Casey said nothing, interested to hear how Lexi would respond.

'No, I'm sorry; I was just scared for Jade that's all.'

'I'd like to bet she'll be swimming in no time. She seems fearless in the water.'

'That's what I'm afraid of.'

He couldn't help himself. 'But why, Lexi? Kids need to be allowed to explore their world and make their own mistakes. That's how they learn.'

'You wouldn't understand.' Lexi glared even harder at him and he kept quiet to allow his peace-keeping brother to pour oil on troubled waters.

'I want to make it up to you,' Riordan said, 'so please, all of you, come to Sunday lunch tomorrow. Our parents are dying to meet Jade and I think we're having lamb.'

Casey wanted to applaud his brother. If he'd suggested it, no doubt Lexi would have thought up an excuse as to why they couldn't go. But the lamb looked as if it was the deciding factor.

'I love lamb,' Craig said.

'Is Craig invited?' Tom asked.

'Of course, Jess too,' Riordan replied.

'Oh, that's really kind of you, so long as you're sure.' Jess's eyes were shining, and Casey smiled at her.

'Will Tom be there?' Jade asked and they all laughed.

'Of course, honey; he lives there,' Riordan said. Tom blushed and munched on his chicken nuggets.

'Okay, then, I'll go,' Jade announced grandly as if she was bestowing a favour on the group. His daughter was enchanting, and he couldn't wait for his parents to meet her.

He wondered why Lexi was throwing daggers at him and then he remembered his promise to run suggestions by her first before making plans for Jade. He grinned mischievously and pointed at Riordan from behind his hand while mouthing, "*It wasn't me, it was him*". It reminded him of the many times when they had been boys, they had blamed each other for their misdemeanours in the way of siblings who loved each other despite their competitiveness.

It made him feel warm inside to think of his family and the love they all shared. He couldn't wait to add Lexi and Jade to their number.

But Lexi had folded her arms and turned her head away.

Chapter Thirteen

Lexi opened her eyes and groaned. The day had finally arrived. Her worst nightmare. The day she stood in front of Casey's parents and tried to justify herself. To explain why they had a gorgeous little granddaughter that they'd known nothing about, and she had caused them to miss out on the first three years of her life. The years that most grandparents treasure; the baby and toddler years.

They were going to hate her, she just knew it.

At least the worst part would soon be over. Once it was, things could only get better, couldn't they? They could only stay mad at her for so long. And maybe, with Jess and Craig there, they'd take pity on her and not humiliate her in front of everyone.

With a heavy heart, she showered, then considered what she should wear. Should she try to look smart? Do the

O'Connors make a big deal of Sunday lunch? It had seemed that way when Riordan had invited them; as if Sunday lunches were a special family occasion. She hoped it wasn't too formal an occasion as she wasn't confident in that type of setting.

It had been nice of Riordan to include Jess and Craig. He came across as a caring man. As Casey did. Would their parents be the same, or would they bombard her with questions and accusations the minute she walked through the door? Or, worse still, would they ignore her completely and lavish all their attention on Jade?

She went downstairs to find Jess and the children having breakfast.

'Hi. Want some juice?' Jess looked at her in sympathy. She knew exactly what this day meant to her.

'Thanks. I don't feel like eating a thing but probably should try some toast. Can't imagine I'll eat much at the O'Connors. I feel like I'm going to my execution.'

'I don't think you have anything to worry about,' Jess said scooping up a forkful of scrambled egg. 'Casey and Riordan are such lovely men. I can't believe their parents are ogres.'

'Not ogres, no. Just grandparents and I've stolen their memories of Jade's early years. That's something I'll never be able to make up for, no matter how hard I try.'

By the time Casey arrived to collect them all, Lexi's stomach was tying itself in knots.

Jade had insisted on wearing her party dress. It was really an ordinary dress, as Lexi hadn't been able to afford a proper one, but she had added wings in sparkly gold fabric, sequins, ruffles and lace at the skirt. She had also made her a wand. The garment was more suitable for fancy dress than Sunday lunch with the relatives, but Lexi wanted to avoid any tantrums and had given in to Jade's demands. By the way her nerves were stretching and her anxiety levels rising, she may be the one throwing the tantrum and not her daughter, before the day was out.

'Wow! Look at you.' said Casey when he saw Jade. He was obviously going to play the role of indulgent father today. Then Lexi could take a backseat and let father and daughter take centre stage.

Soon, they were all safely in the car and on their way.

The O'Connors lived in the oldest, most affluent area of Leytonsfield. Grand old detached houses on wide tree-lined streets, the oaks and sycamores providing shade and a sense of history, the properties had extensive gardens with high hedges and modern conservatories.

Lexi was in awe as they parked outside one of the homes. She hoped Jade would behave well. She really had no idea what to expect, so was amazed and pleased, when there was no one waiting outside to greet them. For some reason, she had expected a welcome committee.

Casey led them around to the side of the house. A boy's bike lay abandoned outside the back door and there was a free-standing basketball hoop on the lawn.

They trooped through to the kitchen, Casey calling out, 'We're here!' as they went through. Jade was holding Casey's hand tightly and Lexi kept as close to Jess as possible.

At the sound of running feet, they all turned as Tom came hurtling into the kitchen, followed by Riordan and a woman who was obviously Mrs O'Connor.

Lexi froze and stood still, letting the mayhem that ensued wash over her. Tom and Craig greeted each other like old friends and started talking at the same time. Riordan said hello to Jess and Mrs O'Connor held her hands out to Jade with a sweet smile on her face.

'And you must be Jade. What a beautiful dress! Are you an angel or a fairy?'

Jade, who had recovered her voice and confidence, said, 'I'm your God-fairy mother.'

Mrs O'Connor beamed. 'How delightful, I've always wanted my very own God-fairy mother.'

She noticed Lexi, hovering anxiously on the edge of the group and enveloped her in a warm hug. 'Lexi, – it's lovely to meet you, dear. Come and sit down and I'll make some tea.'

Mrs O'Connor was a tall woman with greying hair pulled into a bun, but she wore jeans and a baggy shirt under her apron and had sparkling blue eyes and a genuine, sweet smile. She had a serenity about her and a natural warmth. Lexi found herself relaxing. Maybe this lovely lady wouldn't judge her too harshly.

Soon they were all settled around the large, scrubbed wooden kitchen table; everyone talking at once and two or three conversations going on at the same time. Lexi found it a bit overwhelming, so just sat and listened.

'Where's Dad?' Casey asked.

'He's out on a call, but he'll be back in time for lunch. He promised,' said Mrs O'Connor.

'He shouldn't still be doing house calls,' Casey said, 'the NHS has got a service now that takes that kind of pressure off GPs. Why doesn't he use it?'

'Oh, you know your father,' said Mrs O'Connor, 'he still believes in the personal touch. He's known this patient all her life.'

'He needs to start winding down towards retirement. Start taking it easy.'

'Well, don't tell him that, dear, or there'll be hell to pay,' said their mother. 'Anyway, how did you all enjoy the Family Fun Day? I'm sorry I missed it.'

They all started talking at the same time; the children's voices just as loud as the grown-ups. Mrs O'Connor seemed to take it all in her stride, smiling at everyone in turn as they regaled her with details of their day together.

Once again, Lexi began to feel like an outsider, so sat quietly and said nothing. This is what it must be like to be part of a loving family. Unconditional love, acceptance and someone who genuinely wanted to know how you feel about things and who listened with no judgement or criticism, but she knew that she had yet to face the music and explain herself to Casey's parents.

The group started to disperse; Craig and Tom to watch movies in Tom's room, with Jade trailing after them.

'I better go too,' Jess said, 'I'll make sure the God-fairy mother doesn't make a nuisance of herself.'

Lexi made frantic *"Don't leave me"* signals to Jess who smiled and shrugged before disappearing after the children.

Riordan and Casey wandered off to the living-room to watch the rugby, Wales versus the All Blacks, which left Lexi sitting at the table with Mrs O'Connor.

'Right, better get the lunch started. Dan will be back soon,' she said. Lexi could smell the lamb which would have been cooking for a while, judging by the delicious aroma that was swirling around the kitchen.

'Do you want some help, Mrs O'Connor?' Lexi asked. She really didn't think her culinary skills would be up to Casey's mother's high standard, but she had to offer.

'Oh yes, thank you dear. And please call me Eloise. We don't stand on ceremony in this family. Would you like to peel the carrots?'

Lexi waited for the questions and accusations which she was sure would follow now that they were alone, but they never came. Instead, Eloise, as Lexi now thought of her, chatted about nursing and how much it had changed since her day. She asked her about her friendship with Jess and how hard it must have been for her when she found out she was pregnant.

Not once did Eloise mention the fact that she missed out on Jade's early years. In fact, she proved to be such a good listener that Lexi found herself recalling stories of her pregnancy, her struggle to cope as a single parent and so much more.

Eloise put her hand on her arm. 'You don't need to be alone anymore, my dear; you're part of our family now.'

*

It was the semi-final of the Six Nations Rugby and Casey and Riordan were indulging in their ongoing argument about which is better, Union or League. Casey favoured Union and Riordan, League. Casey was just winding up for another attack when Riordan abruptly changed the subject.

'What's the deal with you and Lexi?'

'What do you mean?'

'Are you a couple?'

'No, just colleagues and Jade's parents.' Casey took a swig from his beer, his gazed fixed on the television screen. He wasn't going to admit that he was still wildly attracted to her.

'She's not what I expected.'

'In what way?'

'When you told me about the night of the Summer Solstice Ball and meeting a hot woman with whom you had wild sex, I was picturing a rather different person.'

'You don't think Lexi is capable of hot sex?'

Riordan chuckled and sat forward with his elbows on his knees. 'The women you go for are sophisticated, confident, professional women. Lexi seems rather timid and unsure of herself. She's not what I thought, that's all.'

'To be honest, Bro, I was a bit surprised when I took her to dinner. There was no sign of the kick-ass lady that I met four years ago. Whether becoming a mother has changed her, or she wasn't being herself that night, I'm not sure.'

The men stopped their conversation as Wales scored a try. The All Blacks resumed the attack and Casey became engrossed in the game again.

'Why didn't she swim with the rest of us? And why was she so scared that something was going to happen to Jade? She'll make your daughter as neurotic as she is if she's not careful.'

'She's not neurotic, Bro, just over-protective. She doesn't like to let Jade out of her sight.'

'That will have to change now. You're Jade's father and have rights. Lots of couples share childcare but live separate lives. You can make it work if you stay friendly. Why can't you see Jade on her own? Now that she's been introduced to the family and she seems perfectly happy with us. Think about it. You have options. She doesn't have to have it all her own way.'

'Okay, I will.'

*

Despite Riordan's warning, Casey thought things were going well. Lexi had started to relax and was getting on with his parents, especially his mother. Everyone loved Jade who had taken a shine to Tom, so much so that she never took her eyes off him and copied his every move. If he took a drink, Jade did too. When Tom helped himself to more roast potatoes, so did Jade, even though she hadn't eaten the ones already on her plate.

Everyone found it amusing but realized, from Tom's point

of view, such adoration from a little girl could get old very quickly.

He could tell his parents were delighted with their grand-daughter and couldn't wait for the opportunity to spoil her.

Yes, everything was going well.

He was tucking into his roast lamb, trying not to eat too fast, when his mobile rang. He glanced at the screen. 'It's Raj, my registrar; he's on call so I need to get this, sorry.' Everyone nodded, fully understanding that when duty called, doctors were obliged to answer.

He left the dining-room and went into the hallway. After a quick conversation, he returned to the table.

'Problems?' asked his Dad.

'One of my patients has just been admitted with an overdose. I need to go, I'm afraid.'

He looked over at Lexi who was staring at him, waiting for him to tell her who the patient was. 'It's Shelley. You don't need to come unless you want to. Riordan can take you all home, can't you?'

'Sure, no problems,' Riordan replied, smiling at Lexi.

'Of course I'll come.' Lexi got up and said to Jade, 'Come on, honey, we need to go now.' She seemed eager to leave, almost relieved at the interruption.

'I wanna stay here with Tom.' Her face was set, and Casey looked at Lexi helplessly.

'She's fine here, Lexi, why not leave her with us so we can get to know her a bit better?' said his mother. He saw the yearning in her eyes and recognized how hard it had been for both his parents to find out about Jade and know how much of her short life they'd already missed out on. But, true to form, they were keeping their private feelings to themselves.

Lexi hesitated, doing her rabbit caught in the headlights act, but then she shrugged and talked quietly to Jade, explaining that mummy and daddy would be back as soon as they could. It made him go all gooey inside, hearing her say 'Mummy and Daddy' as if they were a proper family.

'What kind of overdose?' Riordan asked, and Casey knew exactly what he was thinking.

'Deliberate,' he answered.

'Is history repeating itself, Bro?' Riordan asked.

'Not if I have anything to do with it, it isn't.'

Chapter Fourteen

They were silent as they drove towards the hospital, Lexi wondering if she had done the right thing leaving Jade alone with strangers, but they weren't all strangers. She had Jess and Craig, had already met Riordan and Tom, who she was completely obsessed with, and this was the perfect opportunity for her to get to know her grandparents.

So, why did she feel as if she had abandoned her child? Because, once again, she was on the outside. Eloise had been eager to be alone with her granddaughter and Jade had smiled and waved happily at herself and Casey when they left. Her daughter had been totally unconcerned that her mother and father were leaving her. She had been dismissed.

Was this her future? Jade had a nice new family and didn't need her mum anymore? She knew she was being stupid but couldn't help feeling a sense of foreboding.

It had just been the two of them, and Jess and Craig of course, since Jade was born, but now she had to share her. She didn't want to share her. She wanted to keep her all to herself.

She glanced at Casey who was staring at the road ahead and frowning. He must have sensed her watching him as he turned his head briefly before looking back at the road.

'Thanks for letting Jade stay with my parents. It means a lot to them.'

'It's the least I can do,' she replied. After denying them so much of Jade's life. She was still puzzled as to why that hadn't been mentioned. Maybe they were saving it all up for another occasion. Perhaps she hadn't dodged that bullet after all.

They both fell silent again, but Lexi felt the need to talk.

'You must see loads of overdose patients, especially amongst drug addicts.'

Casey nodded but said nothing. Lexi tried again.

'What did Riordan mean about history repeating itself?'

Casey sighed and squirmed slightly in his seat. 'I never told you why I left London, did I?'

'You never told me the full story. You just needed a change, I think you said.' Casey told her very little of his personal life. In fact, the man was virtually a stranger even though they had a child together.

'There was a girl, a lot like Shelley. A heroin addict whose family didn't want anything to do with her. She appeared in A&E every Saturday night, regular as clockwork. Sometimes she was high on drugs, sometimes she just wanted some attention.'

'Poor girl!' muttered Lexi. She couldn't imagine being so desperately lonely that the only place she could find sympathy and a listening ear was the emergency department of a hospital. Thank heavens for friends. She silently gave thanks for Jess.

Casey stiffened beside her, then he sighed. 'As you say, poor girl.'

'Go on,' she whispered.

'It was a frantically busy Saturday night. As well as the usual drunks and addicts, we'd had our fair share of elderly people slipping on ice and fracturing various bits of themselves. It had been a hard winter and when the girl showed up, I thought she just wanted to get out of the cold. But she had taken more stuff than I at first realized.'

Casey paused. The road ahead was blocked with Sunday drivers and they slowed right down at some road works, then came to a complete stop at a set of temporary traffic lights.

'What happened to her?'

Casey frowned and stared ahead unseeing.

'She wanted to discharge herself and I tried to persuade her not to, but I didn't try hard enough. Then I had to leave her alone to deal with a child who was having a bad asthma attack. We nearly lost him but managed to pull him around just in time.'

'That was good.' Lexi could feel the tension in the car as Casey lived through that fateful night all over again.

'Yes. Then we got a code red. The kind that everyone dreads. Three cars were involved. There were fatalities, and one of them was the girl. She must have left when I was treating the child. She walked in front of a taxi that had to slam on the brakes and the two cars behind went into the back of each other. Sadly, he was going too fast to avoid hitting her. She was dead on arrival.' Casey's voice was dull and expressionless, concealing a world of pain.

'Oh Casey. You can't blame yourself for her death. You can't stop patients discharging themselves.' But she knew he did blame himself, as any doctor would in those circumstances. As she would have done if Shelley had walked out of A&E and something had happened to her.

'It was my fault. I should have tried harder. She was my patient. My responsibility. I let her down. I'm not letting Shelley down.' He was silent then and Lexi knew the conversation was over.

The traffic started moving again and shortly afterwards they arrived at Leytonsfield General.

*

'How bad is she?' he asked Raj who looked calm but tired. A&E was full as usual. The smell of lavender permeated the air. He was glad to see the staff were behind his essential oils therapy. Anything that improved the lives of patients and staff was worth trying, in his opinion.

'She's in here.' His registrar led him to one of the cubicles. 'She's asleep but was in a right state when they brought her in. I suspect domestic abuse, so I've contacted Social Services.'

'Good man. I'll just sit with her for a while in case she

wakes up.' He turned to Lexi who was hovering anxiously at the entrance to the cubicle. 'Do you mind staying? She may not wake up for ages though.'

'No, it's okay, I'll stay with you.'

There was only one grey plastic chair next to the bed, so he indicated that Lexi should take that one. He searched around to find one for himself, then set it down next to hers. Raj had disappeared, so they sat side-by-side, staring at Shelley.

She was in the recovery position, surrounded by pillows and Casey didn't know which was paler, his patient's face or the linen. At least she was alive and would remain so if he had anything to do with it.

It was strangely peaceful in the cubicle with the heavy curtains drawn around them. Voices, the sound of feet on linoleum and the clatter of trolleys and equipment seemed distant and unconnected to the three of them huddled together in the tiny space.

Casey sat in silence with his hands in his pockets and watched Shelley breathing deeply, due to the sedation she'd been given. In, out. In, out.

The silence stretched on, punctuated by the background noises of a busy A&E department, to the point where Casey's eyelids started to droop. It wasn't often he just sat and did nothing. Forced inactivity didn't come easily to him. He was a man of action, always wanting to be up and doing.

He didn't like to be alone with his thoughts; they tended to stray to negative things. All the mistakes he'd ever made, his drug addict patient who'd stepped in front of a taxi, Helen and his aborted child. Helen hadn't even told him she was pregnant, yet she had taken it upon herself to make the decision to terminate their baby. His child. His own flesh and blood. Would he have had a daughter or a son? He'd never know.

Casey shifted uncomfortably on the chair, sat forward with his elbows on his knees and placed his head in his hands. He closed his eyes. The small, stuffy cubicle felt claustrophobic suddenly. The smell of lavender was strong. Perhaps he'd stick to citrus from now on.

'I want to tell you something.' Lexi's voice near to his ear was quiet and small, slightly husky from the long period they had sat together, not speaking.

He looked up. She sat huddled on the chair with her arms folded, staring at the floor.

'A confession?' he asked.

'In a way.' Still she didn't look at him, so he sat back on his chair and waited.

'I know you think I'm a wuss because I won't have swimming lessons.'

'Lexi – I don't think anything of the kind.'

'It's okay, I don't blame you. I am a wuss. I'm so scared of drowning.'

People weren't usually scared of things for no reason. He thought of her lonely childhood and wondered about all the pain she kept inside.

'What happened?' he asked. She cleared her throat before she spoke.

'The primary school I went to took us swimming when we were ten. I was being bullied at the time by a kid called Howard. He knew I was scared of him; I couldn't hide it. He threatened me with all the things he was going to do to me, but it had just been talk up to then. He never actually touched me. Until one day.'

A chill ran down Casey's spine, causing his fists to clench and his jaw to tighten. The thought of anyone hurting her was almost too much to bear, but he had to stay calm for her sake and listen.

'Go on,' he said, trying to sound encouraging but hearing the bite in his own voice.

'He pushed me in at the deep end and I sank to the bottom. That was bad enough as I'd never even been under the water before. If he'd just left it there, I might have been alright, but I couldn't rise to the surface. I could see lights, shimmering shadows and figures above me, but I couldn't reach them.'

Lexi's voice was rising, and Casey feared she was going to lose it. He reached out and held her hand. She grasped it tightly.

'He'd dived in after me and was holding my feet, so I couldn't move. I was stuck, and my lungs were burning. I thought I was going to die. Then he let me go.'

She was shaking her head as she relived the terrifying memory. She burst into tears and Casey couldn't hold back any longer. He threw his arms around her and held her tightly while she sobbed. He didn't care if someone came in. Lexi was in a world of pain and needed him. He stroked her hair and murmured to her as he would have done to Jade.

'It's alright, darling, you're safe. No one will ever hurt you again, I promise.' Her body felt slight in his arms and she trembled as he held her close. 'Did you tell anyone about it?'

'No. When we got out of the pool, he said if I told anyone he would keep me down longer next time.'

'Didn't anyone see it?' Casey couldn't believe that no one had gone to her rescue.

'Just the other kids, but no one said anything. I hid in the changing room until everyone had left. From then on, I made an excuse every week to avoid going back to that hateful place. I know I should have got over it by now, and I do want to learn, it's just that...' She trailed off and put her head on his chest. A gesture that meant she trusted him. He wouldn't let her down. He felt a surge of protectiveness towards her but didn't examine it too closely. She was in pain and needed comforting, that was all.

'Listen, we'll sort this out, okay? You're not a wimp, Lexi, you're a beautiful, brave woman who's had a shit start in life, but things will be better now, I promise.' He was about to say more when his phone rang, startling them.

'I need to get this, it's my mother,' he said moving out of the cubicle and Resus. He kept the conversation brief so he could get back to Lexi and their unfinished business. There were things he wanted to say, but by the time he returned to the cubicle, she had got herself together and smiled at him reassuringly.

'Everything okay?' she asked. Casey could see that she

had attempted to wipe all trace of her tears, but her smile didn't quite reach her eyes. The things he wanted to say would have to wait.

'Fine. The kids are in bed and Jess is happily chatting with Mum. Dad and Riordan are having a pint in the Dog and Partridge. He'll bring them back tomorrow morning on the way to the hospital.'

'Oh.' Lexi looked troubled and frowned. 'Is Jade okay? She's never been away from home before now.'

'She'll be fine, don't worry. It'll give you the chance to have a quiet evening to yourself. I bet you don't get many of those.'

'No.' Lexi still looked uncertain, so he sat down again and, the intimate mood of before now dispersed, resumed the watchful vigil at Shelley's side.

It was obvious, however, that their patient was out for the count. After ten minutes, a nurse and a porter popped their heads around the cubicle curtain.

'We're taking Shelley up to the ward now.'

'Right,' said Casey, springing to his feet, 'we'll be off then.'

There was a chill in the air as they wandered across the carpark, but it felt good to breathe clean air after the stuffy heaviness of the hospital.

'Oh, look!' Lexi cried, 'a shooting star, did you see it?'

'No,' Casey said scrutinizing the night sky. 'I missed it. Did you make a wish?'

Lexi looked at him and smiled. 'Of course, but I can't tell

you what it was, or it won't come true.'

He felt his heart turn over at the longing in her eyes. She deserved some luck in her life. She deserved to be loved and cherished, and to have someone think she was the reason the sun rose every morning. He wanted to be that for someone one day. The way his parents were for each other. He had thought once that the woman was Helen but look how that turned out. He didn't know whether he could ever trust a woman again after the pain of her betrayal.

'Well, I hope it comes true for you, whatever it is.

Chapter Fifteen

Lexi put the key in the lock and turned to face Casey, standing behind her. He had been silent on the journey home from the hospital, obviously deep in thought. Was he thinking about Shelley, or had his thoughts turned to more personal matters?

He was a caring doctor, that much was obvious, and he was going the extra mile to make sure Shelley got the help that she needed. But the hunger in his green eyes as he gazed at her now, told Lexi that he had left all thoughts of his patients behind.

The cottage was empty. They were alone. There was nothing stopping them spending the night together. Re-enacting the magical time that she couldn't stop thinking about. Nobody need ever know. Just one night of hot sex with no strings. Would that be so wrong?

'Would you like a coffee?' she asked as her gaze met his.

She wanted him to stay. She didn't want to spend the night alone in the empty cottage, and Casey's nearness was causing her erogenous zones to light up like a pin-ball machine.

He grinned, which made him look younger and transformed his features from serious medical professional to imminently desirable and sexy man. The sexiest man she had ever met.

'I thought you'd never ask,' he replied, 'as long as you make it tea, I drink too much coffee at the hospital. I need something to relax me at this time of the day.'

She returned his grin, thinking of several interesting ways she could relax the good doctor, after she'd driven him mad with desire first. 'Tea it is then, and how about I make us some pasta? There's Bolognese sauce in the freezer. It won't take long.'

They moved into the lounge, which felt distinctly chilly. 'Brrr…' she said rubbing her arms, 'autumn's definitely taken hold. Would you mind lighting the fire, Casey?'

'Sure thing,' he replied and set to work.

An hour later, they had finished their meal and were sitting side by side staring into the flames of a roaring wood fire. Lexi felt herself relaxing in the peaceful ambience and yearned to rest her head on Casey's shoulder. Her thoughts were still with Jade, however. Not just the fact that the little girl had never been away from home before, but what the senior O'Connors really thought about the situation, and when they would have "the conversation", whereby she explained why they had been denied the early years of their grandchild's life.

'Penny for them?' Casey asked.

'Penny? Even with inflation they're not worth that much.'

'You were deep in thought; you're not worrying about Jade, are you?'

'Yes. Well, a bit. But also, your parents' opinion of me. They must blame me for the fact that they've missed out on so much of Jade's life. I like your mum and dad, I don't want them to hate me. But I just don't know what to say to them when we have that conversation.'

Casey chuckled, and Lexi stared at him. 'What's so funny?'

'You, worrying yourself needlessly about something that was not your fault. We've already had "that conversation" as you call it. They blame me entirely, not you. Especially my mum. *"How can you have let that poor girl go through her first pregnancy alone?"* I got plenty of earache from them both.'

'You were angry with me, too, when you first found out. You blamed me.'

'I know I did, and I'm sorry, it was wrong of me. We were both to blame equally, I realise that now. We both made it very clear that night that we just wanted a one-night stand.'

'You asked me once why I didn't stay the following morning.' Casey watched her face and waited for her to say more. 'It's because I didn't think you would like the real me.'

He frowned. 'What do you mean by that? I liked the real you very much, and I thought you liked me.'

'Oh, I did… do. Very much. But I wasn't being myself

that night. I was putting on an act, trying to be sexier, more confident, so I could enjoy myself more.'

'Did it work?'

'Of course. You asked me to dance and we ended up spending the night together. A night I've never been able to forget. Yes, I would say it worked.'

'So, what about now, Lexi? Are you still putting on an act?'

'No, of course not. I don't need to. I'm a different person. Having Jade has given me a purpose in life and an identity. I'm a mother now and everything I do is for her.'

'What about you? Your needs. It's true you're a mother but you're so much more than that. You're a nurse, a friend, and an incredibly sexy woman. You have needs too and they shouldn't be neglected.'

'Are you speaking as a medical professional or something else?' Her heart was beating fast waiting for him to answer. Was Casey telling her that he wanted to satisfy her needs again as he had four years previously? His closeness was preventing her from thinking straight. She was starting to feel turned on by the way his eyes were wide and dark in the firelight, the desperate need she was feeling to stroke his face and kiss him.

'I'm speaking as a man.'

He kissed her. His lips were soft at first, gentle and tender, but when she reached up and ran her fingers through his short hair, tugging ever so slightly, he moaned and deepened the kiss until the heat started to rise in Lexi and she longed to feel his bare skin against hers.

His mouth was hot, and he devoured her with a controlled urgency that reminded her of their first night together. Would this night be the same? They had been complete strangers then, now they were parents, sharing their daughter's care. Would that make a difference to their lovemaking?

His fingers were tangled in her hair and she moved her other hand down his chest and quickly pulled his T-shirt from his jeans, stroking his bare stomach, the muscles twitching slightly at her touch.

'Here or the bedroom?' he asked, his voice husky with need.

It was tempting to stay in front of the fire where it was warm, but Lexi wanted this night to be a repeat of their first one together. She wanted to fall asleep with him in the comfort of her double bed, and more importantly, this time, she wanted to wake up next to him.

'Bedroom,' she croaked.

'Right.' He swept her up easily in his strong arms and carried her carefully up the narrow stairs to the bedroom. Her heart was fluttering madly as he laid her down gently on the bed and pulled his T-shirt off in one swift movement.

When he went to unbuckle his belt, she put her hands on his. 'Let me.'

She undressed him slowly, looking into his eyes and loving the way her touch affected him. He moaned as she stroked his hard length, then took him into her hands, revelling in the feel of his heated flesh and the soft sounds he was making.

Before she could take him higher, he gently removed her hands and undressed her with the same studied concentration and care, kissing every bit of exposed skin, licking and tasting her as if she was a delicious meal he wanted to devour.

They lay down together on the bed. Despite their need for each other, Lexi sensed that this time they would take it easy. He kissed her again, then moved down her body, kissing her throat, her breasts, her stomach. She closed her eyes and let him carry her away on waves of sensation. He explored every inch of her, murmuring occasionally, words that sounded like endearments, but Lexi couldn't be sure.

She felt as if she was on another plane of existence, no longer tethered to the earth. Her body was tingling at each place he touched her, kissing, stroking and licking her skin so that she shivered and moaned in ecstasy. She gave herself up to the feelings and let him do as he wished.

He pushed her thighs apart and kissed her gently. She was so aroused by this time that she felt her climax building steadily and she cried out. He pulled back and paid close attention to the area around her clitoris, taking care not to touch her there until she was writhing and pleading with him to put her out of her misery.

Swiftly and expertly he took her to the edge and held her as she fell into open space. Her orgasm shuddered through her and Lexi felt herself spinning deliciously out of control, as she came, not once, but several times, driven on by Casey's tongue, lips and fingers.

She had never experienced multiple orgasms before and

felt as if they would never stop. She didn't want them to stop. The remarkable feeling of being carried away, like a bird gliding on air currents, not knowing where she was going to land, made her incoherent and helpless.

When she eventually managed to open her eyes, Casey was lying next to her with a smug grin on his face.

'Good?'

'Not the word I'd use,' she said, her voice sounding remarkably normal, in the circumstances.

'What word would you use then?'

'Amazing, stupendous, incredible…'

'That was only the beginning,' he said and kissed her. She didn't think she had any strength left but, as his tongue danced with hers, the tingling between her thighs started up again and she wanted him inside her. She couldn't wait. It had to be now.

Luckily Casey was thinking along the same lines, as he rolled on a condom and entered her. He lifted her hips, holding her with ease, as if she weighed nothing, and she felt him filling her, stretching her inside and she clenched her body around his as if she could merge them together into one person.

She stroked his back and watched his face as he thrust into her hard and fast. She clung to him, her arms and legs wrapped tightly around him as the sensations began to build once more.

There was no more thought as Casey took them higher and brought them both to their sweet release together.

They slept in each other's arms, replete and spent, until one woke the other with a gentle kiss and they started the dance all over again.

*

Lexi woke the following morning in Casey's arms, big, strong arms that held her gently, but firmly. She had her back to him and felt his soft breath on the nape of her neck. She felt something else too – his arousal. A shiver went through her at the feel of his morning erection reminding her, as if she needed reminding, of the night of hot sex they had just shared. It seemed Casey was ready to carry it forward to the next day. The thought made her squirm and his arms tightened around her.

'Oh no you don't.' His deep, sleepy voice murmured in her ear. 'you're not getting away from me this time.'

She turned in the circle of his arms and faced him. He had one eye open, his hair stuck up at the back and his jaw was rough with dark bristles, but Lexi had never wanted a man as much as she wanted Casey at that moment.

'I wasn't planning on leaving,' she whispered.

'Good,' he replied, planting kisses on her lips, cheeks, eyelids and forehead, 'cos I wasn't planning on letting you.'

As he moved over her, she asked, 'What time is it? Don't forget, Riordan is bringing Jess and the kids back early, 'we don't want them to find us still in bed when they arrive.'

'It's early, there's plenty of time.' Casey had reached for a condom as she was talking. He had obviously been ready for a repeat performance of their one-night stand, unless he carried packets of the things as a matter of course. He was an attractive man with a high sex drive. Why would she be surprised if he did? This was no time for her usual self-doubts as Casey rolled her onto her back and pulled the duvet off.

'Time for breakfast as well?' she asked, although food was the last thing on her mind at that moment, as Casey's hand was working its magic on her right breast. She gasped as he teased her nipple.

'Time for everything,' he said before taking her nipple into his mouth. She grabbed a handful of his hair and tugged on it slightly as electricity shot from her breast to the sensitive nub between her legs.

When he entered her, she clung to him and wrapped her legs around his waist trying to pull him in deeper. They moved together, building up a slow and steady rhythm. Lexi was amazed at how little time it took for her to reach the edge of her climax. With each thrust of his powerful body she got closer to the edge. She closed her eyes and revelled in the joy of being carried ever upwards into an infinite blue sky. She was weightless, flying and she never wanted to land.

But land she did. They both did, together, with cries of release, of total satisfaction and pleasure.

When their breathing returned to normal, Casey gently rolled off her and padded to the bathroom to dispose of the condom.

She lay exactly as he had left her. She couldn't move. If she did move, it would break the spell and she would have to wake from the beautiful dream. Wouldn't it be wonderful to be woken like that every morning? To have a partner that was in tune with your needs and desires and who wanted to make you happy? Not because he had a hidden agenda, but because he loved you enough to put your happiness first, above his own?

Casey returned and lay down beside her. Neither spoke. What happened now? Did they go back to the way they were before or had their night of sex moved their relationship on a notch? Did they have a relationship or was the sex a friends-with-benefits type of thing? It couldn't be that, as they had Jade to consider. She was more important than either of them, and her needs came first.

Casey kissed her gently then sat up. 'Right. I promised you breakfast. Full English okay?'

'Perfect.'

He got up and pulled on jeans and a T-shirt.

Okay, so they weren't going to talk about last night, but at least she'd get a decent breakfast; she usually made do with tea and toast.

Chapter Sixteen

When Casey arrived home after another long, tiring day in A&E he put a bottle of wine in the fridge to chill, then gathered the ingredients together for a meal he was going to cook. His dinner guest would arrive in about half an hour.

Dr Catalina Martinez lived in the flat next to his in the doctor's accommodation. She was a paediatric A&E consultant from Spain and had been working at Leytonsfield General for only a few weeks longer than he had. The first night he had stayed in the flat, she had made him a meal to spare him having to get take-out. He'd been grateful for her kindness, surprised at how well they got on and decided, by the end of the evening, that they would be friends as well as colleagues.

It was his turn to cook, which would be a welcome distraction from thinking about Lexi and Riordan's warning not to get involved with her. He hadn't been able to concentrate properly all day and had given himself a stern talking to when he nearly missed an important symptom in a patient that would have affected his aftercare. As it was, he spotted it in time and swore to himself that he wouldn't let it happen again. His patients were his priority, his private life had no right to intrude on his performance as a doctor.

He chopped leeks and carrots and filled the bottom of a casserole dish with the vegetables before laying chicken fillets on the top and, after placing the lid on the dish, shoving it into the oven to cook slowly. He showered quickly and set the small table for two. As an after-thought he added a red rose that he had cut from the gardens on his way in; Catalina would appreciate the gesture, he was sure. She had mentioned that roses were her favourite flower.

He was just opening the bottle of wine when the doorbell rang.

'Hi, Catalina, come in.' She came into the flat and he took the bottle she offered him. 'Vermouth?'

'Yes, it is an aperitif.'

'Would you rather have this than the wine?'

'Oh no, the wine is perfect, and you have already opened it. Are we having chicken? It smells delicious.'

'Have a seat.' He gestured to the old three-seater sofa and, when she was settled, gave her a glass of sparkling white wine. He then settled himself next to her and held up his glass. 'Cheers.'

'*Salud.*'

'So, what kind of day have you had?'

'The same kind we always have, Casey, you know A&E.'

'True. Okay, let's talk about something else.'

'How was the Family fun day? Did you all have fun?'

He wondered how much to tell her. She knew that he had only just found out about his daughter, but he hadn't mentioned his feelings about it.

'All except Lexi who has a water phobia. I just wish she'd told me before.'

'Oh, the poor girl. Did something bad happen to her in childhood? That is where most phobias have their beginning.'

The lady knew her stuff. 'Got it in one. She was pushed into a swimming pool and held down as a youngster and she never got over the fear.'

'That is so sad. If only people realised the damage they did to others when they behave in such a foolish way.'

'Yes.' He wanted to offload, tell Catalina his fears and ask for her sage advice, but he also wanted his dinner guest to enjoy her evening and not be burdened with his problems. He didn't really know her well enough to divulge private information about Lexi.

Catalina sipped her wine thoughtfully and said nothing. He got up and wandered into the kitchen to check on the chicken.

*

Lexi had been on a late and was looking forward to getting home to bed. Something, however, was niggling at the back of her mind. Casey had made love to her with a passion equal to the night they had met. It had been glorious, and she had felt sure that the dynamics of the relationship would change. Casey, however, had carried on as normal. Nothing had been said, no plans to go out as a couple, or to talk about the way they felt about each other.

If Casey thought they would have sex whenever they felt like it and then carry on as if nothing had happened, he needed to think again. She didn't normally indulge in casual sex; he was the only man she had slept with on the first night. Yes, she had thought they could have another night of hot sex with no strings, but now, in the cold light of day, or evening, she realised how irresponsible that was. There would have to be boundaries, for Jade's sake as well as their own.

She decided to have it out with him. The doctors' accommodation wasn't far from A&E, she would call in on the way home and they'd have a serious talk. He had never invited her there, saying there was nothing much to look at. It was small, basic, and Casey only really used it for sleeping in. Well, maybe she could help him make it more comfortable. Perhaps all it needed was a woman's touch.

*

'This is beautiful, Casey, you've gone to a lot of trouble.' Catalina gestured to the rose and smiled. She was a beautiful woman with dark brown eyes, black hair and olive complexion. She was exactly the type of woman Riordan said he went for and his brother was right. Catalina was comfortable in her own skin, happy with who she was. Her gaze was direct and, as he looked into her eyes across the table, he realised that, with a bit of encouragement on his part, they could become lovers.

Is that what he wanted? Should he take his brother's advice and see Jade on his own? The sex between himself and Lexi was wonderful, but was sex enough?

For dessert he had bought a lemon meringue pie and left it warming in the oven whilst they ate the chicken.

'I love this sweet, how clever of you to know it's my favourite.'

'That's one of my superpowers, didn't I tell you?'

Catalina laughed and tossed her hair over her shoulder. 'You are a very accomplished man, Casey.'

They were flirting and Casey was enjoying it. He felt irritated when the doorbell rang. He would send them away pronto so he could continue his evening with the lovely Catalina.

'Casey, hi. I've just finished my shift and I wondered if we could have a talk.'

Caught completely off guard, Casey stood staring at Lexi with his mouth open. He felt guilty suddenly although he had done nothing wrong.

'It's not very convenient at the moment. Could we have a talk another day?'

Lexi frowned and tried to peer over his shoulder to see who was in the flat. He heard the sound of a chair being scraped on the floor. Catalina had finished eating.

'Okay. Come in.' He stood back and let her walk in.

She stopped when she saw Catalina. 'Oh, I didn't know you had company.'

'This is Dr Martinez, she lives next door. This is Lexi Grainger.'

Catalina came forward with her hand out. 'Very pleased to meet you Lexi.' Catalina was holding the rose and twirling it in her fingers. She saw Lexi watching. 'It is beautiful, no? Casey cut it from the garden.'

'Did he?' Lexi's voice was like ice and Casey cringed.

'Catalina was kind enough to cook a meal for me when I first moved in and I was returning the compliment.' Why was he explaining? It was a perfectly innocent meal and he was a free agent.

'Right.' Lexi stood rigidly in the middle of the room, her face like thunder. Suddenly, Casey felt angry.

'You should have rung me, Lexi.'

'Yes, I see that I should have.'

'I'll go, shall I?' asked Catalina, 'I can see that you two have a lot to talk about.'

'No, you won't, Lexi will. We'll talk at a time mutually convenient to both of us, okay?'

Lexi turned to look him in the eye. He was dismayed to see tears in her eyes. 'I'm sorry I interrupted your meal.' Then she turned and opened the front door.

'Lexi, wait…'

She left without turning around.

'Blast!'

'I think that was a bit harsh, Casey, don't you? It's obvious the girl has strong feelings for you.'

'Would you like some more wine?' Maybe he could salvage something of the good mood of earlier.

'No thank you. I think I should go. I have an early start in the morning. Thank you, though for a beautiful meal.' She reached up and kissed him on the cheek. Then she left.

He was alone with half a bottle of wine and the washing up, wondering what had just happened.

Chapter Seventeen

Lexi was on night duty. When she arrived for her first shift, she walked into the middle of a heated discussion between Raj, Theresa and Sarala.

'Just you wait,' Raj was saying as he typed up a patient's notes on the computer, 'it's the worst night of the year. Soon A&E will be full of kids, spewing their guts up from eating too many sweets.'

'It can't be any worse than New Year's Eve with drunks spewing their guts up, and fighting and singing, all at the same time.' Theresa shuddered theatrically.

Sarala caught sight of Lexi and drew her into the conversation. 'Lex, which side of the fence are you on? Halloween - the work of the devil or good harmless fun?'

Lexi smiled and shrugged. 'I'll let you know at the end of the shift.'

They all laughed at that and Lexi joined in. But the truth was, she was worried. Casey, who wasn't on duty that evening, had asked her permission to take Jade, Jess and Craig, Trick or Treating. He was also taking Tom as Riordan was on call. This, as far as Jade was concerned, was the *pièce de résistance*. She loved having her father to herself without her mother around, but to have her beloved cousin at her beck and call too caused her daughter to dissolve into giggles of happiness. Jade was simply in heaven with the chance to dress up and eat sweets.

Lexi had longed to refuse but, how could she? She couldn't break her daughter's heart by playing the heavy and making her miss out on all the fun, but she was worried sick. She hated Halloween, and she was still smarting from the way Casey had treated her when she interrupted his meal with Dr Martinez. He had made it clear that he didn't want her there. She couldn't help wondering if there was something going on, but she pushed it to the back of her mind to focus on the night ahead.

The previous year she and Jess had taken Jade and Craig Trick or Treating; just around the local streets. She'd held Jade tightly in her arms the whole time and refused to put her down. It was a real eye-opener. All the idiots in Leytonsfield, and it appeared that night that there was a hell of a lot of them, were out on the streets dressed in costumes meant to cause the most disgust and revulsion to the local citizens. She had never seen the point in trying to scare people for the fun of it. Life was scary enough in her opinion, why try to make it worse than it already was?

She vowed she would never take Jade again, even though Craig loved every minute of it and even Jess argued that it wasn't as bad as she was making out, but she hadn't reckoned on Casey being part of their lives the following year. He, of course, loved Halloween.

They had been having lunch in the canteen at the hospital when he had asked her about it, and Riordan had joined them briefly, listening in to the conversation.

'It'll be a fun evening, Lexi, the kids will love it and what harm can it do? The four of us always went Trick or Treating. Our parents took us when we were little and then we went alone as we got older. Riordan was in charge and he never let the rest of us get out of line, did you Bro?'

Riordan shook his head. 'Absolutely, and we got tons of sweets. One of the perks of being the offspring of the local GP.'

She had tried to argue with them 'Trick or Treat' isn't the same as Halloween anyway. That's come over from America. It's just an excuse for the confectioners to make lots of money.'

'I never realised you were so cynical,' said Casey grinning.

'Lexi's right though,' said Riordan who always considered people's arguments seriously. 'The original festival was an old Celtic one called Samhain which means the end of summer. Then the Christians took it over and it became All Hallows Eve, a precursor to All Saints Day which is a time to remember the family's departed.'

'I don't care what we call it, I love it and the kids will too.'

'Well, be careful, okay? It seems to me that it's just an excuse for normally sensible, thoughtful people to dress up and scare the living daylights out of each other.'

Casey had laughed at that and, when they all stood up to leave, he had taken her in his arms and kissed her on the nose. And in front of everyone too. And then he had ordered her out of his flat because he was entertaining another woman. Talk about mixed messages.

That was the end of that conversation. Casey had decided and there was nothing she could do but put it to the back of her mind, stop worrying about Jade and get on with being a nurse.

As Lexi checked the cubicles, getting everything ready for the onslaught, Raj was still on his soapbox.

'What other day of the year do we think it is fine to let kids stuff themselves stupid on sugar, run around in the dark behaving like hooligans, banging on people's doors and accept sweets from strangers? It's everything we tell our kids not to do.'

'You really have a downer on Halloween, don't you?' asked Sarala.

'Yes, I do, with good reason, you'll see.'

Lexi secretly agreed with everything Raj said, and it wasn't long before he was proved right.

Their first serious case of the night was a young boy who had run into the road without looking and been swiped by a car. Luckily, he only sustained cuts and bruises as the driver was going extremely slowly, on the look-out for stray kids, he said. But the child's mother was in hysterics, threatening to take the man to court for dangerous driving and shouting about her precious boy.

'Then why didn't she keep an eye on her child?' Raj said in disgust.

The driver, an elderly man with a kind expression and a gentle voice, was clearly in shock. Although he was not strictly a patient, Lexi was concerned for him and made him a cup of sweet tea. This inflamed the mother even further and she screamed at him that the police were going to lock him up. The police, calm and in control as always, managed to pacify the mother and the driver went home in a taxi, too shaken up to drive.

Raj raised his eyebrows but declined to comment. He had plenty to say, however, when another boy was admitted as he had, apparently, eaten sweets containing sugar instead of his usual diabetic sugar-free ones. Another boy had dared him to do it.

Raj was furious but professional and kept his opinions to himself, concentrating instead on treating the boy expertly to prevent him slipping into a hypoglycaemic coma. He stabilized him and had him admitted to the ward whilst the sister in charge spoke to his parents.

After that, there was a steady stream of children being brought in with stomach ache, vomiting and diarrhoea.

'Okay, okay,' Sarala said as Raj looked ready to explode with frustration, 'you win, Halloween sucks.'

She was right. Their A&E department was overrun with overexcited kids in fright wigs. Lexi's thoughts were never far from Jade and how safe she really was in Casey's care. He could behave like an overgrown schoolboy sometimes and, only the fact that sensible Jess was with them, stopped her from constantly ringing to make sure everything was okay.

After one little girl of about the same age as Jade arrived with her mother, Lexi's nerves unravelled and she texted Casey to, casually, ask how things were going.

He replied by texting a selfie of them all in their costumes, with huge grins on their faces. Lexi had to admit, Jade looked sweet dressed up like a black cat, complete with whiskers and tail. Craig wore a skeleton costume and Tom was dressed like Harry Potter.

Jess looked happy as did Casey. Why was she always the party-pooper, unable to join in the fun? Was it fear or because she was knee-deep in the negative reality of Halloween. The A&E department resembled a war zone and there would be a lot of clearing up to do before her shift was over.

She texted back. 'Great! Have fun all of you and be careful.' Then she turned back to the fray.

Raj was still pontificating, and Lexi and Sarala smiled at each other in sympathy.

'What you all need to be on the alert for,' he said, looking more tense than she had ever seen him, 'is a child with something other than sugar overload. Appendicitis or gastritis. You never know, there may actually be a kid suffering from a genuine medical condition amongst that lot and I'd hate for us to miss it.'

'Yes, boss,' said Sarala making a face and rolling her eyes behind his back.

The sound of a child crying alerted them to the arrival of another patient. A little girl of about eight had been bitten by a dog and blood streamed down her arm. She was crying whilst her father shouted blue murder and threatened to kill someone.

'What happened?' Raj asked as they lifted the child onto a trolley and began to examine her arm.

'That bastard set his dog on the kids. They weren't doing anything wrong. He said he got sick of them banging on his door. It's Trick or Treat for God's sake, what does the old fool think happens at Trick or Treat?'

The man was purple in the face and his daughter looked terrified. Whether from the blood loss or her father's expression, Lexi wasn't sure.

After considerable effort, they calmed the father down and he eventually turned his attention to his daughter. He kissed her on the forehead and said, 'Never mind, sweetheart, Daddy will make sure the police arrest the nasty man.'

The wound was superficial, and father and daughter left the hospital soon after. As they left, they heard the little girl say to her father, 'Can we get some more treats now?'

'Yes, darling, of course,' replied her father.

Raj raised his eyes to heaven and muttered, 'Unbelievable.'

*

The stream of child casualties lessened to the odd one or two, then dried up altogether. They were left with the usual broken bones, cuts and bruises and heart attacks that were the mainstay of a night shift in A&E.

Lexi was just starting to relax, hoping the worst of the night was over, when, at the stroke of midnight, the doors to the A&E department burst open while the red phone in Resus started ringing to alert them to a code red. It seemed to Lexi, that the gates of hell had been flung wide and unleashed all the horrors in creation on the unsuspecting staff.

People streamed in, a lot of them covered in blood. They were holding on to each other to keep themselves upright; people were crying, a few were arguing, pushing and shoving, some were making threats and the majority were extremely drunk. The noise level rose in direct relation to the stress Lexi was feeling and her heart rate increased in line with the noise. A fight broke out as two men threatened to kill each other. Chairs were overturned, and trolleys and equipment went flying against the wall.

Lexi feared for the other patients' safety. Security were there instantly, as if they had been waiting for it to happen.

Lexi just stood and stared, helpless in the face of so many injured. Raj stood next to her with his arms folded and a disdainful look on his face.

'Here we go,' he said, 'the fun has started. This is the second act in the Night of the Walking Dead. Brace yourself.'

Lexi, amazed at his nonchalance, stared at him. 'But there's so many injured and an ambulance is bringing in more. How are we going to cope?'

'Umm… look more closely, Lexi, at our patients. See

anything strange about them?'

'Apart from the fact that most of them are covered in blood, and ...' She looked more closely. Really looked. She realized then that they were dressed in Halloween costumes. There was a zombie carrying an artificial hand, a nurse in a blood-stained uniform with a huge red syringe, a surgeon in scrubs splashed with streaks of blood, waving what looked like fake internal organs, as well as the usual vampires, witches and ghouls.

She noticed that some of the patients had made themselves comfortable on chairs in the waiting area, opened cans of beer and appeared to be carrying on the party they had obviously just left. Very few of them were hurt at all. Just anxious to keep drinking.

Lexi felt stupid at her mistake but, in her defence, seeing a crowd of people covered in blood, even though she now knew it was fake or stage blood, had caused her caring instinct to kick in and she had just wanted to help them.

Now she realized the truth, she was relieved that they were just a bunch of irresponsible young people and she was grateful the children had all gone home. She also felt sorry for the real patients, many of whom had already left, obviously deciding that their emergency, whatever it had been, could wait until the morning.

'Come on, let's go and get ready for the real emergency,' Raj said, leading his team back to the relative peace and normality of Resus.

Chapter Eighteen

As they waited for the ambulance to arrive with their real emergency, a young police constable joined them and gave them an update on events. A student party had been gate-crashed by a group of known "druggies" and fights and general mayhem had broken out. There were few serious injuries, mainly cuts and bruises, which were being dealt with in Minors, but the young woman who was being brought in by ambulance, had been badly beaten up.

'With all the people that must have been at the party and are now in the waiting area,' Lexi said to Raj, 'why pick on a young woman?'

Raj shrugged but looked worried.

When the paramedics delivered their patient, they had their answer. It was Shelley.

Lexi was at her side straight away to assess her condition.

Her face was a mess. Her top lip was swollen, one eye was completely closed, and she had livid red marks on the left side of her face.

'Hi – it's Shelley, isn't it?' she asked gently.

'Yeah,' Shelley replied, 'bad penny, that's me.' She passed out.

As the Resus team worked on their patient, checking vital signs, getting a line in for fluids, intubating her and calling out a list of injuries to the other members of the team as they worked, Raj had stepped away and was on the phone. When he returned to Shelley's side, he spoke quietly to Lexi.

'I've told Casey she's here.'

'But Casey's off duty, we can manage, can't we?'

'Of course we can, but those are his instructions. He wants to be informed whenever Shelley is admitted. He must have a special interest in the girl for some reason.' He looked at Lexi and she thought of the story he had told her about the patient who had died whilst in his care.

'He's just concerned. He suspects there's more going on with Shelley than she's telling us.'

'I agree. Domestic abuse victim, I'd say.'

'Do you think so?'

'Oh yes, no doubt about it.'

When Shelley was stabilized and had regained consciousness, she was taken to scanning for a CT of her head. Fortunately, her injuries were superficial, so she was taken back to Resus for observation. Lexi made her comfortable, then prepared to leave the cubicle.

'Wait.'

'Yes, Shelley, what can I do for you?'

'I heard what you said.'

'I haven't said anything.'

'About being bullied, you told that doctor.'

Lexi remembered the night she had sat by Shelley's bedside with Casey. The girl had been out for the count. Or so they had thought.

'What did I say, remind me?'

'About that boy who pushed you in the pool. Little shit.'

So, she had heard and knew everything they'd been talking about. She wracked her brains to remember what else they'd said to each other. Nothing too personal, she hoped, but she couldn't quite recall.

Hearing was the last sense to go in unconscious patients. Even patients who had been heavily anaesthetized. Shelley was gazing at her, waiting expectantly, her bruised and battered face tense and watchful. Now was the time for complete honesty if she stood any chance of gaining her trust.

'Yes, I was bullied as a kid. I was brought up in care, you see, Shelley, I didn't have parents or siblings or anyone else to look out for me.'

'Same,' Shelley said. Her mouth must have pained her as she barely opened it when she spoke. 'I've got no one. My Dad threw me out.'

'So, where are you staying?' Shelley seemed more interested in her life than in talking about herself.

'But now, you're with that doctor, right? The good looking one?'

'We have history but I'm a single mother. I'm independent, it's how I like it. I don't rely on anyone except a close girlfriend. I don't really trust other people, you see.' As she said the words, she realized how true they were. She wished she could be different, but she had never learned to trust.

'Why?'

'Because people let you down.' She thought of the times she'd been fostered out to couples she had grown to like and sometimes even love. She had high hopes for adoption from one or two, but something had always happened to stop it. The foster family's circumstances had changed; once a couple had divorced, one man had become seriously ill, another family had decided to emigrate. And then, occasionally, she thought they must have just got tired of her as she was returned to the home with hardly an explanation. When she was an adult, her ex-boyfriend had dumped her because, in his opinion, she was too needy. No, people couldn't be trusted.

'He loves you.'

'Who? Dr O'Connor? No, he doesn't.' She laughed to show how absurd that idea was. 'We just work together now, that's all.'

Shelley's expression darkened. 'I'm not stupid, I've got eyes. You'd be the stupid one if you let him go. He'll look after you. He's a good man.'

Lexi was just about to recite her usual mantra about not needing to be looked after, when she thought of Jade and the close relationship her daughter already had with Casey, only after a few months. In her innocence, she accepted everything her father offered her and never questioned any of it.

Whereas she, Lexi, was still suspicious of Casey, never being able to completely relax in his company, wondering what he really thought of her. Why couldn't she be more like Jade? But Shelley was spot on about Casey.

'Yes, you're right,' she said, 'Dr O'Connor is a good man, and an excellent doctor, and he's very concerned about you.' Did that sound too patronizing? Shelley had looked away from her and seemed to be struggling with some inner demon. Lexi took a leaf out of Casey's book and stood quietly waiting for her patient to speak. She didn't want to destroy the fragile trust that was starting to build up by asking too many questions, such as who had given her the bruises and cut lip?

Shelley spoke, quietly and with less confidence than Lexi had ever heard in her voice before. 'He did it.'

'Who, Shelley, your boyfriend?'

She nodded but couldn't meet her gaze. 'I want to be like you,' she said, turning then and looking at her eagerly but with frightened eyes. 'I don't want to take no bullshit from anyone. But I'm scared. I'm not as strong as you, I don't know how to do it.'

Lexi was taken aback. Shelley thought she was a strong person. Not an image she had of herself. Other people didn't see her like that either. Casey certainly didn't, he'd told her to stop living in fear. Or words to that effect. She'd been too scared to go swimming, scared to meet his parents, scared of her own shadow. But this poor, battered girl thought she was a strong person. She couldn't let her down.

'I'll help you if you like. You need to get away from him. Is there anywhere you can stay?'

Shelley shook her head and looked sullen again. Lexi knew now, however, that her surly expression hid real fear and it was her way of covering it up. She feigned cheerful confidence, determined to live up to Shelley's belief in her. No one had ever believed in her before, except Jade and Jess. It was a new experience, one she rather liked.

'There are shelters that will take you in. They're safe havens with people who can protect you and make sure he can never touch you again. You'll meet women in the same predicament. Make friends.'

She wondered if she was selling the idea to Shelley. The girl had the reputation for disappearing just when the medical professionals thought they were getting through to her. This time it was different. The belligerence had gone, and the arrogance. In its place was a lonely, battered and defeated young woman. Lexi's heart went out to her. She recognized that look of defeat, she'd seen it in the mirror on so many occasions growing up.

Well, no more. For herself or for Shelley.

When the porters arrived to take her up to the ward, Shelley reached out her hand to Lexi and she took it in both of hers. It was as cold as ice, but her grip was firm.

'Thanks,' she said.

'You're welcome. I'll liaise with the social workers to find you a place to stay. And you need to tell the police about all the violence he's inflicted on you. He shouldn't be allowed to get away with it.'

Shelley squeezed her hand and nodded. Then she looked her in the eyes and said, 'Don't lose that doctor. You'll never find another like him. Trust me. I know men.'

The porters arrived to wheel her out of the cubicle and towards the lifts, to take her up to the ward. Lexi hoped that this time she wouldn't discharge herself before she got the help she so badly needed.

Lexi busied herself with tidying up and getting ready for the next patient. She was weary to the bone; it had been a long, exhausting night but her shift was nearly over. Halloween was drawing to a close and A&E was getting back to normal.

Raj, Sarala and Theresa stopped her before she left the department.

'So, what's the verdict?' Raj asked.

'Yes,' agreed Sarala, 'you said you'd tell us after your shift.'

She smiled. 'It's a bit of both depending on your perspective.'

'That's a cop-out,' said Theresa.

'No, not really. Just the realization that nothing in this world is ever black or white, one or the other. Most things are a mixture or a mystery.'

'You're weird,' said Sarala hugging her.

'Yes, I probably am. Just like Halloween.'

Chapter Nineteen

Murmurs of appreciation spread through the crowd as explosions of purple, green and red erupted into the night sky, and died away in a shower of colourful sparks.

Jade wriggled with excitement in Casey's arms and Tom and Craig expressed their approval whilst keeping the "cool dude" images that they were both cultivating.

'Awesome,' said Craig.

'Yeah, totes,' agreed Tom.

The Leytonsfield Community Bonfire Night Extravaganza was in full swing.

It had always been an unmissable event for the O'Connors, and Casey's parents were there. Dan was well loved in the community and, as an approachable and amiable doctor, knew many of the families who were present in the park that night. Casey felt enormous pride in his father who was his first and lasting role model. His brother, Riordan, was a close second.

He loved these family events, when they all got together to celebrate and acknowledge a milestone in the year of the community. He loved his hometown of Leytonsfield, being greeted by friends and neighbours and, now he had Jade to show off to people, his happiness was complete.

Well, almost.

The only two negatives were the fact that the twins were still overseas, and he missed them terribly. They both loved fireworks and would have enjoyed this event immensely. Though medical professionals, Jay was a paramedic and Josie a midwife, the pair of them had never lost their cheeky, mischievous natures. They lit up a room by their mere presence and Casey couldn't wait for them to be back with the family at Christmas so he could introduce them to Jade.

The other thing that was bothering him was Lexi. He'd been amazed when she'd agreed to join the family for Bonfire Night. There'd been no arguments or excuses, she'd said yes straight away, and had taken it for granted that Jess and Craig would join in the fun.

They hadn't spoken about the night she gatecrashed his meal with Catalina. He had forgiven her, of course, realising he had probably over reacted, but she had been distant ever since, holding him at arm's length. His head was all over the place, one minute he wanted to get closer to Lexi, the next he decided that he should take Riordan's advice and keep away.

She was standing with Jess and his parents, her hands in

the pockets of her thick winter coat, her blonde hair loose and flowing down her back, staring up at the night sky and the fireworks that lit the park intermittently, casting strange shadows and illuminating faces in flashes of light. He couldn't tell if she was enjoying herself or not, but everyone else was, especially his daughter.

'Daddy, I'm hungry,' said Jade, her hand grabbing his chin and turning his face to hers. It was one of her more endearing habits. She wanted to ensure that he gave her his full attention, which he was more than willing to do.

'Okay, let's go get some food.' He was rewarded with approval from the boys so, after asking everyone else and being assured that they would all be along in a minute, he led the way to the market stalls where the vendors were selling the usual fare of burgers, hot-dogs, baked potatoes, candy floss, toffee-apples, treacle toffee, fudge and ice-cream.

'All good healthy stuff,' said Riordan rubbing his hands together.

'Baked potatoes are healthy,' said Casey.

'Hot-dogs!' shouted the three children in harmony.

'Won't do them any harm for one night,' Casey said as they stood in line with the children.

'I'm glad to see you've taken my advice,' said Riordan, 'I think Catalina has the hots for you.'

'We're just friends. We live next door to each other.'

'She's a very attractive woman and she speaks highly of you.'

'When?'

'I was talking to her in the canteen a few days ago. She's exactly the kind of woman you should be with.'

'Spanish?'

'Professional, intelligent, well-educated and sexy. Yes, and Spanish. A hot blooded *señorita*.'

'You don't like Lexi very much do you?'

Riordan frowned. 'I don't know her well enough to pass judgement. I do think she would be high maintenance and I'm not sure that's what you need at this stage of your life.'

The line for the hot-dogs moved slowly and Jade wriggled to be put down, so she could join the boys.

'And what stage would that be, Riordan?'

'Helen?'

Helen had betrayed him. Lexi hadn't. She would have told him about Jade if she'd been able to find him, wouldn't she?

'I have to move on from Helen. She's firmly in the past. Lexi is the mother of my child, that has to count for something.'

'Yes, but you don't need to rush into anything. You know how impatient you are. How often do you see her?' asked Riordan.

'We see each other at work, obviously. I spend as much time with Jade as I can. Several nights a week and every weekend.'

'Maybe that's the problem. You're seeing each other too much.'

'What do you mean?'

'I think you should back off and give her a bit of space.'

'Back off? No way. Jade's my daughter and I've already missed out on too much of her life, not to have been there for her baby years, missing out on her first smile, first word, first steps... I should have been there.'

'Sounds as if you haven't forgiven Lexi yet. You're still holding a lot of resentment.'

'I have forgiven her, just not myself. I should have tried harder to find her.'

'Daddy, I'm sta-arving,' whined Jade.

'Nearly there, chick. Look, there's only two people in front of us.'

The smell of onions made Casey's stomach growl. The mix of aromas in the air; the sickly-sweet smell of candy floss and toffee apples, mixed with fried onions, reminded Casey of the fairgrounds of his childhood. A familiar, comforting smell that took him back in time. He wanted Jade to have the same happy childhood that he and his siblings had enjoyed. Two loving parents who adored each other as well as their kids. Could he and Lexi make a go of it? What if Lexi didn't feel the same way? What then?

'Are you having Ketchup on your hot-dog, Tom?' Riordan asked.

'Yep,' he said, then followed it up with 'please,' when he saw the warning look on his father's face.

'Me too. Please,' said Craig.

'And me,' shouted Jade, 'please, please, please!'

They all laughed.

'Good girl,' said Casey. He adored his little daughter and

wanted her always to be happy and secure.

After they had bought their food and were happily munching on spicy hot-dogs, sauce dripping down the kids' chins, he turned to his brother again.

'What do you think I should do?'

'Give her space, like I say. Not Jade, of course. You've established a routine with your daughter that's obviously working well. Kids need routine, but does Lexi have to accompany her to everything? Jade is perfectly happy with you on her own, so why not spend quality time alone with her? Give Lexi the chance to do her own thing. It sounds to me as if you feel responsible for Lexi as well as Jade, but you're not, she's a grown woman.'

'I want to encourage Lexi to join in, so the three of us can be a family.'

'You're too impetuous, that's your trouble, always were. As a kid you needed instant gratification, wouldn't wait for anything.'

'But if you know what you want, why not go for it?'

'If something's worth having, it's worth waiting for.'

'That's exactly what Lexi said once,' said Casey, remembering the look she gave him as she spoke the words. A look that nearly brought him to his knees.

'There you are then, that's your answer.'

*

Plastic chairs were grouped around the bandstand where a tribute band played eighties songs. Lexi sat next to Casey enjoying the show. They were good and soon the crowd were singing along with them. Even Dan and Eloise tapped their feet to the music.

Lexi had thoroughly enjoyed herself this evening. Surprisingly. She had accepted Casey's suggestion of them all going to the Bonfire Extravaganza together graciously, pushing down any objections and fears that had immediately sprung into her mind, and there were plenty. Fireworks were dangerous as were bonfires, even the organized ones. Things could still go wrong and get out of hand so quickly. She'd worked in A&E long enough to see plenty of burn victims. And don't get her started on sparklers. The heat from a sparkler was almost as hot as lava, apparently. It didn't bear thinking about the pain that one could cause an innocent child.

Bonfire night was worse than Halloween.

But she was determined to stop living her life in fear. Shelley had told her she was strong, and she was going to be from now on. She'd visited her on the ward and Shelley had asked her to go with her when she looked at safe havens for battered women. Lexi had been checking them out and was quite excited to be part of helping Shelley make the first steps to her new life. Shelley was more relaxed with her since Halloween and had started opening up to her more, talking about the brutality of her ex-boyfriend. She hadn't told the police yet though and Lexi was reluctant to push her. She didn't want to damage the friendship that was starting to build between them.

She thought about what Shelley had said about Casey. She was right, she would never meet another man like him. He was kind, thoughtful, gentle, intelligent, a good father, a great lover. He was perfect, in fact. The realisation that there were women everywhere who would snap Casey up if given the chance had come as a wake-up call. Dr Catalina Martinez was quite a catch and more of an equal for Casey than she was. Perhaps she was already too late.

She looked around at the people in Manor Park. It was full of families; kids, parents, grandparents, aunts and uncles, all smiling, singing along to the music, their children playing happily. There were also teenagers, some in couples kissing in dark corners, or brazenly out in the open, not a care in the world.

Isn't this the life she'd always dreamed of? Alone at night in the children's home, spinning fantasies of having a family of her own one day. Reading her romance novels where besotted couples declared their undying love for each other. This was her dream, and it was within her grasp.

She knew Casey was attracted to her, their nights of hot sex and passion had proved that. But did his feelings run deeper than that? The fact that he had never talked about his emotions at all was making her think that it was a personality trait and not because he didn't have feelings for her. Casey was a man of action, not a talker. He was an athlete with a magnificent body who swam fifty lengths every day. Perhaps he wasn't comfortable talking about his emotions. Maybe he was waiting for her to tell him how she was feeling.

If they were both waiting for the other to start the conversation, they were going to be waiting forever. Perhaps she should make the first move and ask him directly. And sitting here in the darkness, listening to music when he would be happy and relaxed was as good a time as any.

'Casey...?'

'Yes? Oh, by the way, before I forget, I'll be in London for the next couple of weeks. It's the "Urgent and Emergency Care Conference" and I'm lucky to get a place as I registered a bit late. Then I'm taking some time off to visit some old friends, so I won't be able to see Jade for a week or so. I'll bring her something back from London to make up for it. Sorry, I should have said something earlier.'

'Yes, you should. She'll be devastated, but don't worry I'll explain it to her.'

'I'm sorry, but this is something I really don't want to miss. I need to keep up to date with best practice in emergency care. It's part of my job, Lexi, you know that.'

'Of course I do, but I just wish you'd given me more notice. I could have prepared her.'

'Yes, you're right, sorry.' Casey did sound sorry, so Lexi decided to let it go, but she wasn't happy.

Jade looked forward to seeing her daddy in the evenings, to read her a story and tuck her up in bed with a goodnight kiss. Still, she understood. Consultants, especially new ones like Casey, needed to stay ahead of the game and keep up to date with the latest techniques for saving lives. He was only doing his job, it wasn't as if he was swanning off on holiday.

Lexi still felt let down. He should have told her earlier, then they could have explained to Jade together. Instead, it was left to her to pick up the pieces.

The night had lost its magic and she was glad when Casey took them home. He walked them to the door of the cottage, watched as Jess and Craig entered, then kissed and hugged Jade, telling her he would see her soon and that he loved her.

Lexi expected a kiss goodbye at least, if only on the cheek, but Casey just waved his hand and told her he'd ring when he was back from London. Then he got into his car and drove off leaving Lexi feeling puzzled and hurt by his offhand behaviour.

Chapter Twenty

Casey was enjoying being back in London. He'd missed the busyness of the place, the constant buzz of traffic and people hurrying everywhere. There was a satisfying blend of old and new with the historic landmarks mixing with the modern architecture, such as the Shard and the Gherkin. He felt the weight of its history in every old building and the promise of the future in the modern, sleek lines of skyscrapers and office buildings.

The hotel hosting the conference was five-star with two good restaurants and three bars. On the second night, he was feeling content having just enjoyed a three-course meal with a group of doctors on the course, one of whom was Catalina Martinez. He had been delighted to find she was attending as well, and they had travelled down to London together on the train. The more he got to know her, the more he liked her. She was gentle with a wicked sense of humour, and they seemed to be on the same wavelength about so many things.

Casey had his back to the door and was telling Catalina about his experiences as an A&E registrar in London, when he realised her attention was wandering. She usually listened as if she was drinking in every word, but this time she kept glancing behind him, over his left shoulder, at the entrance to the bar.

'Am I boring you?' he asked, jokingly.

'No, of course not. It's just that there is a woman over there who is staring at us.'

Casey turned around and looked. 'Oh shit.'

'Do you know her?'

'She's my ex.'

'She's coming over.'

Helen. He had wondered if he would bump into her as she had also been a registrar in emergency medicine when they were together. She hadn't been at the conference and Casey had breathed a sigh of relief that he wouldn't have to face her. He had started to relax and enjoy himself and now she had turned up and was walking towards them.

Catalina was watching him and frowning. 'Do you want me to leave?'

'No… don't you dare. Help me get rid of her.' She smiled at that and sat back in her chair.

Casey stood up as Helen approached, but he didn't move towards her to give her a hug or shake her hand. When she got close, he was shocked at the change in her. She had lost a lot of weight making her face looked gaunt and there were bags under her eyes. Her hair, which was normally shiny with health, hung around her face and looked as if it needed a wash.

'Casey.'

'Helen.' She looked at Catalina and then back to him.

'This is Dr Catalina Martinez. Catalina, meet Dr Helen Fraser.'

The women greeted each other, and Catalina smiled in welcome. Helen didn't smile back and returned her attention to Casey as if dismissing Catalina.

'We work together in the A&E department at Leytonsfield General,' said Catalina, who seemed determined not to be left out of the conversation.

'Oh… you're back home now, I didn't know, I thought you were still in London. I've been trying to find you.'

'Would you like to sit down?' he asked, not wanting to appear rude.

'Can we talk, Casey? In private.' She glanced at Catalina who raised her eyebrows.

'This isn't a convenient time, I'm afraid. Catalina and I were in the middle of a discussion.'

'I'll leave, Casey, I could do with an early night.'

'No, you don't have to…' It was happening again. The second time he had been enjoying an evening with Catalina and another woman interrupted it.

'Thank you,' Helen said to Catalina who said goodnight and moved towards the lifts.

'You two aren't an item then?'

'What makes you say that?'

'Well, she wouldn't have left so readily if you had been, would she?'

Casey suddenly felt hot. He needed air and space. 'Let's go for a walk.'

'Oh yes, how about the South Bank? It's so pretty at night with the lights.'

'Okay.'

They left the hotel and wandered off in the direction of the river Thames. They walked in silence, and Casey grew more anxious with each step. What could she possibly want to talk to him about?

Eventually, when they reached the river and leant on the railing to watch lights flickering on the water, Casey couldn't stand the suspense any longer.

'You said you were looking for me, why?'

'You're still angry I can tell. I wanted to try to explain.'

'What's there to explain? You got pregnant and had an abortion. Without telling me-'

'And I've regretted it ever since. I'm so sorry for what I did, I wish I could turn back the clock, but I can't. I have to live with it every day and it's driving me insane.'

Casey looked at her closely. She really did seem as if she was on the edge. She was crying silent tears, the kind that came from deep inside.

He gestured to a nearby bench. 'Let's sit down.' They sat. 'Now tell me what's been going on.'

'As soon as I had the abortion I realised what a colossal

mistake I'd made. I am so, so, sorry that I didn't tell you, but everything was so good between us and our careers were taking off, we were living the high life in London and… well, I didn't want it to end. You see female doctors all the time, climbing the professional ladder, on the way to being consultants and professors, but then they have children and…'

'There's such a thing as childcare, Helen. Not all women doctors have their careers cut short because they become mothers. I would have helped, done my bit. That was my baby too.' He leaned forward and put his head in his hands. This conversation was bringing back all the bad memories of finding out what she had done. He wasn't over it yet; the pain was still too raw.

'I know, you're right, we would have found a way, together. I miss you so much, Casey, you have no idea how lonely I've been. It's so good to see you again.'

The autumn evening was chilly with a breeze off the river and Casey wished he'd thought to bring a jacket with him. Helen was wearing a coat that she huddled into for warmth. Or comfort.

'Where are you working? Here in London?'

'No. I'm on sick leave at present. I'm living back with my parents. I hate my life. I've lost everything.'

'Why are you on sick leave?' It can't be because of the abortion, that happened over a year ago.

'I had a bit of a break-down. Mental. I've been in hospital for a while.'

'I'm sorry to hear that. But I don't understand why you were looking for me.'

'My psychiatrist says I need forgiveness. I know he means forgiving myself, but I also need your forgiveness. I can't move on without it. Please Casey, I know what I did was wrong, but I've paid the price. I've been to hell and back this past year and I can't get on with my life. I want to be a doctor again, but I don't trust myself around babies.'

'What do you mean?' Casey felt cold fingers on the back of his neck. He shivered. This was more serious than he had at first thought. She was silent and turned her head away. 'What do you mean, Helen, you can't be trusted with babies?'

'I took one.' Her voice was so quiet that he could barely make out her words.

'What? You took someone's baby?' He could feel the anger in his voice and forced himself to stay calm. 'Tell me what happened.'

'I just wanted to hold her. I wasn't going to do her any harm, honestly. I just wanted to know how it felt to hold a baby so I could pretend she was mine.'

'Is that when you went to hospital?'

'Yes. I didn't have to face criminal charges on the grounds of diminished responsibility, but I had to be sectioned. It was a nightmare, Casey, you have no idea.'

'I'm sorry.' He didn't know what to say. 'When were you discharged?'

'A few months ago, but I can't go back to work yet.'

'And you're still seeing your psychiatrist?' She nodded. 'Is it doing any good, the sessions?'

'I suppose so, but what I really need is you to forgive me. And really mean it. I'll know if you're lying.'

Talk about a rock and a hard place. If he said no, he couldn't forgive her, he'd be telling the truth but preventing her healing. If he said yes, she would know he was lying. What did he do?

'I don't know what you want me to say.'

'I want you to forgive me and mean it, Casey. I want you to help me.'

He was a doctor and thereby honour-bound to heal wherever he was able. Was he also honour-bound not to lie?

'All I can say, Helen, is that I would forgive you if I could. I want you to find peace from all this and to be able to forgive yourself. I think that is more important now.'

'So, you're saying you can't forgive me?'

'I'm so sorry, but-'

'You have no idea what you're doing to me.'

She got up and started walking away. He should go after her, tell her what she wanted to hear, but something kept him glued to the bench, watching her figure diminish and disappear into the crowd.

He stared at the water until the lights blurred and the sound of people laughing and chatting all around him receded. What had he done? He should have lied, how hard would it have been? She was obviously mentally unstable, and he had just made the situation a whole lot worse.

Chapter Twenty-One

Over the next couple of weeks, Lexi grew angrier. Casey had been thoughtless. He should have told her his plans to be away for nearly two weeks, then she could have prepared Jade for his absence. She constantly asked where her daddy was and why he didn't come to see her at night and read her a bedtime story. Jade had grown used to their routine and she didn't understand why he had abandoned her.

She attempted to explain that Daddy was an important doctor and sometimes had to go away because of his work. Jade was not impressed.

It reminded Lexi of the lies she'd told Jade about why Casey hadn't been around when she was a baby; that Daddy had needed to go away because of work. Then, of course, she had never met her father, he was simply a name, a shadowy figure who meant nothing to her. Now, Casey was a living, breathing human being; a warm body to hug her, a laughing voice to tell her how beautiful she was, and to read to her, strong arms to hold her and keep her safe. She missed him desperately.

Lexi, whilst furious with him, also missed him. A&E wasn't the same without his confident leadership. Whenever he was the team leader in Resus, the atmosphere was more upbeat, staff worked faster and more efficiently, as if, under Casey's watchful eye, they suddenly had more to prove to the world. She always felt a warm thrill when Casey, often casually and in passing, praised her for a job well done.

After a while, Jade stopped asking about her father and life slipped back, almost imperceptibly, to the way it had been before Dr Casey O'Connor made his appearance in their lives. If nothing else, it made Lexi realise that she and Jade could live without him if necessary. If he got bored with being a father, or met another woman, or decided to move away again, or …

'Hasn't he even phoned?' asked Jess, sitting back on the sofa with a large glass of Lambrusco and a slice of madeira cake she'd brought home from work.

It was Friday night; the kids were in bed and they were kicking back after a particularly long and arduous week.

'No, he's texted a few times but only phoned once. He wanted facetime with Jade but she'd already gone to bed, and I wasn't prepared to wake her up again. Remember that night she and Craig were watching the scary movie we thought was okay for little ones? It was the following night and I put her to bed earlier than usual.'

'Yeah, the poor little mite had nightmares and ended up sleeping in your bed with you.'

'Woke up screaming. Not like Jade.'

'I blame Craig. He must have known what that film was about.'

'No, don't blame him. I'm the negligent mother, I should have checked it out to see if it was suitable. I feel awful.'

'She's fine now though. No harm done.'

Lexi wasn't sure about that. Jade had woken up screaming for her daddy. Who knew what went on in the subconscious of a small child? Fear never really leaves you. She of all people knew that.

It was peaceful in the cosy living room. The open fire crackled as the flames ate into the wood. The curtains were drawn against the darkness and shadows played in the corners. Light and warmth, essential requirements for well-being. Along with food and drink. She poured them both some more wine and cut two more pieces of cake. What more could anyone want? She refused to think about Casey O'Connor. Who needed men anyway? The four of them managed fine on their own.

Although maybe Jess no longer thought so as she had recently joined an on-line dating site and her head was forever bent over her mobile phone, busy swiping left or right. She hardly ever looked up. Like mother, like son.

Lexi had learned that if Jess liked a guy, she swiped either left or right. Jess had told her, but she could never remember which way round it was, and if she didn't like the look of them, she swiped the other way.

'Anyone interesting?' asked Lexi. She hoped Jess could meet a local man to take her out occasionally and spend his money on her, it would do her confidence the world of good. She worked hard and was a great mother, she deserved something for herself.

'Not much,' she muttered, swiping left and then right. 'There is one guy though, do you want to see?'

'Oh, yes please.'

Jess showed Lexi the picture of a thick-set, bearded man with tattoos and intense blue eyes, who looked to be in his thirties.

'His name's Billy and he's a single parent of two boys. His wife died.'

'Ah, that's a shame.' She hadn't seen him around and, like a protective parent, was curious about the man who had caught her friend's eye. 'Have you met him?'

'Not yet. We've spoken on the phone a few times, once for hours. He looks a tough guy from his picture, but talking to him, he comes across as a big softie underneath. Just my type.' Jess's eyes were shining, and Lexi knew that this man must have something special about him to cause that kind of reaction in her friend. She was practical and slightly cynical about men, but she was a young woman with the same hopes of love and romance as any other young woman her age. Herself included. Despite her desire for independence, a greater desire that would be with her for the rest of her life, was the need to be loved and accepted. To have a family of her own and to feel she belonged somewhere and to someone. She and Jess shared the same dream in that respect.

'Are you going to meet him? I think you should. Whereabouts in Leytonsfield does he live?'

Jess moved so that she was sitting cross-legged on the sofa. With her short hair and huge eyes, she looked like a goth-like pixie.

'Yes. Good. And he doesn't live in Leytonsfield.'

'Where's he from then?'

'Edinburgh.'

'Edinburgh?'

'Aye, he's Scorrtish,' said Jess in a very bad Scottish accent. 'Kind of sexy,' she said grinning. Jess had got it bad and she hadn't even met the guy.

'Well, just be careful. Meet somewhere neutral and always tell someone where you'll be and what time. Me, preferably.'

'Do you want to come with me – check him over for me?'

'No, of course not-'

'Joke.'

'Well, you hear all kind of stories about women in these situations. I don't want anything bad to happen to you.'

'Stop stressing will ya? Nothing's going to happen to me, except that I may meet someone to share my life with.'

'Well, just be careful.'

'I will,' Jess replied automatically. 'Right, movie time. Rom-Com or thriller?'

They opted for the thriller, but Lexi couldn't get into it and let her mind wander. She seemed to be telling people to be careful a lot these days. Jess, and Casey when he had Jade to look after. Was she turning into a neurotic who saw danger around every corner? Why? It was almost as if she'd put her life in a straitjacket to stop herself getting hurt. But other people were the ones taking risks, not her.

And, to avoid pain, she was missing out on pleasure. She envied Jess who seemed to have no reservations. She was upfront and honest with her feelings. If she got hurt, which she had been plenty of times in her life, she picked herself up and got on with it. She didn't brood or indulge in a pity-party, she moved forward and got on with her life.

Why couldn't she be more like Jess? Or Casey for that matter as he was the same. He didn't think things to death, analysing situations from all angles; he assessed, made a quick decision and then acted. And he was rarely wrong, was he? His instant decisions as team leader in Resus were never wrong. He had been right about the swimming lessons. All three of them could already swim, albeit slowly and clumsily, but they'd achieved something she had been too scared to even attempt.

She glanced over at Jess, hunched up on the sofa, stuffing cake into her mouth and staring at the TV in absorbed fascination at the action playing out in front of her. She wasn't thinking about something else, silently tormenting herself with imagined dangers, worrying about things that may never happen. Why couldn't she be more like her?

Because she wasn't Jess. She was Lexi Grainger and she needed to start having more belief in herself. Shelley thought she was strong and, if it ever came to it, she would fight to the death for her daughter. She was a mother, and that's what mothers did.

The only area of her life where she was weak was around Casey. He'd proved by his sudden and thoughtless absence that he wasn't perfect after all. She'd been the one to pacify Jade. She would need to be strong around Casey from now on. He wasn't going to be in control anymore. She would be. The feeling made her feel good. It was empowering.

She poured them both some more wine and turned her attention back to the movie.

Chapter Twenty-Two

From the front, the house looked like all the other houses in the street. An ordinary, large, three storey Victorian terrace. It had bay windows with net curtains and a small front garden containing three wheelie-bins in different colours. No distinguishing features that Lexi could see. Which was exactly the way it should be, as this house was a refuge for battered women and Shelley was moving in that morning.

As Shelley didn't have children, Lexi had found it hard to convince the authorities to let her stay in one of the council-run homes, as so many women needed shelter; far more than Lexi had ever dreamed. It seemed the sleepy town of Leytonsfield harboured many violent men who thought it perfectly acceptable to beat up their wives and terrorise their children.

So, she had swallowed her pride and contacted Casey's

father. As a GP, he knew so many people in the community that she was hoping he would know of a charity or privately-run home that would take Shelley in.

Dan O'Connor knew all about Shelley and was delighted to help. Casey obviously talked through the problems experienced by his more difficult patients with his father, and presumably Riordan, so Dan knew exactly what was needed with little input from Lexi. He'd given her a number to ring and the women had told her to bring Shelley to them straight away as there was a vacancy which wouldn't stay open for long.

The safe haven was run by two sisters in their forties and, when Lexi rang the doorbell, a nervous Shelley standing just behind her, both the women opened the door to greet them.

'Can we help you?' one of them said, then waited for Lexi to speak.

'Hi. I'm Lexi Grainger and this is Shelley. I rang you earlier about her, at Dr O'Connor's recommendation.'

They didn't step back to let them in, and Lexi realized by that small act that they took security very seriously indeed.

'Yes, but I still need to see some identification, if you don't mind.'

'Of course.' Lexi showed the woman her driving license and after she had scrutinized it, she handed it back and smiled.

'Good. Welcome.' Only then did she step back and let them into the house. 'Sorry about that, but we have to make sure people are who they say they are.'

'Of course, we understand perfectly.'

'I'm Nina,' said the woman, 'and this is my sister, Hannah.' Hannah smiled and nodded. She seemed happy to let Nina do the talking.

Shelley was standing next to Lexi, gazing around at the hall they were standing in. It looked clean but a bit scruffy. There were toys on the floor and a strong smell of bacon cooking.

'Right. Come and meet everyone. Have you had breakfast?' This was addressed to Shelley who nodded her head without speaking.

Lexi had a strong feeling of déjà vu. It reminded her of one of the children's homes she'd been in for a while. Basic, but warm and with all the essentials. The kitchen was large with old appliances but was cosy and full of the smell of fried food. The women that were cooking breakfast for their children who played on the floor, turned and said hello.

After they'd all greeted each other, Lexi and Shelley sat at the kitchen table sipping builders' tea from large mugs and listening to Nina run through the house rules.

'There aren't many rules, but the ones we have are set in stone, okay?' Shelley nodded so Nina continued. 'No drugs or alcohol. If you want people to visit, please take them into the lounge and get them to sign the visitors' book. No one in the bedrooms but you and your kids.'

'Don't have any,' Shelley said.

'Fine. Just you then. If you have any problems, anything at all, come and speak to me or Hannah. And lastly, don't tell anyone this address without our permission.'

Shelley nodded again and Lexi wondered if she was gearing up for making a run for it as she had so many times in A&E. But then she smiled and picked up a baby who had been crawling on the floor and was trying to climb up her leg. She put her arms around the boy as if he was her own child and Lexi noticed one of the women give a small nod of approval.

'The only other rule is one that you look as if you've already mastered. We look after each other in this house, including kids. If you see a child in need, help them.'

'Sure.' Shelley jiggled the baby on her lap, and he looked up at her with big, trusting eyes.

Lexi would have liked to speak to Shelley on her own, but she needed to back off now and let her settle in.

'Okay, I'll be off now, but I'll come and see you again, Shelley. If you need anything, you've got my mobile number or just send me a text, okay?'

The two women hugged, and Lexi said goodbye to everyone else before being escorted off the premises by an ever-vigilant Nina. Lexi was glad that Shelley was safe, and she turned to Nina at the front door.

'Thanks, I really appreciate this.'

'No problem. She'll be fine.'

Lexi wanted to hug Nina even though she wasn't normally a demonstrative person, but she restrained herself, imagining it wouldn't be welcome. The sisters did a difficult job extremely well, providing refuge for damaged women. She doubted there would be much room for sentimentality in their lives, but there were things she could do to help; the women needed provisions – clothing for themselves and the children, toys, personal effects. They all cost money. Not to mention the food that they must go through each day in that house.

Lexi had found a cause she believed in and something that she could get involved in outside working hours. It would help her to become a less fearful, more confident person. Helping women and children less fortunate than herself, raising money for the cause. Maybe she could ask the elder Dr O'Connor for his advice on how to go about it.

*

Lexi turned her collar up against the biting November wind. Shelley was settled, she had a few hours before collecting Jade from nursery and she was eager to get home quickly and light the wood fire. There was nothing she loved more in winter than the four of them huddled around the huge fireplace, playing games or watching movies.

She stood in the queue at the bus stop her hands stuffed into her pockets and her woolly hat pulled low over her forehead. Across the street, the café called The Sticky Bun was doing a decent trade for a weekday. She sometimes took Jade there as a special treat on a Friday or if they had been out shopping and Jade was asking for stuff as she usually was. The promise of a milkshake and a piece of cake sometimes pacified her and didn't break the bank.

Lexi realized how hungry she was, and thoughts of hot chocolate and toasted crumpets floated through her mind as she gazed at the punters she could see through the large leaded windows on each side of the front door. A couple sat directly in one of the windows. At first, she didn't notice the man as she was intent on watching the woman who was talking quickly and using her hands to express a point. Her fingers were adorned with rings of different sizes. She was dressed in a black power suit and seemed desperate to convince her table companion of something. The man, who listened without interrupting, occasionally nodding encouragement, was Casey.

Lexi was stunned. She had imagined he was still in London. He said he was going to text as soon as he got home and come round to the cottage immediately to see his daughter. He hadn't mentioned her, just Jade. Why hadn't he told her he was back? And who was that woman?

If this was one of her romance novels, it would be the part were the heroine mistakenly thinks that the hero is having an affair merely because he is with a woman. Lexi wasn't going to fall into that trap. She noticed the papers spread out on the table between them, so this was obviously a business meeting of some kind. If they were having an affair they wouldn't be sitting in the window of a café on the High Street, in full view of everyone.

But then, what kind of meeting could he possibly be having in The Sticky Bun?

Should she go over there and find out? The decision was taken out of her hands when the bus trundled up to the bus stop and the people in the queue started to get on. She got on too and sat at the back, staring out of the window at the café until the rest of the passengers were on and the bus started moving. Casey and the woman were still talking.

Lexi mulled it over all the way home. She was still angry with Casey for disappearing for so long and now she was feeling let down because he hadn't told her he was back. Should she ask him about it? Admit that she had seen him and ask who the woman was? But he was under no obligation to tell her everything he did. He was a free agent. They both were. What right did she have to question him? The accusation that her ex-boyfriend had thrown at her that she was too clingy answered her questions for her. She shouldn't care what he did. He could go wherever he liked and have meetings in The Sticky Bun with whomever he liked, it was none of her business.

So, why couldn't she shake off a feeling of unease? Instinct told her there was something he wasn't telling her, something she had the right to know about.

Chapter Twenty-Three

When Lexi arrived at A&E the following morning, she wondered if Casey would be on duty but there was no sign of him. She had expected him to turn up at the cottage the previous night, or at least to text her to tell her he was back, but there had been nothing. If he hadn't phoned or texted by lunchtime, she would phone him.

She nearly fell over a Christmas tree in the patient waiting area as it was lying on its side halfway across the entrance and two men from the Estates Department were clearing a space in a corner to put it up. It was huge. Not the usual six-foot, artificial tree that seemed to be dragged out year upon year, getting tattier and more threadbare every time. This tree looked as if it might touch the ceiling, had been freshly cut from an alpine forest that morning and delivered straight to the department by Santa's little helpers.

'What the heck is that doing there?' Lexi asked.

'It's having a little rest until we can get it moved. What d'ya think it's doing there?' said the younger man.

'There's no need to be snarky but it's right in the path of the patients. Sick people who need urgent attention. I suggest you move it as soon as possible.'

'Yes, ma'am.'

'Is it real?' Lexi asked, touching one of the branches.

'No,' said the older, friendlier man, 'it's an artificial ten-foot Woodland Pine. Nice eh?'

'Has the NHS won the lottery?'

'No, your boss paid for it. And the decorations. Which are over there in those boxes.' He gestured towards reception where tinsel was already tied around the computers, and white fairy lights hung across the counter at the back. Christmas appeared to have started early.

'When you say my boss, who exactly do you mean?'

'He means me,' a familiar voice said behind her.

'Casey. You brought the tree? Why?'

'Because we needed a new one and I wanted to contribute something to the department. It's my first Christmas as A&E consultant and as a dad. I want to celebrate in style.'

'Ah, congratulations, mate,' said the older estates man, grinning at Casey. 'I've got four kids and let me tell you, Christmas is such a magical time when they're little.'

'I can't wait.' Casey said, grinning back and Lexi's stomach dropped. They hadn't discussed arrangements for Christmas yet. Lexi had, naively, she now realized, thought that Christmas Day would be spent as usual: Jess, Craig, Jade and herself. Casey obviously thought otherwise. But that was a conversation for another time. There was work to be done.

'See you later,' she said to Casey as she turned and started to walk away.

'Lexi, we need to talk.'

'Okay. Later though.' No doubt he wanted to tell her that he was having Jade on Christmas Day. Well, he wasn't, and she would never leave Jess and Craig to spend Christmas Day alone. It was too early to have this conversation. It was too early for trees and stupid tinsel tied around everything in sight. Even the IV stands were decorated with them.

She wondered when, exactly, she'd turned into the Grinch? She used to love Christmas. But that was when Jade was a baby and didn't really know what was going on. Now, she was a little smarty-pants and knew too much for her age. She knew how to get around her father, that was for sure. And Casey had a habit of spoiling her.

Christmas was becoming just another source of stress. Didn't she have enough of that already?

*

Lexi was working in Resus, and Casey was Team Leader. About an hour into their shift, a patient was brought in who made Lexi's heart break. She would rather face all the drunks, student Halloween parties and battered women in the whole of Leytonsfield than to watch little Mrs Maisie Williamson try to smile bravely at her husband, Walt. Lexi just stood watching helplessly at the bottom of the bed the patient had been transferred to. Maisie clutched Walt's hand tightly. Even though the paramedics, nurses and the junior doctors had each grabbed a piece of the sheet she was lying on and moved her ever so slowly and gently onto the bed, the emaciated woman had cried out in agony and Walt's face had crumpled with the grief of watching his wife in so much pain.

'This is Mrs Williamson, eighty-eight and in the terminal phase of stage four small cell lung carcinoma. She has extensive bone, liver and brain metastases and has suffered a myocardial infarction. She also has suspected pneumonia and pleural effusion.' As the paramedic gave his report, Lexi moved automatically to Casey's side. He was staring at the floor with a frown on his face as he listened.

'The most important thing, apart from her need for increased analgesia, is the DNR order.'

DNR. Do Not Resuscitate. The patient had made the decision not to have CPR in the event of another heart attack. Which meant they could do nothing for her but make her comfortable and stand by and watch her die. Lexi felt like weeping.

'Okay,' Casey said when the paramedics had gone. 'I need a nurse to make sure she is comfortable and has all the morphine she needs. Lexi? Could you find an appropriate cubicle for Mr and Mrs Williamson please?'

'Of course.' He started to turn away. 'Casey?'

'Yes?' Lexi had never seen Casey so sombre. She knew how much he hated losing a patient. Even one like Maisie with a terminal disease.

'Are we going to drain the pleural fluid? And should I fix her up to the ECG? What else can we do for her?'

'Honestly? Not much. I'm not prepared to inflict more pain on her by doing an invasive drainage and the tumour would just cause her chest cavity to fill up with fluid again in a short time. She'll need oxygen and I'll get the SHO to insert a line for the syringe driver. Just make her as comfortable as you can, catheterize her and don't hesitate to come and get me if you need help.'

'Okay.' She watched him walk away, his head down and his shoulders slumped. She knew exactly how he felt.

It was terrible watching the SHO, a young woman called Shirley, who didn't look old enough to be out of school, and who was fighting back the tears, try to insert the syringe driver on the old lady. Nurses were usually the ones to set them up, but Casey wanted his junior doctors to have experience with all the procedures that were done to his patients. He said that was the only way to learn, but Lexi could tell how nervous she was and wished Casey had let her do it this time.

Maisie had lost so much weight and had obviously been bedridden for so long, she was like a little skeleton. But it was essential she succeeded as the patient would need a constant supply of pain relief and she had lost the ability to swallow tablets. The fluid in her lungs was causing her severe shortness of breath and, although she was calm enough at the moment, could become distressed very quickly. Casey would probably prescribe Midazolam if she became agitated. She would also need an antiemetic to stop the feeling of nausea that she was constantly fighting.

Lexi glanced at Walt, standing watching intently and wringing his hands. She just wanted to hug him and tell him everything was going to be alright. But, of course, it wasn't. He was losing his beloved wife and it was tearing him apart.

'Mr Williamson? Can I have a quick word?'

As they stepped outside the cubicle, he gave Lexi his full attention, a look on his face that was a mixture of hope and dread.

'Mr Williamson-'

'Walt, please.'

Lexi smiled. 'Walt. Your wife is very ill, and we are doing our best to make her as comfortable as possible.'

'I know, and I'm grateful, we both are. She's been through a lot this year.'

'So have you I imagine.'

He shook his head and frowned. 'It doesn't matter about me. She's all that matters. I want to be at her side when she passes, like I've been for the last seventy years. We were childhood sweethearts. You all know about that order thingy, don't you?'

'Yes, of course. Your wife's wishes are for a natural death. We won't try to bring her back, I promise.' Lexi was relieved that Walt understood the implications of Maisie's condition, but she felt helpless in the face of the man's bravery and grief. She just wished there was something more she could do. Casey's words came back to her, that patients deserved a good death as much as a good life and she knew that all her nursing skills would be brought into play over the next few hours, to make little Maisie Williamson as comfortable and calm as she could.

'I'll make you a cup of tea. How do you take it?'

'Milk two sugars. Could you make Maisie one as well? I know she can't swallow as well as she used to, but she could have sips, couldn't she? She loves her tea, that one.' He looked at her hopefully and Lexi nodded.

'Of course. I'll put it in a plastic feeding cup and she can have sips.' It would help to prevent her mouth from becoming uncomfortably dry from the oxygen.

'She has milk and two sugars as well. We're two peas in a pod me and Maisie.'

Lexi smiled again and hurried away to the staff kitchen before Walt saw the tears that were welling and threatening to spill down her face.

As she made the tea, Lexi wondered how it would feel to be with the same person for seventy years. According to her admission form, the couple didn't have children, so it appeared that Walt was truly her other half. The thought of what would happen to the poor man afterwards was unbearable and Lexi tried to banish such thoughts from her mind. Her remit was to look after her patient as best she could. There was nothing she could do for Walt but be around to answer questions or to hold his hand when he broke down, as he invariably would.

But Lexi was wrong. After a long, stressful day, spent checking Maisie's medication to ensure her pain relief was adequate, making tea for Walt and leaving them alone for brief periods to attend to other patients, the end, when it came, was peaceful.

She had only nipped out of the cubicle to use the bathroom and get herself a bottle of sparkling water, expecting the situation to be the same when she returned. Instead, she found Maisie lying still with her eyes closed and Walt, clutching her hand and talking to her gently. He was telling her how much he loved her and how much she had enriched his life. How she was everything he had ever wanted. A final outpouring of love from a devoted husband.

This was an intensely private moment, but Lexi was rooted to the spot at the entrance to the cubicle. She needed to move away and leave Walt and Maisie alone for one last time.

When she went back, Walt was calm although his eyes were red from crying and he looked exhausted.

'She's gone,' he said.

'Oh, Walt, I'm so very, very sorry. I wish there was more we could have done.'

'Can I just sit here for a while? I won't be in your way?'

'Of course you can. Stay as long as you like.'

He was still sitting there at Maisie's side when Lexi went off duty. Nobody had the heart to ask him to leave.

It was a good job it was Friday night, the time she and Jess allowed themselves a bottle of wine when the kids were in bed. She felt like getting roaring drunk. Totally off her head. But she knew she wouldn't, and she also knew that her dreams that night wouldn't be pleasant ones.

Chapter Twenty-Four

Casey managed to press the doorbell, even though his arms were full of parcels. Presents for everyone and bottles of booze. He thought Lexi would probably need a drink after the day they'd both had. He knew he did. He hoped she would ask him to stay the night, so he could dull the edges of the pain of losing a patient and not have to drive home. Somehow, he doubted it.

She had left before he had got the chance to talk to her. The death of a patient was never easy, no matter how many years of experience a person had. Sometimes patients arrived in A&E DOA – dead on arrival – and then, tragic as it was, the staff didn't feel so responsible. Then there were the patients that were teetering on the brink and were saved by the quick actions and skill of the medical team. They were the most satisfying cases. Those people were the reason he had become a trauma consultant. And then there was the third type. The ones who, like Maisie, had been admitted to A&E to die and there wasn't a thing anyone could do about it.

Little Maisie Williamson had been a sweetie: brave, uncomplaining, gentle, one of the old school of patients who were grateful for every little thing that was done for them instead of the younger ones who treated A&E like their own private clinic and complained about everything from the price of chocolate in the vending machine to the unreasonably long wait they had to endure, as if they were in a five-star hotel.

God, he was tired. And crabby. And still shaken from his encounter with Helen. He wondered if he would ever see her again. But the thought of seeing Jade again cheered him up.

'Casey, I wasn't expecting you.' Lexi had dark circles under her eyes and had lost her sparkle. He doubted he looked any better.

'I wanted to see how you were and to see Jade as well, of course.' He could hear his daughter's excited chatter inside the cottage and his spirits lifted.

'Come in.' She stepped back and he entered a world of cooking smells, a crackling wood fire, children's laughter and, the best sight in the world, his little girl running up to him and throwing herself into his arms.

'Daddy!'

'Hello gorgeous. I've missed you.' He swept her up in his arms and hugged her wriggling little body to him. Immediately, he felt some of the tension start to drain away.

'Did you buy me a present?'

'I sure did. Do you want it now?' He looked at Lexi with raised eyebrows and she nodded. She was standing watching them and her expression was unreadable.

'Yeah.'

'Okay then. Let me see if I can find it.' He had placed the presents on the floor before he picked Jade up, so he put her down, then made a big show of rummaging through them even though he knew which one was hers; the biggest one, wrapped in pink.

'Here we go.' He glanced at Lexi who was still watching him. Something was wrong. This was more than the fact that a patient had died. She was annoyed with him over something. 'I got you a present too.' He handed her a box, gift-wrapped by the man on the perfume counter at the department store. 'I hope you like it.'

'Thanks.' She opened it while glancing at Jade opening hers. He rather liked being the bearer of gifts for his girls. It made him feel like a real husband and father. Although technically they weren't even boyfriend and girlfriend yet. A situation he wanted to change as soon as possible. He'd waited long enough.

'Christian Dior, wow. That's expensive. Thanks Casey.'

'No probs. I've got something for Jess and Craig too.' Right on cue, the two of them emerged from the kitchen.

'Hello stranger,' said Jess, 'did I hear someone mention my name?'

'Here – catch!' He lobbed a soft parcel at her, and she caught it deftly. He handed Craig his game and ruffled his hair. 'That's for you, pal.'

'Cool, thanks.' A boy of few words. Which was probably just as well, as Jade had enough for the both of them.

'Daddy, you've got me a dress.' She was holding up his gift and examining it closely.

'Not just any dress, honey, that's the dress that Sleeping Beauty wears. You know that story, don't you?' He knew she did as he had read it to her plenty of times. It was one of her favourite fairy stories which she was happy to hear again and again.

'Yeah.'

'Thanks, Casey, that's kind.' Lexi was still standing, almost as if she wanted to say something but not knowing how.

'That's not all. Have you ever been to a pantomime, Jade?'

'No.'

'Would you like to go to one?'

'I don't know.'

'She doesn't know what they are, Casey,' Lexi said with a frown. Of course, Lexi wouldn't have been able to afford to take her. The tickets for the best performances were expensive.

'It's like a movie but on the stage.' Craig spoke from the sofa where he was absorbed in something on his mobile. He looked up briefly then blushed as if he had surprised himself by speaking up.

'Well, we are going to see *Sleeping Beauty* at the Opera House in Manchester. And you can dress up for the occasion and wear your very own Sleeping Beauty dress. What do you think of that?'

'Yeah!' Jade started jumping around the living room as Jess came back wearing the *I heart London* T-shirt he had brought for her. He hadn't noticed her absence as he had been so engrossed in watching his daughter.

'This is great, Casey, thanks mate.'

'Glad you like it.'

'Craig, set another place at the table for Casey, would you? We're having cottage pie,' said Jess.

'Great. I love cottage pie.'

He glanced over at Lexi to see her reaction to this and was glad to see she was talking to Jade and explaining further about pantomimes. He wondered if she'd ever been to one. He'd have to ask her later. There was something else he wanted to ask her too, but he needed to catch her in the right mood, and tonight wasn't looking favourable.

*

Lexi started to feel better as the evening went on. The meal had been pleasant enough. Jess made a superb cottage pie and Casey finished his first. He declared that he had been starving and Jess promptly took his plate and loaded it with more food. He grinned like a little boy and tucked in again.

Lexi spoke little, preferring to listen to the talk around the table which was easy-going and amusing. She didn't want to have to deal with anything serious tonight. The image of Maisie and Walt Williamson kept drifting across her inner vision and, instead of pushing it away, she let it drift. They had all done the best they could for Maisie and there was no point in going over old ground. She also knew that she would never forget her.

The evening continued with their usual routine. She and Jess did the washing up while Casey put Jade to bed. Craig had disappeared straight after the meal to his mother's bedroom so he could have some time alone on his computer before going to bed when Jade was asleep. It was difficult for an eight-year-old boy to share a bedroom with an almost four-year-old girl, but he never complained. Lexi loved him for that.

When Casey came downstairs, Jess went upstairs to enjoy facetime with Billy. She did this nearly every evening now; their relationship was moving forward at an alarming rate. At least, Lexi found it alarming; Jess seemed to find it exhilarating. She had a new spring in her step and a permanent grin on her face. Lexi just hoped it didn't come crashing down around her ears.

Casey collapsed on the sofa next to Lexi. 'She's finally asleep. Too excited about the pantomime to listen to any other story but Sleeping Beauty, and I had the heck of a job convincing her not to sleep in that dress.'

'Thanks for the tickets. When is it again?'

'Saturday. It's the matinee and starts at 2.30 so I promised her we could go to MacDonald's first. Is that okay with you?' He glanced at her and she smiled. He was asking her permission after he had told Jade, again. She had almost given up on getting him to run things by her first. It was a concept that he completely failed to grasp. But what did it matter? She was too tired and depressed to care tonight.

'It's fine,' she said. 'Shelley seems happy in her new

home. I took her to Nina and Hannah's and left her cuddling a baby and eating bacon butties. That was on Wednesday.'

'Yes, Dad told me what a great job you'd done finding her a place. I'll go and visit tomorrow. I'm on a late, so I'll have time to call in beforehand.'

'She'll be happy to see you. Your dad was very helpful, I appreciated it.' She sipped tea from her favourite mug and settled back on the sofa.

'He's Nina and Hannah's GP and has treated many of the women they help. It's one of his pet obsessions, helping women who are victims of domestic abuse.'

'I'd hardly call it an obsession, Casey, more of a calling.'

'Dad can get very passionate about the causes he supports.'

'So that's where you get it from, then.'

'Me? Do you think I'm like that?'

'I think you can be very passionate, Casey, yes.' Passionate in his work and in his bed. The thought made her want to move nearer to him, put her arms around him and lay her head on his chest. But they needed to talk. She had to ask him. Even though she had made the decision to say nothing, she needed him to be straight with her. If he lied, she wanted to know why. But she couldn't just blurt it out and had to lead up to it slowly.

'How was the conference?'

'It was good. I learned quite a lot.'

'Great. Then you spent the rest of the time in London?'

'Not all of it.'

'Oh? So when did you get back to Leytonsfield?'

'Thursday. I would have called round straight away, but I didn't get back until late.'

'Thursday? Are you sure? Not Wednesday?'

He looked at her. He had been staring into the fire, answering her questions half-heartedly. Was it Lexi's imagination or did he now look a bit shifty?

'What is this, Lexi? Why all the questions? Does it matter when I got back?'

'I saw you.'

'Pardon me?'

'When I left Shelley, I waited at the bus-stop on the High Street. I saw you and a woman in the window of The Sticky Bun. That was Wednesday.'

He put his head back and closed his eyes. He had nowhere to hide now. He couldn't deny it. Was he about to confess all? But what was he going to confess? That he had a flat white and a toasted teacake with a business associate? She may have been a family friend or the O'Connors could have businesses she knew nothing about. It wasn't the woman she was bothered about, just the fact that he had tried to cover it up.

He sat up and looked her straight in the eye. He had a half-smile on his face. Lexi felt irritated with him. If he was in the wrong, he should at least have the decency to look guilty. Instead, she was the one who felt guilty, for questioning him like a nagging wife.

'Okay, Miss Marple, you want to know who the woman is?'

'I don't care about the woman, Casey, I just want to know why you lied to me.'

'Fair enough. I didn't lie when I said I came back on Thursday, but I did lead you to believe it was this week when in fact it was last week.' He waited for her reaction.

'You've been back a whole week? Why didn't you say you were back? Jade has really missed you and has been constantly asking when you were coming home.' Not exactly true; she had stopped asking after about a week. At the mention of Jade, however, he rubbed his face with the palms of his hands.

'I'm sorry about that, I missed her too, desperately, but I didn't want you to know I was back until it was finalized, and I had the keys. That's what we were doing in The Sticky Bun, exchanging contracts. She's an estate agent.'

'I don't understand.' Casey had obviously bought himself a house, but why was that such a cause for secrecy?

'I need to show you then. Let's go now. Jess can look after the kids. Come on.' He grabbed her hand and pulled her to her feet. 'Go and tell Jess and put your coat on.'

Chapter Twenty-Five

This wasn't the way he'd planned it. For a start, he wanted to show her the house in the daylight when he could point out all the best features, as the estate agent did for him. But she had seen him and was understandably angry at him for lying to her. He hated lying and being lied to. Maybe he'd handled this all wrong, but it was too late to backtrack, he just had to convince her that he had acted with good intentions.

They pulled up outside a large detached house a couple of blocks from his parent's house. It was ideally situated for the hospital, schools, shops – okay, enough. She could see for herself.

The house was in darkness and would remain so as the electricity was switched off. He had brought a torch with him and that would have to suffice.

She had been silent during the drive here, occasionally

throwing him glances and then looking away again. Lexi was a lady who kept her thoughts to herself and he found her hard to read at times, but he was getting used to her ways and the little tells that she unconsciously gave out. When she frowned, it didn't necessarily mean she was angry, it could just as easily mean she was thinking. She was a great thinker was Lexi. And a worrier. He would need to be the one to re-assure her.

Casey could think of several ways to do that. It seemed ages since they had made love and he was desperate for a re-peat performance, but that wasn't going to happen tonight. Tonight was for talking. About their future.

'Stay by my side as there's no electricity and we'll have to use the torch,' he said as they got out of the car and walked carefully up the path to the front door. There was a large gar-den surrounded by a hawthorn hedge, about which the estate agent had enthused. The mayflower was a delight when it was in bloom, apparently, but now, in the dark, the garden was full of weird, black, unidentifiable shapes and shadows.

Casey put the key in the lock, and it turned easily. There was an inner porch and two steps up to the front door. This key turned easily as well, and he pushed the door open. No creak thank goodness.

The smell, when they entered the hallway, was of lemon air freshener. He would have been mortified if it had smelt musty. The house had been empty for a few months, had bare floorboards, ancient wallpaper and no curtains. This was only his second visit and he'd fallen in love with the place almost immediately. It was exactly what he had been searching for. Foolishly, he hadn't taken a lot of notice of the smaller details. Now, with Lexi by his side, he saw it through the eyes of a woman with a child. The woman and child he wanted to live with him and turn this house into a home.

He shone the torch down the length of the hallway. There wasn't much to see except the doors leading off, and the stairs, which were bare of carpet, leading to the first floor.

'Do you want a quick look in each of the rooms?'

'Okay.' Lexi had hold of his elbow as he had suggested, and he liked the feel of her hand on his arm. He opened the first door.

'This could be the drawing room, maybe.' He shone the torch around the walls, and they peered into the room, which was a decent size with a large bay window. The house was similar to the one he had grown up in and he tried to imagine what it would look like full of furniture, books, knick-knacks and the clutter of family life. The thought excited him.

'Okay, let me show you the kitchen. You're going to love it, it's such a great size and room for one of those large wooden tables like my parents have got.'

They looked at every room, both downstairs and upstairs. He tried to sell it to her the way it had been sold to him, but he was no estate agent and, as it was pitch black apart from the beam of light from his torch, he didn't think she was seeing it at its best.

When they were in the master bedroom, the one he had earmarked for himself and Lexi, he pulled her into his arms and hugged her. She hugged him back but then stepped out of his embrace and stuffed her hands into her coat pockets.

'What do you think?'

'I think it's a very nice house, Casey.'

'A family house, yeah?'

'Yes, I suppose it is. I'm sure Jade will enjoy staying here with you when it's your turn.'

'Or maybe she'd like to live here permanently. Make it her home. It's close to a good primary school and my parents, and-'

'No. She lives with me. Is this your way of telling me you're going to apply for custody of her? Because if it is, I'll fight you all the way.'

'What? No! Is that what you think? I'd never do that.' He tried to reach for her, but she backed away from him.

'Get away from me, Casey. I thought I could trust you, but you go behind my back, make decisions for Jade without consulting me...' She was walking backwards, and Casey was following her when suddenly she cried out and tripped in the darkness, falling on her bottom onto the bare floorboards. 'Ouch!'

'Careful... here, let me help you.' He helped her up and put his arm around her. 'Are you hurt?'

'No. I can't believe you're being so devious. You're not taking my daughter away from me.'

'Lexi listen to me. You've got the wrong end of the stick. Of course I want Jade to live here permanently, but I want you as well. I want the three of us to live here as a family.

Together. Wouldn't that be great? I want you both to move in when I do.'

*

Lexi couldn't believe what she was hearing. He'd bought the house for the three of them, not just for himself. He wanted them to be a family. He was looking at her eagerly as if he expected her to be leaping around the house with joy as Jade would have done. All she felt was immense sadness.

'Oh Casey, why do you always do this to me?'

'Do what to you? I thought you'd be happy. Don't you want to be with me?'

The answer, of course, was yes, more than she had ever wanted anything, but not like this. Not because it would be convenient, the next logical step. Would he be asking her to give up work next and become a full-time mother and look after the home? The wonderful home he had bought without even consulting her. She'd become a glorified housekeeper to the successful doctor. He would make all the decisions for his home, his daughter and his… what?

'What am I to you, Casey?'

He looked puzzled, as much as she could tell in the torch-light. He shone it on the ceiling, so it wasn't in their eyes and he was merely an indistinct figure in front of her and a voice coming out of the darkness.

'What do you mean? You're the mother of my daughter, my lover, a respected colleague, my friend – I hope.' He laughed. He just didn't get it.

'Do you love me?'

'Come here, you,' he tried to make light of it and reached for her, but she backed away, making sure she didn't fall on her butt again.

'You don't, do you?'

'Yes, of course I love you. I thought you knew I loved you.'

'How can I know when you never tell me? You've never said it, not even when we make love.'

He gave an irritated sigh. 'I'm not good with the emotional stuff, Lexi, but it doesn't mean I don't feel it inside. I think the world of you, you must know that.'

'You tell Jade you love her all the time. That comes easily to you.'

'She's my daughter, that's completely different.' His voice was stern, and she wished she could see his face properly.

'I've always dreamed of living in a house like this, with Jade and maybe more kids, with a man who adored me and who I adored back.'

'And now I'm offering that to you. It's not a dream anymore, Lexi, it's a reality now.'

'No. You're only offering me half of it. Unless you can offer the second half, I'm afraid Jade and I are going to have to decline your kind offer.'

Chapter Twenty-Six

On Friday, the day before the pantomime, Lexi was on duty in Minors.

On the way in, she stopped in the patient waiting area to admire the tree, now standing proudly in the corner, adorned with the decorations that brought it to life. There were gold and silver baubles, tiny boxes wrapped in multicoloured paper to represent gifts, red and gold tinsel and a shiny silver star on the top. It was bright and cheerful, and Lexi hoped the patients would gain some pleasure from it.

Casey had good taste. Had he bought a similar tree for his new home, the one he expected them to share? She pictured the three of them decorating it together as, seen through the window, snow fell gently, turning the garden into a winter wonderland. Inside, they were warm and cosy with the smell of ginger-bread baking and Jade beside herself with excitement. It would be a dream come true. A scene straight out of her romantic novels.

But there was a vast difference between a dream and reality. She had lived in the real world since Jade was born; a world of frugality, struggle, worry and stress as well as the sheer unadulterated pleasure of watching her daughter grow and thrive.

And there had been friendship too, and laughter. Jess was her best friend; the four of them together had made a good team. They'd been happy and content until Casey had re-entered her life and turned it upside down.

If she knew for sure he loved her, things would be different, but she didn't. She'd never been in love, so she didn't know how it felt. What they shared wasn't love. Good sex and shared parenting wasn't enough for a relationship. There had to be more.

'Are you going to stand there all day, or are you planning on doing some work, Nurse Grainger?' The voice of the sister-in-charge caused her to whirl around in horror. But it was only Theresa who stood laughing at her.

'Don't do that, you scared the living daylights out of me.'

'You were staring at that tree as if it held the answer to some deep meaningful question.'

'I was simply admiring it, that's all.'

'Right. Come on then, before the real Sister comes after us.'

*

The morning was surprisingly uneventful. She treated a few sprains and breaks where people, especially the elderly, had slipped on the icy pavement. The temperature had dropped suddenly, causing the wet ground to freeze overnight, catching people unawares.

She was treating a knife wound, sustained by an elderly man who had been preparing chestnuts for his wife to add to the stuffing for the turkey they were having on Christmas Day. The knife had slipped and cut him across three of his fingers. Fortunately, the wounds were superficial and would heal completely in time.

'She wanted to get organized this year as they're all coming to us for Christmas,' he explained, 'get the veg peeled and the chestnuts cooked, then stuff it all in the freezer 'til Christmas Eve, she said.'

'Sounds like a plan,' Lexi said, carefully cleaning his wounds.

'Aye,' he said, 'and it would have been if I hadn't cut me bleedin' fingers.'

'Oh, I'm sure your wife will forgive you. It was an accident, after all.'

'Have you met the wife? Happy bloomin' Christmas.'

Lexi tried not to laugh as she bandaged his hand. It was true he wouldn't be doing any more work in the kitchen for a while.

She considered family life as she worked, and how much of a minefield it could be for some people, especially at the festive season. Arguments about whose family to spend it with, having to invite elderly relatives that you never saw from one month to the next, the forced jollity of trying to live up to the adverts on television. Was it worth it? Perhaps being single was a better option.

She saw in her mind's eye a pair of soulful green eyes gazing at her with a look she had always interpreted as lust. But, looking deeper, behind the forest green with the black ring around the irises, there was another emotion swimming in the depths. Was it love? She wished she knew.

*

There was something about the lead up to Christmas that caused people to hurt themselves, by accident or on purpose, and it seemed to Casey that this day they had all found their way to Leytonsfield A&E. He had never known it so busy. It reminded him of his previous job in London, but without the gang warfare.

Lexi was in Minors, so he didn't even have her company that day, but when a woman was brought in with a suspected overdose, he was glad she wasn't around.

At first he thought she was another case like Shelley and was happy to leave her in the expert care of his team, leaving him to administer to a road traffic accident victim who had been brought in at the same time. The Sister-in-Charge was a middle-aged Scottish woman who took no prisoners, neither patients nor staff. She was, however, one the best nurses in A&E and Casey was happy to leave the woman in her care. He had just turned away when she called his name.

'I found this in her handbag addressed to you.'

'Me?'

'It says Dr Casey O'Connor on the envelope. That's you isn't it?'

He skimmed over the note, after ripping open the envelope, then screwed it up and shoved it into his pocket.

'Does that note give us any clue to her identity?'

'Her name's Dr Helen Fraser and she's under psychiatric care. What's she taken?'

'A mixture of painkillers and Diazepam. Not enough to kill her but she's barely conscious. She's a doctor?'

'I used to work with her in London.'

'The poor wee lassie. So what's she doing here in Leytonsfield I wonder.'

'I was wondering exactly the same thing,' said Casey. The note, however, had given him the answer to that. It had simply read *"See what you've made me do."* If Helen thought that her cry for help would make him feel guilty and responsible for her welfare, she was right on both counts. He was devastated to think he had driven her to this, and all because he couldn't bring himself to lie to her. If only he'd just told her he forgave her, a few simple words, then this would never have happened.

'Let me know when they take her up to the ward, please Sister.'

'Of course.'

'He left the cubicle feeling worse than he'd felt for a long time.

*

'Lexi, there's someone to see you. She's over there.' Lexi turned to see where the receptionist was pointing. At first, she didn't recognize the woman who hovered around the

Christmas tree, gazing up at it. She had blonde hair with purple and pink streaks and wore a suede coat and a white scarf. But when the woman turned as she approached, she was surprised to see it was Shelley.

'Shelley, hi, lovely to see you. Loving that hair.'

'Hi. It was Gemma's idea. She's a woman who lives in the house. She's a hairdresser and said she'd do mine for nothing. Do you like the coat? Hannah gave it to me.'

'Well, Gemma's done a great job, and the coat suits you. So, how are things?'

'Oh great. Couldn't be better. I haven't taken any drugs since I moved into the house. Oh, and I told the police about my ex and they've arrested him. I've got to testify in court.'

'How do you feel about that?'

'Terrified, but Nina is going to come with me. I have to do it. I've heard some stories in that house and mine isn't the worst, but they all say the same thing. If you don't tell the police, nothing changes, for you or them. I'm frightened he'll come after me. I'd rather face the scumbag in court than live in fear.'

'Oh Shelley, I'm so proud of you.' The frightened, battered young girl was gone and, in her place, stood a woman with strength and pride in herself. Lexi hugged her and Shelley hugged her back.

'I've got something for you. The biscuits are for the staff here in A&E, but these are for you.' She shoved four tea-towels tied with a red ribbon into her hands. Lexi recognized them as the same ones she had bought once from the Pound

Shop. Four for a pound. Blue and white check.

'Thanks. You can never have too many tea-towels.'

'Casey told me you were moving in with him, in his new house. I wanted to get you something for the kitchen. I haven't got much money, or I would have got you something better. I'm still looking for a job.'

Casey. So, they were on first name terms now and Casey was telling her his private business. She wasn't sure what to think about that.

'No, they're great. It's what you said about moving in with Casey. It isn't definite, you know.'

'Really? That's a shame. He wanted to know what I thought about it. I told him to go for it. I think you two are perfect for each other.' Lexi didn't know what to say so she said nothing. 'Anyway, I've got to go. My turn to cook the tea tonight so I need to do some shopping.'

'Well, it's lovely to see you again, Shelley, and thanks for the presents. I'll come and see you again soon.'

'Cool. Bye Lexi.'

Lexi watched as Shelley walked out of A&E with her head held high. What a transformation. It was good to see. She'd buy her something nice for Christmas and take it round next week. Maybe she'd make up a hamper of food for the women, full of Christmas goodies. She hadn't forgotten the pledge she had made to herself to help the cause of battered women. She needed to talk to Casey's father first.

Casey. It had surprised her that he'd asked Shelley's advice. Apart from his immediate family, she couldn't imagine

Casey asking anyone's advice. After Shelley telling him to go for it, was her rejection of his idea more hurtful? Maybe they needed to talk so she could try to see it from his point of view. Not that it would change her decision. She could never live with a man who didn't love her.

Chapter Twenty-Seven

Casey had never seen Jade in such a state of excitement. From the minute he'd arrived at the cottage to collect his girls, Jade had squealed and shouted, jumping about and bumping into furniture. Lexi had told him she'd been like that from the moment she'd got out of bed. She'd hardly eaten any breakfast and had to be told to calm down umpteen times to no avail. Jess and Craig would be glad to see the back of them for the day, so they could enjoy their Saturday in peace.

She looked lovely in her Sleeping Beauty dress with her blonde hair shining and her eyes bright. Casey adored his little daughter and wanted to make her happy. His first Christmas as a dad and Jade's first pantomime. It was perfect. He still had a mammoth task on his hands; to win round her mother.

He had hoped to have the chance to talk to Lexi on the drive to Manchester City Centre. He needed to clear the air and to apologise for his thoughtlessness. Of course she would want a say in choosing a home for the three of them, any woman would. But he was impetuous and, having made the decision to ask her to move in with him, he wanted to have a house ready for her to move into, fully furnished and looking its best. He hadn't anticipated being caught in a lie and having to show her the shell of a house, in the dark. No wonder she hadn't been impressed.

Riordan had tut-tutted and shaken his head when he'd confided in him. Not only had he ignored his advice to back off and give Lexi space, he'd gone all out and backed the poor girl into a corner. He deserved everything he got. Playing the caveman was not the way to behave if he wanted to win her trust.

Maybe a pleasant family day at the pantomime would go some way to making amends.

'Are we there yet?' Jade's voice from the child car seat in the back made him laugh.

'No, darling, we haven't left Leytonsfield yet.'

'Can I have an ice-cream?'

'Yes, at the interval, we can all have an ice-cream.'

'Yay!'

Casey glanced at Lexi. She was dressed in a casual but smart shirt in pink and grey check over tight black boot-leg jeans and grey suede ankle boots. Her hair, like Jade's, was loose and flowing, healthy and shiny with a slight hint of co-conut shampoo that he caught a whiff of whenever she turned her head.

Lexi was gorgeous and he loved her. He wanted her. Not just sexually, although the thought of how long it had been since they'd made love was driving him nuts. No, he wanted her in his life forever. He wanted to marry her. The thought of not having her by his side permanently was unthinkable. The memory of Helen's betrayal was already fading, to be replaced by the truth and honesty of his love for Lexi. It was time he found some way to tell her how he felt.

As he drove up the slip road onto the motorway, he thought of all the things he loved about the woman sitting next to him quietly watching the scenery go by. She wasn't a chatterer, but when she spoke it was always worth listening to. She'd grown in the last few months becoming a more confident person. She was braver now, sassier, funnier and she stood up to him, told him exactly what she thought. He needed that. A woman who was straight with him and wasn't afraid to put him in his place. He had tremendous respect for her.

Then he thought about Helen. He had always considered her to be a professional, competent, intelligent woman who knew what she wanted from life. Recent events had shown him that, inside, Helen was an extremely damaged young woman. She had become vulnerable so easily it had shocked him. Regretting the abortion had sent her over the edge. And the overdose was down to him. Once this weekend was over, he needed to talk to Helen and do what he could to help her.

Today, however, belonged to Lexi and Jade. Right on cue, Jade piped up from the back seat.

'Daddy? How many sleeps did Sleeping Beauty have?'

'She means how long was she asleep for,' whispered Lexi.

'Uh… well, a long time probably.' He glanced over at Lexi to find that she was laughing at him.

'Good answer. In the fairy tale it was a hundred years, but in the movie, as long as it takes the prince to defeat the wicked fairy.'

'Artistic license.'

'Exactly.'

'So, what's your wicked fairy, Lexi?'

'What do you mean?'

'If I'm the prince, and I like to think of myself in that role, than I need to defeat your wicked fairy in order to win your love. But I'm struggling with that. I don't know who, or what, the enemy is here. I don't know what I'm doing wrong. I need you to help me.'

Lexi was silent for ages before she spoke. 'I don't think this is the right time for this conversation, Casey.'

'Are we there yet, Daddy?'

'Getting closer, honey. Not long now.' He lowered his voice when he spoke to Lexi. 'But we will have this conversation soon. I'm not giving up. Just so you know.'

*

Manchester City Centre a few weeks before Christmas and it seemed the whole population were of the same mind. Shop 'til you drop. Lexi had never seen so many people, all hurrying along, wrapped up in coats, scarves and hats, many of them on mobiles, not looking where they were going, staring at the pavement and relying on others to move out of their way.

Most of them ignored the rough sleepers who sat against the walls on blankets, with plastic cups next to them. Lexi wished she had money to give them. Maybe, on the way back, she could find some change to hand over, or maybe she could convince Casey to buy a few coffees, but there were so many of them. How do you decide who to help?

There was a girl with a dog who reminded Lexi of Shelley. Maybe she'd give her something.

Casey had left the car in a multi-storey carpark and they had joined the crowds streaming down Oxford Street. Both herself and Casey held one of Jade's hands tightly and she seemed to accept this willingly as people jostled each other, some risking life and limb by stepping onto the gutters to avoid the crush.

Lexi was grateful when they reached MacDonald's. The warmth hit her as they struggled through the doors, fighting their way passed baby buggies, people trying to leave, carrying bags of food and cartons of drinks, whilst steering their children ahead of them.

Eventually, after holding the doors open for a family of four, the father thanking them in a distracted fashion, they managed to get inside.

'Mummy look, that girl's got my dress on,' Jade said indignantly.

'They're going to the pantomime too.'

'Grab that table quick, the family's just about to leave.' Casey herded them over to the window, where moisture ran down the glass and collected in pools at the bottom. It was cold outside, hot and airless inside. Lexi was starting to feel a bit claustrophobic from the noise and all the people. She squashed herself into the booth and tried to ignore it. How much worse was it going to be in the theatre?

'They've made a mess,' Jade said with disdain as she surveyed the table that looked like a disaster area. The family who had just left had ignored the rule to clear up after yourself and the table was littered with crumbs, empty cartons and trays.

'Don't worry, sweetheart, I'll get rid of this in a jiffy.' Casey proceeded to pile everything onto a tray and whisked it away to the disposal area. Lexi marvelled at how similar father and daughter were. They both liked things just so. She would have just pushed it all to the end of the table. She had enough of clearing up after people at the hospital, but it was nice of Casey to think of their comfort and to clear it up himself. It seemed he couldn't do enough for them today.

'Right. What's everyone having?' he asked when he returned.

After he had taken their order, chicken nuggets for Jade, cheeseburgers for the grown-ups, fries and milkshakes all round, he hurried off to join the queue for the food.

'Mummy?'

'Yes, darling?'

'Why doesn't Daddy live with us?'

'Daddy has his own home and we live with Jess and Craig.' Where had this come from? Surely Casey hadn't told Jade she was going to live with him? He wouldn't use her in that way, would he?

'Mabel says her new daddy is going to live with them. I want my new daddy to live with me too.'

'You can go and stay with daddy whenever you like.' In his brand-new house with no furniture.

'That's not the same,' whined Jade.

'We'll talk about this later, okay? Daddy's gone to a lot of trouble to make this day really special for us, so let's just enjoy it and not think of anything else.'

'I'm hungry,' Jade said. Lexi was beginning to realise that her daughter enjoyed getting the last word. Now who did she get that from, herself or Casey?

Casey returned with the food. They ate their meal without further comments from Jade and didn't linger when they'd finished. They cleared away all evidence of their meal, struggled out of MacDonald's as there seemed to be more people trying to get in than when they arrived, and emerged into the cold, but fresh air. They grabbed Jade's hands again and made their painstaking way through the crowds down Quay Street to the Opera House.

*

Boy, this brings back memories. As they approached the Opera House, Casey had a feeling of déjà vu. His parents had brought them all to see a panto every Christmas when they were kids. He must have seen every fairy story ever written and put on stage. His favourite had been Jack and the Beanstalk.

Jade was staring intently at all the children who lined up outside, waiting to go in. A lot of them had costumes on, mainly Sleeping Beauty for the girls, but a few were dressed as the prince; boys and girls. And why not? He was all for gender equality. The children were also sporting headbands with flashing lights. Casey hoped they wouldn't induce epileptic fits in any of the kids. He was off-duty and would prefer it if he could stay that way. He wondered if Jade would ask for flashing lights. Silly question.

'Daddy, can I have some of them?'

'Some of those you mean,' Lexi corrected her.

'Yeah, them,' agreed Jade.

And this was before they'd even made it inside.

'We'll have to see how much they cost, Jade, they may be too expensive.' Lexi frowned at him, no doubt expecting him to back her up.

'Daddy?' His daughter turned a pleading face to him.

'She can't have everything she wants, Casey.'

He put his arm around Lexi and hugged her, then whispered, 'She can today. Indulge me? Just for today?'

Lexi made an exaggerated angry face, so he kissed her. 'Please? It's our first pantomime, there'll be time for common sense and austerity after the festivities.' He knew Lexi was right but couldn't bear the thought of having to say no to Jade today. He wanted this day to be magical for them all. He felt Lexi relax against him and he hugged her tighter before letting go.

'Come on then, let's get inside.'

He led his family into the foyer, after the tickets had been checked at the door by a member of the front-of-house staff, to be met with a cacophony of sound, a sea of colour and the aroma of sugar, coffee and perfumes. There was an energy vibrating in the air and barely controlled excitement. Casey was loving every minute.

'Right – twinkling lights, a programme, sweets and – what shall we get to drink?'

'Bottled water,' answered Lexi.

Jade had been vocal, chattering away ten to the dozen, right up until the time the music started and the curtain went up, when she suddenly went still and quiet. Casey's heart sank. Maybe she'd eaten too much at MacDonald's and felt sick. Did she need the toilet? Was she frightened by all the noise? The music was very loud.

He leaned over Jade to ask Lexi if she knew what was wrong. Lexi had the same look on her face. Then he remembered that neither of his girls had ever been to a pantomime before. They must have seen them on TV, but this was a completely different ball game.

There he'd been, being blasé, taking it all in his stride, thinking back to his childhood and these two had been thrust into wonderland and were sitting in their seats like stunned mullets.

When the chorus of little girls came on and started dancing, Jade said, 'Oh…' quietly to herself. She was lost in the magic and so overcome, that she crept onto his knee and sat as still as a little mouse staring at the stage, mesmerized.

He hugged her tightly, his throat dry and his heart full. He remembered when Riordan had taken Tom to see *The Lion*

King and his brother had red eyes when they returned. He said he was just tired, and Casey had accepted that explanation without question then. But now he wondered.

To be able to share such happy times with your own child was one of the best feelings ever. And he was sharing it with Lexi too, the woman he loved more than life itself. If only he could convince her of how much he loved her, his happiness would be complete.

*

At the end of the performance, when they had sung, shouted and screamed, "He's behind you!" at the tops of their voices, with the rest of the audience, he carried his emotional little daughter out of the theatre, with Lexi following close behind.

'Daddy, I didn't want it to end,' Jade whispered, which were the best words he could have heard.

In the car, driving away from the city, Jade said, 'I'm going to be a dancer when I'm older.'

'Are you, darling?' he asked, as she yawned hugely, 'not an astrophysicist or a brain surgeon?'

'No, a dancer.'

'Have you thanked Daddy for taking you?' asked Lexi.

'Thank you – it was the best day of my life.' She fell asleep.

'You can thank me, too, if you like, but I'd like my payment in kind.'

'Oh, would you now,' she said as she tried to stifle a yawn, 'okay, but not tonight, I'm exhausted. But thanks, Casey, it was a lovely day.'

He wondered if this was his chance to ask Lexi to move in with him again. They had about an hour's drive back to Leytonsfield, plenty of time to thrash out any doubts she may have and put her mind at rest. When he glanced over at her, wondering how to broach the subject, he realized that conversation would have to wait as well. Lexi was fast asleep.

He drove away from the city and towards the Cheshire countryside, enjoying the peace after such a hectic, noisy day. It was quiet in the car with both his girls asleep, giving him time to think.

He was going to suggest they go Christmas shopping the following Saturday. The Christmas markets were always worth a look and Santa would be in the Precinct all day. A golden photo opportunity. He intended to take as many snaps of Jade as he could. He wasn't making up for lost time exactly as that wouldn't be possible. He would need a time machine to recapture the images of her babyhood that were lost to him forever. He was a reasonable photographer and she was so photogenic.

Maybe Lexi would be willing to help him with his Christmas shopping. He had always been hopeless at it and had usually resorted to asking his mother to help out. It was his parents first Christmas with Jade too and everything would have to be just right. This year was going to be so different to previous years.

One thing, however, weighed heavily on his mind. The problem of what to do about Helen.

Chapter Twenty-Eight

Casey approached Helen's bedside with some trepidation. He needn't have worried though, as she smiled widely when she saw him and held her arms out to him.

'Casey, thank you for coming to see me.'

He hugged her, and she clung on to him. Gone was the sophisticated lady he had once known and in her place was a desperate, sad person with mental health issues.

'How are you feeling?'

'A lot better thank you. And thanks to you I didn't die.' She watched him with pain-filled eyes.

'Have you seen a psychiatrist yet?'

'Yes. A very nice man called Dr Moreton who talked to me about counselling. He speaks highly of you.'

'Really?'

'Oh yes, I told him of all the problems we're having that

led to my breakdown. He was very understanding.'

'Helen, what are you doing in Leytonsfield?'

'Because you live here, of course. It's my home now, too.'

'Where are you staying?'

'Well, that's the thing. They want to discharge me, and I'll continue to see Dr Moreton on an outpatient basis, but I need a secure place to live. I said I was going to stay with you, I hope that's okay?'

Everything inside him screamed, "No!" but he couldn't bring himself to say it out loud. She needed professional help, but the hospital were discharging her. He wondered if he could persuade the head of the psychiatric unit to admit her for longer-term care.

'Is there nowhere else you can go? I live in a one-bedroom flat here in the hospital. Standard doctor's accommodation. I can't look after you properly as I work long hours. Helen, you'd be better with people who can care for you. Like your parents, aren't they worried?'

'I'm not going back to London, Casey. I belong here, with you. Isn't that what you want too? You said you loved me once.'

'Like I said, there are rules about the doctor's residences, they don't like us to have people staying as it disturbs the other residents.'

'What about your house? The one near your parents? When are you moving in?'

'How do you know about that?' Casey hadn't told anyone except Lexi and his family that he had bought a house.

'I saw you when the furniture was being moved in. It is your house, isn't it?' Helen smiled as if she knew secrets about him.

'Have you been following me?' She'd been stalking him it was the only explanation.

'No of course not. I was simply walking in that area and I spotted you. I was going to say hello, but you looked busy, so I left. Is there something wrong?'

Yes, there was something extremely wrong. Casey had a bad feeling about Helen. She might be suffering from a psychosis as her version of reality was different to his. If he told her she couldn't stay, she'd probably turn up on his doorstep anyway and that would be a lot worse.

'Okay, you can stay for a few nights until you get a place of your own, okay?'

'I knew you'd say yes. Thank you Casey. Everything's going to be fine now, you'll see.'

Somehow Casey doubted that very much.

*

Casey was forced to expedite the move into his house. He wanted to wait until Lexi agreed to move in with him and then the three of them could go shopping for furniture and things for the home together, just like a proper family. Now that Helen had moved in, that would have to wait. He had bought beds, the kitchen was fully fitted so all he needed was a sofa, television and a table and chairs. The rest would have to wait. He had lived in sparser accommodation when he was a student, but he knew Helen would be used to better things.

He collected her from the ward and escorted her to his car, hoping that he wouldn't bump into Lexi. Fortune was on his side because he didn't see any of the staff he worked with.

Helen seemed happier. She smiled and chatted away about inconsequential things, then, when they arrived at the house, she exclaimed at everything, declaring it a perfect family home.

'Yes, well, that is the reason I chose it.'

'Oh, poor Casey, I am so sorry about the baby, I know how desperately you want to be a father. If there was any way I could change history-'

'I am a father.' He had to tell her sometime, now was as good a time as any.

Helen spun around in the middle of the half-empty lounge and stared at him. 'What? What do you mean?' The happy, light-hearted attitude had gone, and she looked angry.

'I was going to tell you about my daughter. Sit down, Helen. Do you want tea or coffee?'

She shook her head and perched on the edge of the sofa. 'What do you mean? You haven't got children. Have you been lying to me all this time?'

Helen was starting to get agitated, so Casey explained about Jade. She listened intently, shaking her head occasionally as if she didn't want to accept what he was saying. She looked away from him as if she couldn't bear to look him in the eye.

'Helen? Are you okay? Do you want to go and lie down for a while?'

'Jade. That's an unusual name for a child.'

'She has green eyes like mine.'

Helen was rocking slightly, and Casey was growing concerned. 'Have you taken your medication?'

'No.'

'Right, then I think you should.' He went into the kitchen and filled a glass with water, then picked up the bottle of tablets and brought them back into the lounge. 'Here. Then you need to have a lie down, okay?'

She took her tablets obediently then sat back on the sofa with her arms crossed. 'What are our plans for the weekend, Casey? Shall we go shopping? Christmas shopping?' Helen now seemed happier, animated almost, but Casey was about to burst her bubble.

'I've already made plans for the weekend. I'm taking Lexi and Jade Christmas shopping. I'm sorry, but we made plans a while ago. Maybe you could use the weekend to find yourself somewhere to live.'

'But… I've only just arrived. I was hoping we could be together, like in the old days. You remember how good it was? Casey, I want us to give it another try. I know I messed up with the abortion, but I am truly sorry. You must know how sorry I am. I've never stopped loving you and I know you still love me, so it would be stupid to ignore our feelings. We're good together, aren't we?'

Casey felt his spirits getting lower and lower as Helen pleaded with him. He should never have brought her here, for he realised with a cold certainty that it wouldn't be easy to get rid of her. She was incapable of facing facts and whatever he said she would ignore. He had to try.

'Helen, we did have something special but that's in the past. I've moved on, made a new life for myself. Jade is my priority now. And Lexi.'

'Do you love this woman? Even though it was just a one-night stand? It was just sex, Casey, not a relationship. It wasn't as if you wanted to see her again. Four years later you find out she deceived you by not telling you about the baby. I can't believe you love her.'

'Well I do.' As he said it, he realised how true it was. He loved Lexi and wanted to spend the rest of his life with her, and not just because she was Jade's mother. He now knew that she was the only woman he would ever love unconditionally, as his parents loved each other. As he wanted her to love him.

'So, where are you taking them?' Helen seemed calmer. Maybe the meds were kicking in.

'Just to the town centre. Jade wants to see Santa.'

'Nice.' Casey listened for a note of bitterness in her voice, but she just sounded indifferent. The way she used to sound when he suggested she join in with his family on one of their get-togethers. She had never fitted in with the O'Connors because she had never made the effort. Family had meant little to her.

'I think I'll go and lie down now; I'm feeling a bit tired.'

'Good idea. And when you wake, I'll make us a meal. Do you have any preference?'

'I'll leave it up to you. I know you remember the things I like.'

He did. And he remembered so much more, not all of it good. The thing he would never forget, though, was the pain of knowing she had been pregnant and hadn't bothered to tell him.

Chapter Twenty-Nine

Lexi was exhausted. She'd had a strenuous week in A&E with a constant stream of patients through Minors with insignificant or fabricated illnesses; things they could easily have gone to their GP with or treated themselves. One patient came in because he had a verruca. Lexi patiently wrote down the name of a topical application that could be bought from the local chemist and sent the patient on his way.

All day there was a background of sirens as the serious cases were rushed into Resus. Raj was team leader for some of the week and Casey for the rest. Lexi wished she could join them. She didn't feel she was stretched enough in Minors and had too much time to think while she was cleaning cuts and applying bandages. She found herself listening to the patients with only half her mind on what they were saying. The other half seemed permanently fixed on Casey.

The day of the pantomime had been such a lovely day. For the first time she felt that they were a real family unit, out for a day of family fun. Casey had been so sweet last Saturday, telling her that he wanted to win her love and that he wouldn't give up. It made her question why she was hesitating to move in with him. But deep down, she knew the real reason, because he had yet to tell her he loved her.

When they arrived back at the cottage, he had carried the sleeping Jade inside and put her to bed. She wondered if he would stay the night, but he didn't suggest it. Instead he told her he wanted to take Jade to see Santa and asked her to help him with his Christmas shopping the following Saturday.

So, here they were, in Casey's car, driving around Leytonsfield Town Centre, trying to find somewhere to park. Casey was keeping remarkably cool in the circumstances. Men weren't supposed to like shopping, were they? He was exhibiting just as much excitement and enthusiasm as Jade. Although he wasn't jiggling up and down in his seat like his daughter was. Lexi kept asking her if she needed the toilet, she was wriggling so much.

'Don't worry,' he'd told Jade when she asked him if he was going to buy her Christmas presents, 'your Daddy's got his credit cards all ready. Just let me know what you want, sweetie.'

Lexi sensed that she and Casey were going to clash over their daughter's Christmas. She had always tried to keep the expense down to a minimum; mainly because she'd never been able to afford to do anything else. She'd tried to instil in

Jade a sense of the magic of Christmas rather than the commerciality of the event. She'd had carols playing on the radio, they went on walks into the local woodlands to cut holly and mistletoe to decorate the cottage, they made mince pies and Christmas cake together, attended the Christingle service at the local church and Lexi encouraged Jade to be happy with a few special presents that she could treasure.

This year, she just knew that Casey would want to celebrate Christmas with his daughter by throwing money around and buying her everything she asked for, thereby spoiling her rotten.

She remembered, with a large dose of guilt, that this was Casey and Jade's first Christmas together, and the two of them adored each other. They'd formed a bond that was so strong, nothing would ever be able to break it. Lexi certainly didn't want to do that.

Yes, Christmas was going to be different this year.

One thing that wouldn't change was Christmas day itself. That was sacrosanct. Herself, Jade, Jess and Craig spent Christmas day together, as they had every day since Jade was born. It was tradition, because they were family, the four of them, not having any other.

If Casey wanted to spend time with Jade, he could visit Christmas day night, or Boxing Day, when he could have her all day if he so wished. Of course, there was no "if" about it, the whole O'Connor clan would be desperate to have Jade for the whole of Christmas and New Year too probably. Well, they couldn't, that was all there was to it. Jade was her daughter and she would say how and where she spent Christmas.

'Wow, Jade, will you look at that?' Casey's voice interrupted her thoughts as they wandered towards the town centre, having found a parking space in one of the side streets.

Market Street, a pedestrianized thoroughfare that ran through the length of the main shopping area of the town, had been transformed into a world designed to tantalise the senses. Small wooden cabins, looking like an advert for Swiss chocolate, lined the street, one after the other, stretching right to the town square. Each one was decorated with fake snow and white lights hung from the roofs like icicles. The smell of food wafted over their heads, and colourful lights twinkled everywhere.

Each cabin was an Aladdin's cave of delights, containing a myriad assortment of products. You didn't know where to look first, and Jade ran from one to the other, shouting, 'Daddy, look!' and 'Mummy, come and look at this!'

They looked and admired whatever it was that had caught their little daughter's attention.

'So, what's the order of play today?' asked Casey.

'Well, we have to fit lunch in somewhere between shopping for Christmas presents and a visit to Santa.'

'Looks as if there's plenty of places to eat around here. Jade and I are going to need some time alone to choose your Christmas presents, so you'll have to make yourself scarce at some point.'

Lexi's stomach dropped as something occurred to her.

Something she hadn't thought of before. She couldn't afford to buy presents for all Casey's family.

'Listen, I don't think we should buy each other anything, just the kids. That's what Jess and I do, we just buy something for the children.'

'I'm not Jess.' His expression was serious as his gaze swept over her face. 'I want to buy you something, Lexi, and I want to buy Jade something to give to you as well. Something special. That's what Christmas is all about, isn't it? It's a time to buy people things they'd never think to get for themselves.'

Great start. Casey's definition of Christmas is the complete opposite to hers.

'Is that what Christmas is all about? And here's me thinking it's about peace on Earth and goodwill to all men.'

'Ha, ha, very funny.'

'That wasn't a joke, Casey-'

'Mummy, Daddy, come on!' Jade grabbed each of her parents by the hand and tried to drag them along the pavement where they had stopped to argue. This was Jade's day and they needed to keep the bickering down if they didn't want to spoil it for their daughter.

After they had looked at every single cabin and Jade had declared that none of the things they sold were on her Christmas list and asked how Santa would find all the things she wanted, Casey decided to look for the toy shop he remembered from his childhood.

'But how, Daddy?' asked Jade, not willing to give up until she'd received a satisfactory answer.

'Santa doesn't buy the toys, darling, he makes them in his workshop in the North Pole.'

'All of them?' Jade's eyes grew wide with amazement at the thought of all the toys he must have to make. Lexi's heart turned over at the look on her face and the wonderment in her voice.

She wanted to say, *"This is what Christmas is about, Casey, the magic of it all, seen through the eyes of a child."* But she said nothing.

Casey, however, was in full flow. 'Yes, Santa's a very busy man, which is why he relies on all the mummies and daddies to help him with some of the presents that are on your list.'

And what about the children who don't have mummies and daddies? Casey must have read her mind, for he shot her a slightly embarrassed look and shrugged.

'Oh, but I've got a separate mummy and daddy list,' said Jade importantly.

'Have you, darling?' Casey looked at Lexi and she nearly burst out laughing at the expression on his face. She should take pity on him, after all, he was new to all this, but she was having too much fun watching him tie himself in knots.

'Santa can bring me all the presents on *his* list, and you can get me all the presents on the mummy and daddy list.' Jade grinned as if she had, single-handedly, solved an extremely complex puzzle.

Lexi took pity on Casey and said, 'Jade, honey, you won't be able to have everything on your lists, you know, because you have put a lot of things on them and we did say, didn't we, that you could just choose a few from each. Do you remember?'

'No.' Jade frowned, and Lexi sensed her gearing up for a tantrum, the last thing she wanted to happen in the middle of Market Street on a Saturday, surrounded by Christmas shoppers, but she was giving Jade boundaries and teaching her to appreciate the things people gave her. Even Santa.

Jade had an ally in her father, however, and she'd learned already how to twist him around her little finger.

'Daddy, that's not fair. I want *everything* on my lists.'

'Look, there it is – Jeffersons. It's still there. Come on guys!' Casey, excited that he'd found the toyshop of his childhood, started striding off. Neither of the female contingent of the shopping expedition followed him.

'Daddy!' screamed Jade, causing people to turn and stare. A few harassed mothers smiled at Lexi in sympathy. Casey stopped, turned back and looked at them both in bewilderment.

Okay, hotshot, let's see how you handle this.

'What's up?'

'Your daughter wants absolutely everything on both her Christmas lists, and I was just trying to explain that-'

Casey returned and swept Jade up in his arms and lifted her high in the air where she gasped then giggled in delight.

'You, my little princess, can have anything you want. Just say the word and it's yours.'

What? No. 'Casey – that's not helpful.'

He was already striding away with Jade, still giggling. She had no choice but to trudge after him. This was the last time, the very last time, she would ever go shopping with Casey O'Connor. The man had no idea of moderation. All the good work she'd been trying to do with Jade, all her motherly wisdom and advice, was going to be totally ignored now as Jade would know exactly how to get whatever she wanted. Her authority over her daughter was slowly unravelling along with her patience. And she had absolutely no idea what to do about it.

*

Jeffersons turned out to be a high-class toy shop with handmade puppets, soft toys and dolls. It stocked the latest games as well as some from the past that sent Casey into paroxysms of nostalgic glee.

'I remember playing that with Riordan,' he said turning over a complicated board game and examining it closely, 'and I sometimes beat him. Well, okay, not that often. My brother is a nerd with a photographic memory, what chance did I have?'

'Daddy, I want a bike,' said Jade who had found a pink two-wheeler with ribbons hanging off the handlebars.

'Okay, sweetie, we'll ask them to deliver it.'

Lexi was horrified. 'You don't even know how much it costs.'

Casey grinned. 'Sod the price. I want her to have everything she wants this year. If everyone in my family bought her a couple of items on her list, we'll have everything covered.'

'That's sending her the wrong message. She'll think that she can have everything she wants all the time. I don't want her growing up believing that.'

'No, she'll grow up believing she's loved and cherished, surrounded by people who care about her.'

Lexi felt as if he'd slapped her. 'How dare you insinuate that Jade hasn't been loved and cherished. No one could love her more than I do.'

'Lexi, God, I'm sorry, I didn't mean that, please don't think-'

'And she has *always* been surrounded by people who not only care about her physical welfare but have adored her since the day she was born. She has always had family around her, and they will always be there for her.'

'Please, Lexi, forgive me.' He looked stricken and Lexi's anger started to dissipate. He had been thoughtless with his words, but not malicious, yet Lexi still felt the sting in the centre of her being. She was sensitive where Jade was concerned, anxious that she be the best mother she can be and any suggestion that she had fallen short of the mark hurt her deeply.

'Daddy, I want this.'

'Oh, look Lexi, a rocking-horse. We used to have one of those, then Tom had it when he was little.'

Casey appeared to have recovered quickly and was busy admiring yet another thing that Jade wanted to add to her rapidly growing Christmas lists. Why did she have to choose the most expensive things in the shop?

Her bitterness at Casey's words lingered in her mind and she had to get out of his way. They agreed to part company for an hour and a half and meet up for an early lunch. Even then, they couldn't agree on where they would meet.

'I want doughnuts,' Jade insisted, her good manners disappearing with the last shreds of Lexi's patience. She was getting sick of hearing her daughter start every sentence with "I want…" Time for Mum to take charge.

'Right, listen up you two. Here's the deal.' Casey and Jade gazed at her in trepidation. 'We'll meet at the Fruit and Fish Bar for fruit salad and juice. They also do tuna or salmon salad sandwiches for you, Casey. Then, if you're good, Jade, and stop asking for everything you see, later on this afternoon, *I'll* decide if we have doughnuts and hot chocolate. Okay?'

Jade watched her with a frown, considering the deal. Then a beatific smile spread across her face and she looked more like the little girl Lexi adored. 'Okay, Mummy,' she said.

Lexi hugged her, feeling the familiar warmth spread through her at the feel of her daughter's arms around her. 'I love you so much.'

'I love you, too, mummy.' Lexi kissed Jade and, without even as much as a backward glance at Casey, she strode out of the shop.

*

Casey watched her go. How was he managing to get everything so spectacularly wrong? He'd just been given a hard lesson in parenting, one he richly deserved. Jade was now behaving beautifully, standing next to him with her hand clutching his, not even bothering to look at any other toys.

'Right,' he tried to adopt the same tone of voice that Lexi had used, but when Jade looked up at him, her green eyes so very like his own, he melted. 'Would you like to help me choose a present for Tom? And one for you to give him as well?'

'Yes, please.' At the mention of her favourite cousin, his daughter became animated again and Casey asked her to pick some things she liked so they could decide on the best. Whilst she was distracted, he phoned Riordan.

'Hey, Bro, I need your help.'

'Of course you do. Some things never change,' Riordan sounded amused. 'What can I do for you?'

'Well, how do I stop Jade from asking for everything she sees?'

'Shopping trip going well, then?' Riordan paused. 'You can't, she's a child, it's what they do.'

'I hate saying no to her. I love her and want her to be happy.'

'You don't want to be cast in the role of villain, is that it?'

'Exactly.'

'Well, tough, that's parenting. What does Lexi say?'

'She's not happy with me at the moment, we're not really communicating.'

'I feel sorry for you, Casey, you have so much to learn. Okay, you want my advice. Firstly, you have to say no to your kids sometimes. Trust me, they don't love you any less for it. Secondly, listen to what Lexi says. After all, she's got a head start on you.'

'Right. Thanks. One more thing. Is that rocking horse still in the loft? Jade has seen one she likes but, instead of spending money on a new one, I wondered if I could have that one?'

'Ah. Okay, this was supposed to have been a surprise, but Dad's way ahead of you. He's had it repainted and resaddled. They're going to give it to Jade on Christmas Day.'

'Brilliant. Glad I asked now. Thanks Bro.'

'Have you had the difficult conversation with Helen yet?' Casey had seen Riordan for a drink after Helen moved in so he could get his advice. His brother wasn't happy with the situation and told him he was a fool and to get rid of Helen as soon as he could.

'No, but she seemed a bit happier this morning before I left. I'll tell her tonight.'

'Just be careful how you approach the subject. She's already tried to take her own life, she's obviously unstable.'

'I'll tread carefully. I just want her out of the way so I can concentrate on Lexi. Thanks for everything, Riordan. See you soon.'

'Happy to help. Enjoy the rest of the day.'

'Daddy, I've got Tom's presents for you.'

'Good girl. Wow, he's going to love these.' She'd done well, choosing a Lego Marvel Universe set and a basketball. Even at such a young age, his daughter had Tom sussed.

'Okay, how about we go and buy Mummy's presents now?'

'Yeah.'

Chapter Thirty

The Pound Shop had been heaving. She'd bought a few sweets and small items that could be added to Jade's and Craig's stockings. Craig knew that Santa wasn't real, but he kept up the pretence for Jade's sake.

As much as she tried to fight it, she was still angry with Casey. He had no idea how inadequate he made her feel when he splashed the cash and gave in to Jade's demands. He must have maxed out his credit cards by now and the day wasn't over yet.

They were so different the two of them. It would never work, them being together, she couldn't imagine why she ever thought it would.

She arrived at Fruit and Fish Bar to find Casey and Jade already tucking into lunch. They both looked happy and she started to relax.

'We got you salmon, hope that's okay?'

'Fine, thanks. Did you get everything?'

'Yes. Jefferson's is going to deliver everything next week.' They were being terribly polite but that was better than biting each other's heads off.

'Good.'

'Are you working Christmas Eve?'

'Yes, an early. You?' Lexi bit into her salmon sandwich.

'Same. I'll come and pick the pair of you up afterwards then.'

'Pick us up? For what?'

He looked at her in surprise. 'For Christmas, of course. Unless you want me to collect you early Christmas Day morning?'

'Casey, I have no idea what you're talking about. Jade and I will be spending Christmas Day at home as we always do.'

'What? I assumed you'd want to be with my parents on Christmas Day. They're all looking forward to it so much. The twins will be home next week and-'

'You have never mentioned this to me before. If you had, I would have explained that it's our tradition to spend Christmas Day together, just the four of us. I'm not leaving Jess and Craig on their own, not on Christmas Day.'

'Mummy, why are you fighting again?'

'We're not fighting, darling, we're just talking.'

'Can we go and see Santa now?' asked Jade.

'Not yet. Soon. Finish your juice, there's a good girl.' Jade obediently picked up her glass and took a drink.

'Jess and Craig can come too. The more the merrier.' Casey sat back as if he'd solved the problem.

'No, Casey, that isn't going to happen. Jess wouldn't want to intrude like that. Christmas is for families.'

'Exactly.' Casey said, 'and you and Jade are my family, so we should all be together. Jess'll understand.'

'I'm not part of your family.'

'You are. If you knew how often my parents talk about you, how much admiration they have for you, you'd know they want you to be part of the family.'

What about what I want? She wanted to be a member of a big, energetic all-embracing family, where she could feel wanted, accepted, and safe. A family like the O'Connors, and she wanted to be married to a gorgeous sexy man who loved her more than life itself. Just like the man sitting opposite her. So why was she holding back all the time?

A cold, clammy hand clutched her heart as she realized that Jade's chair was empty and she hadn't heard her voice in a while, so engrossed was she in the argument she was having with Casey.

She looked around the café frantically but couldn't see her. 'Where's Jade?'

*

At first, his mind still intent on winning the argument, Casey didn't understand the question. Jade was sitting in the chair to the left of him, playing with the fruit left in her bowl, as she always did when she'd had enough to eat and had food left over. Only she wasn't. The chair was empty.

He got up and looked around but couldn't see her. 'Maybe she's gone to the toilet.'

'She'd never go on her own, she never has.'

He felt a twinge of concern, but nothing more. Jade was a sensible little girl, she wouldn't just wander off. He walked around, glancing under tables to make sure she wasn't hiding from them as a game, but that wasn't like her either. Jade wasn't a tease.

Lexi was doing the sensible thing and asking the staff behind the counter if they'd seen her. He approached the customers on the table nearest to theirs.

'Have you seen a little girl? She's nearly four, blonde, wearing a red coat?'

They looked at him blankly. 'Sorry mate, no,' said the man.

Lexi hurried over. 'We need to contact the Help Desk. They'll alert security. We need as many people as possible looking for her.'

Casey stared at her. He was having trouble processing the words. She wasn't missing, she'd be around somewhere, all they had to do was keep looking.

'Come on, let's go and find her.' He paid for their meal, glancing around him the whole time as he fully expected Jade to turn up at any moment. He was waiting to hear her voice and then he and Lexi would feel silly for panicking.

How should he play it when they find her? Should he be angry with her for running off? He didn't know how a parent should behave in such circumstances. He'd take Riordan's advice and follow Lexi's lead.

Lexi was already outside the café, staring anxiously up and down the walkway, first to the right and then the left. She disappeared suddenly and he hurried out after her. She had dashed into a clothing shop but came straight out again.

He put his hands on her shoulders to try to calm her. 'It's okay, we'll find her. You need to keep calm.'

'Calm? How can I keep calm? Where is she, Casey? Anything could have happened to her.'

'Nothing's happened to her. She's around here somewhere. She was here a few minutes ago, she won't have gone far.' He was convinced they would spot a little blonde girl in a red coat amongst the crowd at any time. She was here, nearby, he just knew it.

'It's our fault. Jade hated to hear us arguing.'

'We weren't arguing.'

'Of course we were. We've been doing it all day.'

'I thought we were having a disagreement.'

'She's a child. Raised voices to a child is arguing.'

Casey's stomach turned over as the truth of what Lexi was saying hit him. It was his fault Jade ran off. Because she had a totally self-absorbed father, caring only about getting his own way. He should have put her needs first, but he was too busy being right about everything.

Lexi's face was drained of colour and her eyes were huge and brimming with tears.

'I'm sorry,' he whispered.

'Where is she, Casey? Where's my baby?'

At her words, the sickness that had been growing

threatened to erupt and he thought he might be in danger of losing his lunch. He swallowed hard, then pulled Lexi into his arms for a reassuring hug. Her body was stiff against his and she didn't hug him back.

'We'll find her, I promise. Trust me.'

He felt lightheaded as he thought of the size of the shopping mall. It had three storeys, linked by escalators in the middle of each floor, hundreds of shops and there were thousands of Christmas shoppers swarming all over the enormous building. Who knew what kinds of people were amongst them?

He'd never thought of a shopping mall in terms of danger before, but now it was all he could think about.

Okay. Think logically. 'Did she say anything to you? Anything that might give us a clue?'

Lexi looked distraught and kept her hand over her mouth as if she, too, felt like throwing up, or screaming.

'No. She just wanted to go and see Santa.'

'Santa?' The first flicker of hope gave him a rush of adrenaline. That was a clue, wasn't it? 'So, she might be trying to find Santa?'

'Possibly, but she has no idea where Santa is, or where anything is. She's only three. Oh, God, she's all alone and terrified. We need to do something. Why are we just standing here when we should be doing something?'

Lexi was beginning to lose it, so they had to keep moving, but Santa was the only clue they had, and he was going to run with it.

'Come on, let's go back to the Precinct.'

'What if she's not there?' Lexi was crying now, her whole body shaking as they speed-walked towards the exit.

'Then we'll try somewhere else.'

'I'm scared. What if something's happened to her?'

'Nothing's happened to her.'

'How can you be so sure?'

'Because I can't deal with the thought that something has happened to her right now.' He was shouting and people turned to stare at them as they hurried by. He wanted to scream at them to stop staring and help them look. Jade was their precious child and he was going to find her. One step at a time. It was the only way he was going to hold it together.

On the way, he stared at every red object he saw in case it miraculously became a child's coat. Once, he thought he saw her, but when the girl turned around, she wasn't Jade. The disappointment stopped him in his tracks. Then sheer panic started him moving again.

As he started running, he heard Lexi calling him to slow down.

Chapter Thirty-One

Lexi's phone rang as Casey disappeared into the crowd. She tried to retrieve it from the bottom of her handbag whilst running but stumbled and dropped both her handbag and the plastic Pound Shop bag, the contents spilling on the ground.

'Casey!' she screamed but he had vanished. She grabbed her stuff and shoved it all back in the bags. The phone had stopped ringing now and she started walking whilst checking who had been trying to contact her. The only person she could think of was Jess and she hated missing her calls, but now wasn't the time to chat. It was an unknown number, so she ignored it.

She started running when she saw that Casey had stopped at the exit to wait for her. Her phone rang again and this time she answered it.

'Hello?'

'Is that Lexi Grainger?'

'Yes. Who's this?'

'A well-wisher. I've got your daughter. Don't worry, she's quite safe.' Then the line went dead.

'No!' Lexi didn't know she was screaming until she felt strong male arms holding her and a deep voice telling her everything will be okay. How could anything be okay when someone had kidnapped Jade?

'Tell me what happened,' said Casey, his voice soothing. Lexi couldn't be soothed.

'A woman… she's got her… help her Casey, please…'

'What woman? You're going to have to calm down, sweetheart and tell me the whole story.'

So Lexi took a deep breath and told him about the phone call and what the woman had said to her. Casey took his phone out of his pocket and started punching numbers.

'Are you ringing the police?'

'No, not yet. We may not need the police.'

'Of course we need them! She's been taken by a mad woman. God knows what she's doing to her. Ring the police, Casey or I will.'

'She won't hurt her.'

'How do you know what she'll do?'

'I think I know who it is. Blast it keeps going to voicemail. She's not going to pick up.'

'You know this woman? How? Who is she? What the hell's going on Casey and where's my baby?'

Lexi could feel the hysteria mounting in her again. Jade

abducted by a woman Casey knew. She'd be frightened, poor little mite, calling for her mummy.

'Who is this woman!' she shouted at the top of her voice indifferent to the people who had stopped and stared, some even taking photos of her on their phones.

'Come on, let's go.' Casey grabbed her arm and dragged her towards the exit. 'We need to get to my house, I think that's where they'll be.'

'How will they have got there so quickly?' Lexi was trying to make sense of it all and keep herself from falling apart.

'She probably had a taxi standing by.'

'She planned this? How do you know her and why has she targeted Jade?'

'She's my ex and Jade's my daughter.'

They reached the car and Casey pulled out of the narrow space, narrowly missing scraping the car in front and they sped off back to the area of Leytonsfield where Casey's new house was. Lexi was trembling and she was fighting the need to be sick. Casey wouldn't appreciate that in his car along with everything else they were facing.

'I never told you this, but Helen and I were an item. She got pregnant and had an abortion without telling me about either one. I couldn't forgive her. Still can't.'

'What's that got to do with Jade?' Lexi was sorry for Casey but all her thoughts at that moment were with their child.

'She regretted the abortion and I think she's had some kind of nervous breakdown. She turned up in Leytonsfield a couple of weeks ago with an overdose. I said she could stay with me until she got a place of her own. I realise now, how stupid that was.'

'She's living with you? For how long! And why did she ring me and not you?'

'She must have copied your number from my mobile. She's not dangerous. She didn't hurt the baby she took, so-'

'What? She took a baby! Oh my God, Casey, this just gets worse. Why is she walking the streets if she snatches kids? She should be locked up.'

'She needs help. Professional psychiatric help. I'm going to phone Joe Moreton and get her admitted.'

'You should have done that before!' Lexi was yelling in his ear, but she couldn't help herself. She was frantic with worry over Jade. Everything Casey told her made her think her darling daughter was in danger from this mad woman. And Casey knew all about it. Knew she was dangerous.

'Calm down, Lexi, Jade'll be fine.'

'You don't know that. Did you tell this woman where we were going to be today?'

'Yes, I'm afraid I did mention it. She could have followed me, she's done that before.'

Lexi couldn't believe what she was hearing and sat in stunned silence until they reached Casey's house. All the way there she prayed to God to keep Jade safe. She didn't even know if she believed in God, but in that moment, He was all she had.

'Right. Stay in the car while I go in and talk to her,' said Casey.

'Not on your life. I'm going to get my daughter so don't try to stop me.' Lexi got out of the car and slammed the car door, then marched up the path to the front door.

*

Casey followed Lexi, feeling dread in the pit of his stomach. This was all his fault. All of it. He had handled things so badly, he didn't know what he was thinking.

Lexi waited at the front door almost vibrating with fear and rage. He opened the door and tried to go in first, but Lexi pushed passed him shouting for her daughter.

'Mummy!' Jade ran into the hall and hugged Lexi, who broke down into loud sobs and held the little girl so tightly, she started to wriggle.

Casey went into the lounge to find Helen sitting on the sofa as if she was enjoying afternoon tea with friends. A glass of juice was sitting on the coffee table next to a plate of biscuits.

'Helen. Why did you do it? You scared us half to death.'

'I wanted to meet your daughter and I knew if I asked you'd say no.'

'Yes, I would, but that is no reason to steal a child.'

'I didn't steal her. Anyway, it should be me playing happy families with you, not her.' She gestured at the doorway where Lexi was standing with Jade in her arms.

'Lexi is Jade's mother, not you. You gave us such a fright.'

'Well, she's not looking after her properly, neither of you are. The poor little thing had to listen to you arguing while you ignored her. No wonder she preferred to come with me.'

'You followed me.'

'Yes. I was bored here on my own. I wanted to join in the fun too. So I got the bus. It was easy to find you; I just looked in all the toyshops and found you in Jeffersons. Then I followed you. I didn't intend to take the girl, but she came willingly, so I thought she'd be better off with me.'

'You're a liar!' Lexi said. 'My little girl wouldn't have wandered off if you hadn't enticed her.'

'Think what you like. She was happy here with me, weren't you love?' She smiled at Jade who looked to Lexi for direction.

'No. I wanted to be with Mummy and Daddy.'

Lexi looked triumphant and Helen shrugged as if she didn't really care.

'Well, there's no harm done, is there? You've got her back now, so that's an end to it.'

'Not quite,' said Lexi, 'the police will be here in a minute.'

'Why did you call the police,' asked Helen in exasperation, 'I haven't done anything wrong.'

'Kidnapping is a criminal offence, I'm afraid, Helen. If, however, you agree to be sectioned, I will ask Joe Moreton to admit you. And this time, you need to stay in until you're better.'

'Are you abandoning me again, Casey?' Helen looked at him imploringly.

'No, I'm helping you.'

They looked up as the doorbell chimed. Casey went to answer it. Both the police and an ambulance had arrived.

Fortunately Helen went willingly. In the doorway, escorted by the paramedics, she turned to look at Casey and Lexi.

'Oh, by the way, Jade told me she wanted to spend Christmas day at her grandparents which is why she ran off in the first place. Nobody was listening to her. Just thought you should know.'

*

Lexi felt as if she was coming down from a momentous high. The adrenaline pumping around her body had left its mark. She felt nauseous, dizzy and tearful. All she wanted to do was to take Jade home and lock the door against the world. Before she did, however, she needed to tell Casey a few home truths while she still had the courage.

He had made them both a mug of tea and Jade was happy in front of the television watching the Disney channel.

'I need to talk to you.'

'Can't it wait, I feel so shaken up I don't think I would make much sense in a serious discussion.'

'Then shut up and listen for once in your life.'

He looked at her to see if she was joking. She wasn't. She'd never been more serious.

'Because of you, our daughter was put in mortal danger-'

'I think that's a slight exaggeration.'

'Because of you, Jade was kidnapped by a woman who is mentally ill and who had already taken a baby.'

Casey didn't speak.

'I have never felt so frightened in my life, Casey. This day makes all the other horrible days I've had in my childhood pale into insignificance. I will never, as long as I live, forget the feeling I had when that woman rang me and told me she'd got Jade.' Lexi stopped as tears threatened to overwhelm her.

'I'm sorry.'

'Being sorry isn't enough, I'm afraid. I can't trust you Casey, not anymore. And when you include everything else, I don't think you and I have any kind of future together.'

'Everything else? Like what?'

'You never listen to me. I tried to tell you last Saturday not to spoil her, but you didn't listen. You like everything your own way; over Jade, the house – everything. You asked me to move in but never thought I'd like some say in choosing where we were going to live. We could have looked at houses together.'

'I just wanted it to be perfect for you.'

'You're a naturally confident person who likes to be in control and I can understand why. You're a team leader so you have to be seen to be confident and know what you're doing, but being a father is new to you and, trust me, you really have no idea what you're doing.'

'I didn't think I was doing that bad a job.'

Then he sighed deeply and turned his head to look at her. 'You're right. About nearly all of it. About me not knowing what the hell I'm doing as a parent anyway. And yes, I should ask your advice and I will start to do that, I promise. But you're not right about me being a naturally confident person. I have to work at that every day to appear confident in front of the team. I live in fear that one day they'll see through me to the quivering wreck underneath.'

'I find that hard to believe.' Lexi took a sip of her tea.

'It's true, I'm afraid. Did you know I nearly gave up medicine?'

'Really? No, I didn't. When was that?'

'You remember the patient I told you about? The young woman who walked in front of a taxi?'

'Yes, of course.'

'It was my fault. She died because of me. I couldn't face it. I went to my GP and got a sicknote for a month. I came back to Leytonsfield to discuss alternative careers with my parents and Riordan. I was thinking about being a physio or something else in the medical world where I couldn't kill anyone. I just lost all my confidence. Hated myself. Was on the verge of handing my notice in when Riordan told me about the job going at Leytonsfield General. I told him he was mad. If I couldn't cope with being a registrar, how could I cope with the post of consultant? But my training was nearly over and that was the next step. And, of course, he was right. A smaller, quieter hospital was exactly what I needed. And when Shelley was admitted, this time I was ready.'

'So, that first day you appeared in our A&E Department looking as if you were ready to conquer the world, you were really shaking in your boots?'

'My legs were like jelly, but then I saw you and I took it as a good omen that I'd made the right decision.'

'And what do you think now?'

'The same. You and Jade mean everything to me. I know

it may not seem that way after today, but it's true.'

Lexi sighed, suddenly weary to the bone. 'We need to go home. I'm exhausted.'

'I'll drive you.'

'No. Could you just pay for a taxi for us? I want to be on my own now.'

'Okay, if that's what you want. One more thing though.' Casey called Jade over and sat her on his knee. 'Darling, did you run off when we were arguing? And then you saw the lady?'

'She told me to go with her. She said she was your friend, Daddy.'

Casey asked, 'Where did you tell that lady you wanted to spend Christmas day, can you remember?'

Jade suddenly looked serious and Lexi braced herself. 'I want to spend Christmas Day with Daddy and Nanna and Granddad and Tom and Uncle Riordan.'

He looked at Lexi but said nothing.

Lexi's heart sank. Casey had won. Her daughter would rather be with her new family than her old one. As she looked back at two pairs of green eyes gazing at her expectantly, she sighed. 'I'll have a word with Jess, but I'm not promising anything.'

*

'Billy's invited us to Edinburgh for Christmas and New Year. Hogmanay, they call it.'

'That's great! Don't need to ask if you too are still loved up.'

'We're as loved up as two people who've never met can be.'

They were sitting in front of the open fire in PJs and dressing-gowns, sipping hot chocolate. Jess was still glowing from her nightly facetime with Billy and the kids were in bed. Lexi had told Jess about her horrendous day and then said she didn't want to talk about it anymore.

'I was expecting a lecture about being careful or meeting him first before Craig meets him,' said Jess before blowing on her hot chocolate to cool it.

'You've obviously thought it through and decided he's worth the risk. Just leave me his address and phone number, okay?'

'Okay. And you'll be with the O'Connors. So, it's all worked out well in the end.'

'Yes, I suppose it has.'

'You don't sound very sure.'

'Practically, it makes sense. Jade'll be over the moon. And Casey. It's just that, after today, I'm not sure how I feel about him.

'It must have been terrifying losing Jade. For both of you, I mean. I'm sure Casey wouldn't deliberately put Jade's life in danger. He loves his daughter to bits.'

'I know, but he never even told me that she was living there. If he had, we could have been more vigilant.'

'Maybe. Is that all that's worrying you?'

'No… Jade has settled into the O'Connor family so easily. She's one of them now. But me… well, I still don't feel I belong in their family. I'm still the outsider. You and Craig are the only family I've ever known.'

'You're not going to lose us, we'll always be there for you and Jade.'

'I know. Thanks.' She put her arm around Jess and hugged her.

'Anyway, what about you and the sexy doctor? Are you going to move in with him?'

'No, I don't think so.'

'Why? It makes sense to me.'

'That's the problem. I can't live with a man merely because it makes sense. He wants me there for all the wrong reasons. Because it'll be convenient for him mainly. He'll have Jade there permanently and me to do all the running around and looking after the place.'

'Is there nothing between you two then? You know, in the bedroom?'

'Oh yes, the bedroom has never been a problem. In fact, it's a distraction. I think Casey is confusing lust with love. We are attracted to each other and when we get together…'

'Fireworks?' suggested Jess with a grin.

'Skyrockets!' agreed Lexi.

Jess laughed out loud. 'Cool, as my son would say.'

'Yes, but not enough for a permanent relationship. If I ever live with a man, then I want the real thing. All of it. I want romance, commitment, loyalty and trust. And I want love. Real, unconditional, abiding love.'

'Did you get all that from your romance books?'

Lexi drained her mug of the last bit of chocolate and placed it on the coffee table in front of them. She sat back and stared into the flames.

'Do you think I'm asking too much? Am I being unrealistic? Maybe all those things don't exist except in novels.'

'Our problem, you and me, is that we never had parents who showed us how a marriage should be. We don't know what's real and what isn't.'

They fell silent, listening to the crackle of the fire. It was warm and cosy with the curtains closed to shut out the night. She was happy in the cottage and part of her wanted time to stand still; to stay like this forever, safe and secure in the now. But, if things worked out with Billy, Jess and Craig would be moving to Scotland and she'd have to advertise for a tenant. She couldn't afford the rent on her own.

Jess spoke again, her voice quiet in the stillness. 'It's not easy for me either, you know. I want Billy to be someone I could have a future with, but at the moment the man's a stranger. We've never even met. I'm just trusting that we'll hit it off.'

'I hope it works out for you, too, Jess, I really do. You deserve to be happy.'

'Thanks. I appreciate that. Sometimes you have to take a chance. And like you say – Jade is an O'Connor already. And if you don't want Casey, there'll be plenty of women ready to step in and snatch him up.'

Lexi felt a sudden chill, despite the heat from the fire. That thought had also occurred to her. They were tied together because of Jade. They would always be in each other's lives. But in what capacity? If they weren't together as a couple, it wouldn't take long for Casey to find someone else to love him. She knew she would never feel for another man the depth of longing she felt for Dr Casey O'Connor.

Chapter Thirty-Two

The Leytonsfield Hotel was dressed for the festive season, like the grand old lady she was. The outside of the building was lit by the silver fairy lights around the main doors and festooning the shrubs that sat snugly in their pots on either side of the entrance.

Walking up the steps and passing through the heavy wooden doors, into the warmth and noise of the interior, was like emerging into a party-animal's Christmas paradise.

It seemed that every department at Leytonsfield General had booked their Christmas party there. Casey had chosen this venue because of the long association his family had with the hotel. His parents had celebrated their fiftieth wedding anniversary there, the twins celebrated their twenty-first birthdays, not to mention myriad lunches, dinners and tête-à-têtes over the years. Their food sat neatly between pub-grub and fine dining. Casey was looking forward to the meal immensely.

There were tables set in every available corner, some already occupied by people wearing paper hats or Santa hats and unfurling party blowers annoyingly in their colleagues' faces, while other tables were empty. Neat piles of crackers sat invitingly in the centre of each, with party poppers, cutlery and glasses untouched and pristine, waiting expectantly for the revellers to arrive.

After a brief search, Casey gave up and asked a passing waiter to show him to the A&E table. There were two of them, in pride of place in the main dining-room, adjacent to the lounge, temporarily converted to a disco for the duration of the Christmas parties.

One table sat sixteen and the other fourteen. Some of his team had arrived and had plonked themselves down on the larger table, joyfully opening the wine and examining the crackers. They'd made a special effort with their attire, the men wearing suits or open-necked shirts and jackets, matched with casual trousers. No jeans. The women looked gorgeous in low-cut dresses, heels and sparkly earrings. How pleasant it was to see the staff looking happy and relaxed, dressed like normal human beings instead of stress-heads in shapeless scrubs.

Would Lexi be coming tonight? She hadn't confirmed by email as requested and he'd paid her deposit himself just in case. They'd seen very little of each other since last Saturday, being on different shifts and their paths had seldom crossed.

They had waved to each other occasionally but had not found the chance for conversation. The nights he managed to get to the cottage to see Jade, Lexi had been on a late shift. He couldn't help thinking she was avoiding him.

When he'd found out that Jade was his daughter, his only wish was to be the best father a little girl could have. He hadn't reckoned on how difficult that simple-sounding task was going to be. All he'd succeeded in doing was to annoy Lexi and make her life harder than it had been before he arrived back in Leytonsfield.

So far, he'd proved himself to be a hopeless dad. Incompetent, scared of saying no, desperate for Jade to love him. Then the fiasco with Helen. Being a parent was the hardest job he'd ever had in his life. He didn't know how other people coped. He couldn't do it alone, he needed Lexi's help but, as she'd pointed out to him, he never asked for it; he just assumed he knew best. What an idiot.

And another thing he was equally ashamed of was the way he'd asked Lexi to live with him. It was a miracle she hadn't run screaming from the house. He just wasn't the romantic type and had no idea how to tell Lexi how much he loved her.

So, the only noble thing he could do, was to give Lexi space. He wasn't sure what she intended to do with the space, but just hoped it didn't involve filling it with a more attentive boyfriend. Hopefully, he hadn't blown his chances completely.

'Evening,' he said forcing a smile to his face as he joined the people already seated. He was going to let his hair down with his team tonight. They had all earned a good night out and, as team leader, it was his job to make sure they got it.

'Hello, Casey – on your own?'

Catalina Martinez was already drinking white wine and looked ready to party.

'Yes. You?'

'I am. Young, free and single. Well, the second two, anyway.' They laughed.

'Great! Then will it be okay if I sit next to you? Two singletons together?'

She grinned and pulled the chair out for him to sit down.

He wasn't flirting, but suddenly Catalina was looking at him with real warmth in her eyes. Under different circumstances he would have been happy about that, but he didn't want the others to get the wrong idea. They all knew about Jade and Lexi.

Oh, what the heck… It's Christmas and people will think what they want anyway.

He poured himself a glass of wine and when he looked up again, he noticed Lexi on the other table, glaring at him. He hadn't noticed her arrive. She was sitting with Theresa, Sarala, Raj and their partners. She looked stunning in a dark blue wrap-around dress with three quarter sleeves and a low neckline, and her hair was long and loose. The dress looked familiar. Casey thought it may be the same one she had worn to the Italian Restaurant, when he'd just found out that Jade was his child. So much had happened since that night.

*

It had been a last-minute decision. As usual, she had been torn between wanting to get dressed up, so she looked her best and go out and kick ass as Jess described it and stay at home in front of the fire with a romance novel and a cup of cocoa.

Jess and Craig were off to Edinburgh the following day, which was Christmas Eve, and Tom and Riordan were collecting Jade to stay for the duration of Christmas, as both she and Casey were on duty and there was no one else to look after her.

She knew Casey would be here tonight, and she had hoped that he would, at least, want to sit next to her. He was on the other table, getting cosy with Catalina Martinez who was all over him like white on rice. He hadn't even noticed her. Lexi's cheeks burned, and she fumed as she stared hard at the pile of crackers.

'They won't go bang unless you pull 'em,' said Theresa, pouring two glasses of white wine.

'Pardon me?'

'The crackers – you look as if you are trying to use mind control on them.' She handed Lexi a glass and clinked hers against it. 'Cheers.'

'Cheers,' Lexi responded, taking a large gulp.

'So – what's going on?'

'We had a bit of a falling out. It's a long story which I will tell you one day. Tonight I want to forget all about men and ex-girlfriends and have a good time.'

'Maybe you should tell your face that, you look a real misery-guts for someone who intends to have a good time.'

'I just need some more of this,' Lexi said holding her glass out for more wine.

Theresa poured and Lexi knocked back half the glass.

'Hey, easy tiger, we've got a long night ahead of us.'

'Yes, you're right.' Lexi smiled at the others around the table. 'I'm the only one on my own,' she said finally, the smile slipping.

'No, you're not. There's lots of single guys here tonight. You never know who you might meet. That is, if you're sure you and Casey are finished.'

'I told him I didn't think we had a future together.'

'And what did he say?'

'Nothing much, I didn't really give him the chance. I let him have it with both barrels.'

'Have some more wine.' Theresa filled their glasses again and Lexi realised she was filling them right to the top. They'd gone through a full bottle already - just the two of them.

'I'm working tomorrow.'

'Me too. Anyway, it's Christmas. Let your hair down. If what you say is true – and, I would like to add at this juncture that I think you're wrong – but if you're not wrong, then there are plenty of eligible single men here tonight to flirt with and make the good doctor seething with jealousy. You can have Pete for a start. If he doesn't stop flirting with Sarala I'm going to send him to A&E myself, so he can see what it's like on the other side of the fence.'

'Poor Pete.' She giggled. Pete was a Senior House Officer and was being sized up by Theresa as potential husband material. Somehow, she didn't think he'd last the course. Or even the night, judging by the way Theresa was eyeing up one of the consultants from orthopaedics on the other side of the room.

She just hoped that Pete would still be around at the end of the evening to give her a lift home. She doubted Casey would offer. They'd made eye contact twice now and he hadn't even bothered to come over and say hello.

*

Casey detached himself from Catalina's soulful gaze and wandered over to the other table. They all looked up at his approach. All except Lexi who wouldn't meet his eyes.

'Hi, guys – how's it going? What did you all have for a starter?' He wasn't really interested in what they'd eaten, but as an ice-breaker, it was as good as anything else he could come up with on the spur of the moment.

'I had the prawns,' said Theresa.

'Garlic mushrooms,' said Sarala and her partner together. They glanced at each other and smiled as only lovers could do.

He hadn't been introduced formally to the plus-ones, so Sarala's boyfriend stood up and shook Casey's hand solemnly.

'Pleased to meet you,' Casey said, forgetting the man's name immediately. He was too eager to get Lexi to look at him to be interested in anyone else at that moment. 'Lexi – what did you have?'

She turned her head from contemplating the wall at the far

end of the room and gave him a social smile. 'Oh, hi Casey. I had the soup. And what did you have? I'm sure we're all dying to know.'

Theresa had just put her glass to her lips and taken a sip of wine. She spluttered indelicately and put her napkin to her mouth.

'Actually, I had the soup too.'

'And Catalina?'

'Uh – the soup.'

'And did she enjoy it?'

'Yes, very much.'

'I'm so glad,' Lexi said, her voice dripping with sarcasm.

Lexi was still mad that much was obvious. There was only one thing to do. Retreat. 'Well, I'd better get back as the waiters are serving the main course. Have fun, team. See you later.'

Chapter Thirty-Three

'You're reading too much into it.' Theresa speared a sprout with her fork and stuffed it into her mouth.

'Urgh!' Sarala said with a shiver, 'I don't know how you can eat those things, they taste disgusting.'

'Love 'em,' said Theresa chewing.

'Well, you can have mine, then.' She scraped all the sprouts off her plate onto Theresa's.

'Cheers.' Theresa continued shovelling them into her mouth, their conversation apparently forgotten.

'Well, how would you read it? It looks to me as if he's with Catalina and not me. How else can it be interpreted?' She stumbled over the last word, realising how much she had drunk.

'He's just sitting next to her. He's probably just doing his duty as team leader and making sure she has a good time.'

'They don't have to sit *that* close. And why is it his job to make sure she has a good time? And what about me?'

Theresa pointed her fork at Lexi and gravy fell off the sprout, held captive on the prongs, and dripped onto the white tablecloth.

'You know what your trouble is?' she said, waving the fork in front of her, 'you don't know what you really want.'

'What d'you mean?' Lexi watched, mesmerized, as another sprout disappeared into Theresa's mouth.

'I mean,' she said belching quietly, 'Casey's yours for the taking but you don't do anything about it. He's perfect for you but you keep sending him mixed signals. Just go after what you want. Now would be the perfect time.'

'What if he doesn't want me? I did say some very harsh things to him. What if he's gone off me and has set his sights on Catalina?'

'Yes, but what if he hasn't? Anyhow, you were there first. Finders keepers, losers weepers and all that.'

'I don't know how. Seriously. I'm no good at this kind of thing.'

Theresa pushed her plate away and sat back with her hands over her belly. Pete was nowhere in sight and Lexi wondered if Theresa had forgotten all about him.

'So, tell me something. How did you two get it together that first time?'

'Well… we were dancing, and-'

'Bingo!' Theresa leant forward and thumped the table, making the neat arrangement of crackers collapse in a heap.

'That's your answer. Get him on the dance floor. Work your magic. Charm him. He'll be putty in your hands.'

'Who will?' asked Pete as he returned to the table and grabbed a cracker, pointing it at Theresa. 'Pull this with me?'

She pulled and the whole table were joining in, pulling crackers, screeching at the bangs, reading the jokes aloud and groaning, playing with the novelties, until all the crackers had been pulled and the debris scattered all over the table.

As she joined in the fun, Lexi watched the other table out of the corner of her eye. Casey and Catalina were talking quietly, their heads together. Casey was frowning, and Catalina was gesturing a lot with her hands. It reminded Lexi of the time she saw Casey in the Sticky Bun with the estate agent. That woman had used her hands a lot when she talked as well.

She hadn't felt the slightest bit jealous then, so what had changed? Why did she feel such red-hot resentment of a female colleague? Because it made her realise that she was on the verge of losing the best thing that had ever happened to her. Apart from Jade. And the two were indistinguishable. Casey had done everything he could to convince her of his feelings. And she had rejected him. It was all her fault. She thought she could never forgive him for letting Helen kidnap Jade but was finding it hard to hang on to her conviction. She knew deep down that Casey had been as scared as she had been. It was time she forgave him.

She loved Jade and she loved Casey. She wanted them both. Needed them both. Together. She should be the one sitting next to him tonight, as his partner, so close they were breathing the same air. The thought of him desiring another woman was like a knife to the heart. Theresa was right. She needed to do something before it was too late, and she lost him forever.

*

'I'm a good listener, but you can tell me to mind my own business if you want.'

Casey sighed. 'It's complicated.'

'Isn't it always with affairs of the heart?'

So Casey told Catalina the whole story. Helen, the abortion and how it sent her into a psychotic episode, her taking Jade and Lexi telling him she couldn't trust him and that they had no future together. She listened intently without interrupting. Casey was grateful for her friendship and the opportunity to offload. He felt better when he had finished.

'And how do you feel about Lexi?' Catalina asked.

'I love her. I want us to be together as a family. I want her to be my wife eventually. My parents have got an incredibly strong marriage and I've always wanted the same. They talk every issue through, they share everything: good times and bad. Neither makes a decision that affects them both without checking it out with the other.'

He fell silent as he pictured his mum and dad in the kitchen at the end of the day, in their dressing-gowns, chatting easily and companionably, before going to bed. They were madly in love, but their love had always been built on friendship and trust.

'Casey?'

'Umm?'

'Are you okay? I just asked you a question.'

'Sorry. What did you say?'

'I said you talk a lot about what you want, but what does Lexi want?'

Casey was silent, then he frowned. 'I think she wants the same. She's never known family life as she was brought up in care. Doesn't everyone want to be part of a loving family?'

'Have you ever asked her what she wants?'

'Well…' Had he? Surely he must have done. 'Maybe not in so many words…' He realised that he never had.

'Have you ever told Lexi how you feel? Women today have many and varied talents, but I'm afraid mind reading does not feature amongst them.' Casey loved the way Catalina expressed herself. Her English was impeccable and poetic. Her questions, however, were too close to the bone and were beginning to make him squirm.

'Yes, I've told her. I bought a house and asked her to move in with me.'

'And she said yes?'

'Well no, not exactly. She said she would have liked the chance to choose somewhere herself.'

'What do you intend to do?' Catalina sipped her wine. He couldn't read her expression and she hadn't offered any advice. He needed advice. Badly.

'I don't know. What do you think I should do?'

'Are you asking my opinion?'

'Yes. Please.'

'Then tell her. Tell her exactly what you have just told me. That you love her and can't live without her. If your parents' marriage is your role model then you must have as your foundation, trust and friendship, yes?'

Casey felt a wave of gratitude for Catalina, mixed with a twinge of guilt. She was looking at him with concern.

'You're right, and I just want to thank you for listening. You came here for a good night out and ended up as my agony aunt, listening to my problems. Let me apologise for that.'

'No need to apologise. What are friends for? And I hope we are friends as well as colleagues.' She put her hand on his arm and leaned closer. 'Would you like a quick dance before the disco gets too crowded? I know what these Christmas parties are like. Soon everyone will be trying to get on the dance floor, and it will be like a tin of sardines.'

He grinned. 'Great idea.'

*

'He's dancing with her now.' Lexi felt wretched. Casey had his hand on the small of Catalina's back as they passed their table. He had barely glanced her way.

'Doesn't mean a thing,' said Theresa who was yawning, 'he's being a good host, that's all. Don't stress it.'

'He's not the host, though, and he's hardly spoken to anyone else all night, including me.'

Theresa leant forward and held up three fingers. 'You have two choices,' she was slurring her words and seemed to be having trouble focusing, 'you can sit there being a miserable party popper and feeling sorry for yourself,' she put down a finger, 'or…' she paused to swig some more wine.

'Party pooper, you mean.'

'You got that right. You've had a face like a slapped arse all night, or,' the fingers came up again, 'you can fight for your man. Get onto that dance floor and show him your moves, girlfriend. Give it the old shimmy-shimmy and the poor man won't stand a chance.'

'Come with me?' she pleaded.

'Okay.' Theresa stood up then grabbed hold of the table and sat back down again, abruptly. 'Oh God, I'm drunk. Think you'll have to go alone.'

'Right. Then I will.' She would. In a minute. Just as soon as she'd worked out a strategy. Should she go up to him and start talking, as if she hadn't been furious with him all night? But what about Dr Martinez? It would be too rude to interrupt them. Heck no, he was her boyfriend, the father of her child, she had every right to join them. What if they were slow dancing, or worse, kissing? Would she just stand there suffering the bitterest humiliation she could think of, or would she take a swing at him, or her, or maybe the pair of them? Perhaps she should stay here where she was safe.

'What are you waiting for?' asked Theresa.

'Courage.'

'Have some more wine.' Theresa poured the last of the bottle into Lexi's glass and she knocked it back in one go.

'Don't leave it too long,' Theresa said.

'I'll just nip to the ladies first, freshen up a bit, put some lippy on.'

'Good idea.' Theresa leaned back in her chair and closed her eyes. Lexi wondered how long it would be before she started snoring.

The ladies was packed with women standing three deep in front of the mirrors, mouths contorting as they applied lip gloss and eyes wide as they repaired the damage to their mascara. The harsh lights were unforgiving, so Lexi merely pulled a comb through her hair and sprayed on some more perfume, to add to the growing bouquet of aromas making the air thick and difficult to breathe. She looked pale, so pinched her cheeks as she'd forgotten to bring her blusher. She could have asked one of the women if she could borrow theirs, but it was unhygienic to share make-up and she was beginning to feel claustrophobic. She fought her way out of the confined space and made her way to the lounge.

The DJ was playing lively Christmas songs and people were singing along loudly and tunelessly, kicking their legs up and whooping with laughter. Everyone wore either a paper hat from their cracker or one of the mass-produced Santa hats. Raj still wore his flashing antlers and Sarala had acquired a hat that was huge and Christmas tree shaped, but, if it had been a different colour, say, black or brown, could have been mistaken for a witch's hat. Lexi was sure she hadn't been wearing it during the meal.

She wasn't really in the mood for dancing, so wandered around the periphery of the dance floor, searching for Casey. After two circuits, she admitted defeat. He wasn't there. And worryingly, neither was Dr Catalina Martinez.

There was only one thing to do. She made her way out of the lounge to return to the tables. If Casey was there, she was going to talk to him and make him talk to her, whether he was alone or not.

As she was leaving the lounge, a blast of cold air made her turn her head to look at the front door, and she caught sight of Casey carefully helping Catalina on with her coat and escorting her out. Casey was wearing his coat too and Catalina linked him as they hurried out into the night.

*

The temperature had dropped dramatically during the evening, so Casey left the car heater on. He had dropped Catalina off, then said he was going back for Lexi. He had to speak to her before he lost the chance of them being reconciled. Catalina was right, he had to tell Lexi he loved her. Even if she rebuffed him, he had to try and he had to do it now, he couldn't wait any longer. Unfortunately, when he got back to hotel, Sarala told him Lexi had already left. Pete was giving a few people lifts home as he had volunteered to be a designated driver.

So Casey had parked near the cottage, but a few doors down on the other side of the road. He would see Pete's car when it arrived, then he would make his presence felt and tell Lexi he loved her. At least, that was the plan.

It would have worked perfectly if he hadn't fallen asleep. He had only drunk one glass of wine, but had eaten a hearty meal, including Christmas cake and mince pies. In fact, he remembered eating a few extra mince pies that his colleagues had piled on his plate. He was stuffed, and tired after a long day and evening, and the car was like a hothouse.

He woke to voices and Lexi waving goodbye as Theresa leaned out of the car window shouting "Merry Christmas" in a loud voice as the vehicle sped away. He turned off the engine and scrambled out of his car, fumbling with the key. By the time he strode up to Lexi's cottage she had gone in. The lights downstairs were switched off and a light came on in the front bedroom. Lexi's room. She had gone straight to bed. He stood on the doorstep wondering if he should ring the bell, but then realised that he risked waking everyone in the cottage and scaring them half to death.

He would have to wait to declare his undying love. Maybe it was for the best. Lexi had been drinking, he was tired, and they were both on duty the following day. He had the whole of the Christmas period in which to tell her. And he would. He had to. Somehow he would convince her that he was sincere and that he loved her more than life itself.

Chapter Thirty-Four

Lexi was glad to be back at work. Despite the organised chaos of bright lights, the flurry of people dashing all over the place, the incessant beeping of machines monitoring the patients' vital signs and the underlying smell of vomit and worse that even Casey's essential oils couldn't mask, today she caught the notes of cinnamon and spicy orange, Lexi felt completely at home and confident of her place in the pecking order.

Christmas Eve in A&E was notoriously busy at Leytonsfield General. To add to their woes, the temperature had dropped overnight to below zero and the sky was a heavy, grey blanket that threatened to fall on their town at any moment.

The odds for snow on Christmas Day had just increased tenfold. The kids would be pleased but the adults went about their business with furrowed brows, wondering if their cars had enough anti-freeze, cursing for putting off the annual central heating boiler service and, in Lexi's case, wishing she'd stock-piled more wood for the fire.

She'd be away for two whole days at the O'Connors, the cottage would be freezing by the time she and Jade got back home. Jess and Craig weren't returning until after the New Year.

For now, though, she had other things to worry about. She was late and was on duty in Resus all day with the likelihood of having to work with Casey for most of that time.

As she threw her things in her locker, Theresa arrived silently, and stood next to her, like a wraith appearing out of nowhere. Her face looked as green as the sprouts she'd been demolishing the previous night, and she stared ahead, unseeing.

'Hi - are you okay?' Theresa shook her head slowly but said nothing.

'Do you want a coffee before we start?' Really, there wasn't the time, but she couldn't let Theresa go on duty looking like that.

'I'll be fine,' she whispered, then dashed into the toilet cubicle.

When she emerged, looking too ill to work, Lexi left her sitting on a bench nursing a mug of black coffee she made for her.

'I'll tell Sister you'll be out in a minute,' said Lexi wondering why they had all drunk so much the previous night.

She didn't have time to beat herself up as, when she made

her way to Resus, she heard the familiar crash alarm and automatically started running. *"Cardiac arrest, resus bay 3, cardiac arrest, resus bay 3."*

The first person she saw when she arrived was Casey, standing at the bottom of a patient's bed and barking orders. He was wearing purple scrubs and looked alert and completely in charge. She grabbed some gloves and waited for instructions. A doctor had secured the patient's airway, and another had started chest compressions, so Lexi made sure there was IV access to take bloods, while another attached the defibrillator pads.

After two minutes, Lexi took over from the doctor doing the compressions. The patient was still not breathing when the anaesthetists arrived and took over the patient's airway.

Lexi glanced at Casey. His face was serious, and his jaw clenched. Looking at him, Lexi had a bad feeling about the outcome for their patient. The longer it took to bring a patient back, the worse the prognosis.

Her fears were realised after fifteen minutes when there was still no pulse and an x-ray taken earlier confirmed that the shortness of breath the patient had attended A&E with was caused by a large mass in his lungs.

Casey, his expression closed and his eyes sad, went to discuss the situation with the man's relatives. Lexi knew that the team were fighting a losing battle. Even if cardiac function could be restored, with the disease in his lungs, the man's quality of life was likely to be severely limited.

There was no pulse after fifteen minutes and further tests. The prognosis was looking bleak.

Casey decided to call it. The family and the rest of the team agreed. Lexi wished there was something she could say but words weren't enough. As the staff drifted away to leave the patient and his family together for one last time, she looked around for Casey. He had disappeared.

*

Casey filled a glass from the tap and drank deeply. Would he ever get used to losing a patient? And if he ever did, would that be the time to quit medicine?

The man's family had been brave; stoical. He had been elderly, but loved life, his family had told him. He had been looking forward to spending Christmas Day with his grand-children. Simple pleasures that could suddenly be taken away, with no warning.

Spending quality time with loved ones and making memories that stayed with you the rest of your life; they were the important things.

Suddenly, he wanted to see Lexi, to apologise for not spending time with her at the Christmas party. Never mind giving her space, he should have been with her. She was the woman he loved, the only woman he would ever love, and he couldn't lose her.

When he hurried back to Resus, he was met with a code red that tested all his skills as a trauma consultant. Four young people, no more than teenagers, had been involved in an RTA. A young girl hadn't been wearing a seat belt and had serious head injuries. She was transferred to intensive care. A young man had a thigh bone fracture and was prepared for surgery.

The other two, it turned out, weren't seriously injured but had been drinking and started to make nuisances of themselves to the extent that security had to be called to keep them in line. Casey wasn't a bit surprised when, later, the police turned up as the car they had been driving had been stolen. A teenage prank gone wrong, or were these kids serial offenders?

As Lexi was about to go off duty, she came looking for him.

'What time are we leaving?'

'I'll pick you up later, okay? I'm sorry we won't get home for hours yet, but…'

'I know, it's been mad today. Glad I'm not on duty tomorrow.'

'Yeah, me too.' He gazed at her dear face, wanting to kiss her, to hug her, to tell her that he loved her. 'We'll have a good time this Christmas, I promise. I texted the twins – they've already been enslaved by Jade and are loving every minute of it.'

Lexi grinned. 'I can't wait to meet them.'

'They'll love you.' As he did.

'Right. See you later then.'

He watched her walk away, wishing he could have left with her, but would be in A&E for a while longer yet. There were still too many patients in Resus. His work was far from over.

*

As Casey would be picking her up that evening, and she didn't want to risk a spark jumping out and setting the cottage alight while they were all away, Lexi didn't bother lighting the fire.

She brought the cases downstairs and placed them on the floor in the middle of the lounge. Then she brought the carrier bags of Christmas presents and put them next to the cases. She hadn't spent much money but had bought small, novelty tokens for everyone. Casey knew her financial situation and had, no doubt, warned his parents not to expect much from her. She just hoped they appreciated the gesture.

Gradually, she was starting to relax from the horrendous day they'd all had. What a shift! Christmas Eve was notoriously busy but today had tested them all. Especially as they were one nurse down with Sister sending Theresa home to bed. She'd taken one look at her and shooed her out of the door. She'd be fine after rehydrating with a few glasses of water and a long sleep.

Casey was more of a concern. They hadn't had the chance to talk at the hospital; it had been frantic from start to finish. And losing that patient … the poor man had looked shattered. He took every loss as a personal affront, but the patient had been very sick even before he'd been admitted.

Maybe there'd be the chance to talk in the car. She was going to tell him how she felt. She loved Casey and they should be together. She didn't know why she had ever doubted that they were perfect for each other. Watching him with Dr Martinez at the Christmas party had made her realise how foolish she was being. She had never experienced such jealousy at the thought of him wanting someone else. She assumed they had left together because Casey gave Catalina a lift home.

The air in the cottage was icy. She got up and walked to the window. The sky was full of snow. There wasn't much traffic on the road and no sounds of people chatting as they walked past or kids shouting in the distance. It was eerily quiet.

She shivered and turned around to look back at her cottage. As it was open plan, she could see straight through to the window at the back and then outside to the tiny garden. The cottage was immaculate. All the toys had been packed away out of sight and there were no slippers or shoes on the floor or dirty mugs on the coffee table, as there usually were.

It came to her suddenly that this was the first time she had ever been entirely alone in the cottage. She felt as if she was leaving for good instead of just two days. Moving on with her life. She couldn't wait to see Jade again but, surprisingly, hadn't been concerned with their brief separation. Jade was in the loving arms of her doting family and would be showered with care and attention. She'd be lapping it up and playing the Princess for all she was worth.

Lexi smiled at the thought of her gorgeous daughter. The next moment, the doorbell rang, and her heart leapt. It was Casey. Her first real family Christmas was about to begin

.

Chapter Thirty-Five

Lexi had been prepared for the overwhelming surge of noise that the O'Connor clan produced whenever they were together, but not to her own reaction to it. The first time she had experienced them all talking at once, their voices getting louder as they fought to make themselves heard, she'd wanted to slink away into the shadows.

Now, as she and Casey stepped through the kitchen door into laughter, light, carols on the radio and the delicious aroma of spices, she wanted to dive right into the middle of this marvellous, hyperactive family.

'Mummy! Daddy!' Jade came hurtling towards them and threw herself into her arms. She hugged her tight, the familiar feeling of all being right with the world that she experienced whenever she held her daughter washing over her in waves.

'We're face painting.'

'Yes, I can see that – with glitter, by the looks of it.'

As Jade hugged Casey, Lexi noted a young woman hovering at the kitchen table. She had long dark hair and hazel eyes.

'I'm Josie.'

'Hi, I'm Lexi, you've obviously met Jade.'

Josie laughed, and Lexi warmed to her straight away. 'Oh, yes – quite the little poppet. She begged us to let her open one present, so we gave in, but unfortunately, she chose the glitter face paint and it's gone everywhere…'

'I hope you're going to clean up the mess,' Casey said hugging his sister.

'You're the daddy, mate, we've saved that for you. I'm Jay, by the way, seeing as no one is going to introduce us.'

Jay was a shorter and stockier version of Casey but with the same colour eyes as his twin.

'Hi, Jay, I'm Lexi.' She had barely finished her sentence when she was lifted off her feet by a pair of strong arms and swung around the kitchen.

'Put her down, Jay. He thinks he's Tarzan,' said Josie.

'He did that to me, too!' shouted Jade happily.

The rest of the family came into the kitchen, and Lexi got lost in all the voices and banter. She didn't try to keep up with it all, just sat back and watched. Someone thrust a glass of mulled wine into her hands, then the doorbell rang, and she heard a voice shout, "Carol singers!"

They all trooped out to the hallway to listen to the choir from the local church. They sang *Once in Royal David's City* in four parts and a lump formed in Lexi's throat at the beauty of their harmonisation. Dan, who was standing next to her at the back was singing quietly; he had a lovely bass voice. She turned her head to watch him and noticed he also had glitter on the side of his face and adorning the shoulders of his woolly jumper.

He moved closer to her and whispered, 'I'm so glad you're going to be with us this Christmas, it wouldn't have been the same without you.'

The lump in her throat grew bigger, but she managed to murmur, 'Me, too.'

Then the choir sang, *Oh Come, All Ye Faithful* and the whole family joined in. Casey was holding Jade, the twins had their arms around each other, Eloise had one hand on Tom's shoulder and the other around Riordan's waist and Lexi's lump dissolved, the tears spilling over and running down her cheeks. If anyone noticed, they were too polite to say anything.

*

The room was warm, the murmur of conversation soothing, and the home-made mulled wine was working its magic. Casey felt his eyelids drooping.

An enormous Christmas tree stood in the corner of the living-room, decorated with all the old family heirlooms. Things their parents had bought early on in their marriage, misshapen and strange ones the four of them had made as young children, and some they had been given by patients. His father had collected a whole box-full over the years. He, himself, had one he was rather proud of. It was a tiny set of blue scrubs with a red stethoscope. The wife of a patient whose life they had saved had made the whole team one each. Casey treasured it and would like to see it on his own tree one day. Maybe next year if things went well.

Josie had told him they had left a dozen or so decorations for Jade to put on the tree, so she could feel she'd played her part. His daughter and the twins had bonded already.

Tom and Jade were on the floor with the twins playing a board game. The rest of the adults sat in armchairs and sofas, sipping wine and talking quietly. His father had his eyes closed. He looked tired. Casey worried about him; he worked too hard. Maybe he'd have a word with Riordan later.

He also needed to talk to Lexi. She looked happy and had lost the rabbit-caught-in-the-headlights look she usually had whenever she was here. In fact, she looked at home, as if she belonged. At last.

Jay had been staring intently out of the French windows at the garden. It was lit by solar powered security lights that stood around the perimeter of the lawn. Nearest the house was Casey's favourite; a light that resembled an old-fashioned streetlamp. It had been a present from Riordan and himself two years previously, when they had been at a loss as to what to buy for their parents. Fortunately, it had been a resounding success as it served as a security light as well as being an attractive piece of garden furniture.

'You owe me a tenner,' Jay said, laughing at the expression on Riordan's face. 'He said it wouldn't snow until tomorrow, but, guess what?'

Casey returned his grin. 'It's snowing?'

'Yay! We can build a snowman on Christmas Day. Can we go tobogganing, Dad?' Tom was beside himself with excitement.

'It may not stick,' Riordan said with a frown.

'It'll stick,' said Jay, 'come on, give.' He held his hand out for the money and Riordan, sighing, slapped a ten-pound note onto his open palm.

'If it melts, I want that back.'

'No way, a bet's a bet.'

Casey listened with half an ear to his brothers' bantering. He was watching Lexi who gazed out of the window with a look of wonder that lit up her face making her look almost angelic.

'Isn't it beautiful? Look Jade, at the way the snowflakes dance in the light from the lamp.' Jade looked. Seeing the two of them, their blonde heads together, their expressions of joy at so simple a sight, touched something deep inside him.

I love you, Lexi Grainger. I love you so much. And before this Christmas is over, I'm going to find a way to tell you. Somehow.

Chapter Thirty-Six

'Mummy, get up, Santa's been.'

Jade, who had been sleeping in the lower bunk in Tom's room, came through the door, dragging the stocking that she and Casey had put at the end of her bed the previous night. It had been a poignant moment, watching her sleeping in a strange bed and she'd wanted to linger or kiss her cheek, but Casey had whispered, 'Don't wake them,' and they'd left.

Outside the bedroom, he had put his arm around her and murmured, 'We need to talk. I want to explain about the Christmas party.' She didn't want to spoil the mood she was in, which was surprisingly mellow, by talking, and she was scared of what he was going to say. Nothing was going to ruin Christmas for her this year. All the serious stuff would have to wait.

When he'd picked her up from the cottage on Christmas

Eve, she'd tried to talk to him then, but there hadn't been enough time before they called in to the safe house to give them a box of food and small presents for the children she'd been collecting. Shelley was pleased to see them, and they'd stopped for a coffee and a mince pie. She'd looked happy and content with her new friends and hugged them both when they were leaving.

Casey had told her what a wonderful job she'd done with Shelley which made her feel warm inside. They then spent the short time before arriving at the O'Connors talking about the patient who had died. Casey had still been upset and said he needed the drive home to unwind and could they leave any personal stuff until later? She'd agreed. How could she not?

And now it was Christmas Day and, once again, there would be no opportunity to be alone, to sort out their feelings for each other.

'Mummy, look at everything I've got.'

'Aren't you a lucky girl?' She looked at all the toys and trinkets that emerged from the stocking, making suitable ooh and aah noises at everything.

There was a knock on the bedroom door and Casey came in with a mug of tea. 'Happy Christmas, gorgeous girls.'

They both said Happy Christmas back and he kissed them both and Jade showed him her stocking.

'Am I the last to get up?' Lexi sat up and sipped her tea.

The bedroom was at the back of the house and the view through the window showed a thick layer of snow covering the garden. It looked so pretty with the sun shining on it. Like a film set or a Christmas card. It must have snowed all night.

'Yes, sleepyhead, but don't worry, everything's under control.'

'Where is everyone?'

'Mum, Dad, and Josie are at church, Riordan, Jay and Tom are making breakfast – pancakes and maple bacon. An O'Connor tradition.'

'And we're here,' said Jade bouncing up and down on the bed.

'So we are, darling. And I think we should go downstairs now and let your mummy get dressed, don't you?'

'Okay.'

'I didn't know your family were religious,' Lexi said.

'We're not, but as Dad is a family GP, he likes to show his face at Christmas and Easter. It's another tradition. A lot of his patients are in the congregation. Josie goes with them to get out of making breakfast. She's not terribly domesticated, my sister.'

'I love the twins.'

'And they love you. And I love you.' He leaned down to kiss her, and she slipped her arms around his neck.

'Do you really?' she said, her tone more serious than she intended.

'Of course. How could you doubt it?'

'Daddy, come on.' Jade was at the door, eager to get on with the celebrations.

'I love you too.' She watched his eyes soften. If Jade hadn't been around she would have pulled him into the bed with her, but he gently removed her arms from around his neck and kissed her again.

When they'd gone, she dressed quickly and went downstairs to join her new family.

*

Tom and Jade gave out the presents, while the adults sat in various places in the living-room, like patients in the waiting room, as Dan commented. Lexi was concerned that her presents wouldn't pass muster. They were simple, cheap things, but all the O'Connors thanked her profusely as they hugged and kissed her.

She had bought Casey a watch and he looked shocked when he opened the box. 'Oh my God, Lexi, this is perfect. How did you know I wanted this one?'

She winked at Riordan across the room and he winked back.

She opened her present from Casey. It was a gold locket with a tiny photo of Jade inside. It was exquisite and perfect. He put it on her and fixed the clasp at the back. Then he turned her around and she waited for him to say something profound.

'Don't lose the box,' he whispered, but when she looked inside to see if there was something she'd missed, it looked empty.

'Right,' Riordan said, rubbing his hands together, 'who's for a snowman building competition?'

The noise was deafening as the younger contingent shouted their approval and Jade jumped up and down in her excitement.

'Then may I suggest we split ourselves into teams of three and nominate captains? My team will consist of Tom and Jay. I, of course, will be captain.'

'Okay, then I want Jade and Lexi,' said Casey as he picked Jade up to stop her squealing.

'So that leaves the veteran snowman builders and a midwife who's used to working fast and thinking on her feet,' said Dan. 'You lot don't stand a chance.'

They were already thundering up the stairs to put on their coats and gloves and when everyone was ready, they donned wellington boots at the back door, then ran outside and divided the garden into three.

'Who's going to judge?' asked Lexi, feeling a rush of nervous energy at being on Casey's team. She'd never done anything so childish or exciting in her life. She grinned at Jade who looked flushed with happiness.

'No one,' said Tom, 'it's the first to finish.'

'Finesse doesn't come into it,' Casey said laughing as he gave out shovels, small spades for the children and brought out a box from the garage that contained old tatty scarves and hats. The family had obviously done this before and were fully prepared. Was this another O'Connor tradition? If so, it was one she heartily approved of.

'Ready, steady, go!' shouted Dan.

There was a flurry of activity with the captains shovelling snow into a pile whilst the other two members of the team tried to make it into something that resembled a snowman.

Lexi was at a disadvantage as she had never built a

snowman before. She didn't want to let her team down, however, so cast surreptitious glances at the others and copied what they were doing. Soon, their mound of snow began to assume a recognisable shape and Casey was shovelling like a demon, obviously trying to beat Riordan. They were so competitive, but today Lexi found it rather endearing.

When the large mound had acquired a small mound for a head, they fished about in the box for clothes for it to wear. They had a carrot for the nose, and small pieces of wood for the eyes; coal obviously being in short supply, then the fun part began. Jade took ages to choose the right hat and scarf, the colours having to match, whereas Tom just shoved anything on their snowman's head.

Inevitably, Riordan's team won and the three of them were like football supporters, high fiving each other and running around the garden with their arms out as if they were playing airplanes. Dan's team came second with a rather dashing snowwoman complete with a large straw hat and a pair of sunglasses. She sported a colourful silk scarf and looked quite the fashionista.

Lexi felt guilty that they came last and wondered if Casey had wished he'd chosen a better team, but he was beaming with pride as he helped Jade choose pebbles to stand in for buttons and found a red velvet bow tie at the bottom of the box. There was no top hat, but their snowman did have a rather natty fedora to wear.

'I'm sorry we lost,' she whispered to Casey.

He put his arm around her and hugged her. 'There are no losers today.'

'Well done, team Riordan,' said Dan, 'and your prize is…' he paused like they did on the gameshows on TV, 'the privilege of loading the dishwasher after the wonderful meal we are very soon to enjoy.'

'Ah, Granddad, that's not much of a prize.' Tom looked disappointed and Riordan put his hand on his shoulder.

'It's how you play the game that counts, not the winning.'

Casey guffawed and whispered to Lexi, 'Says the most competitive man I've ever known.'

'Pot, kettle, black,' she murmured. Casey grinned at her.

The garden, having been a pristine white blanket, now looked like a bed that a couple had been wrestling in. Or making love. The thought made her steal a look at Casey. He looked so happy today, in the company of all the people who meant the most to him, enjoying laughter and innocent fun. This is what she'd been missing all her life. But no more, she was part of this big, crazy family and she was loving every second of it.

*

As usual, he ate too fast at lunch and finished before everyone else.

He and Jay had helped their mum cook the meal, Jay telling amusing stories of his time in the States. The rest of them set the table and Team Riordan loaded the dishwasher afterwards.

When the meal was over, he was desperate to get Lexi alone, but she disappeared upstairs with Jade to phone Jess and Craig and wish them a Happy Christmas. Everyone else settled in the living-room to watch television or fall asleep. He, however, felt far too restless to join them.

She hadn't mentioned the note. Had she found it? He'd poured his heart out to her, telling her how much he loved her, how he wanted her. He had said things he could never have told her face to face. He had to find the box.

It was there, next to her pile of presents, but when he looked inside, the box was empty. That meant only one thing, she'd read it but didn't feel the same way about him. He'd made a fool of himself for nothing. Or, he took a deep breath, she hadn't read the note as, somehow, it had fallen out of the box. He needed to find it before anyone else did.

He went into the kitchen and tipped the box of paper for recycling on the floor, frantically rummaging through all the wrapping paper, cards and envelopes.

'Daddy, I'm going to draw a picture.' Jade came into the kitchen and knelt down next to him.

'Good idea, sweetie, what are you going to draw?'

'A snowman like the one we made.'

'Have you got paper and crayons?'

'I've got this paper, but I don't know where the crayons are.'

'Okay, I'll help you...' He looked up and saw his carefully compiled love note about to be turned into a snowman. 'How about we get you a better piece of paper and you let me have that one?'

'Okay.' Jade relinquished his note and he breathed a sigh of relief.

*

Lexi had spent more time upstairs on her phone than she had intended. She didn't want the O'Connors to think she was rude, disappearing for so long, but she wanted Jade to thank Jess and Craig for her lovely Christmas presents personally. It was good manners. After she had done that, however, Jade escaped to find her beloved daddy and Lexi caught up on all the news from Scotland.

Jess looked and sounded happy and strangely excited. Loved-up was probably the only way to describe it. Edinburgh, and especially Jimmy, had obviously lived up to her expectations.

After their face-time conversation was over, she quickly texted Theresa to find out if she was feeling better. She received a text back to say she was enjoying Christmas day with her family and was feeling much better. Her text was littered with festive emojis, so she was obviously back to her old self.

Tom and Jay had retreated to Tom's bedroom to play computer games. The rest of the family were in the living-room watching Christmas movies on TV. Dan was asleep, his paper hat over his eyes. Eloise and Josie were cuddling up on the sofa and Riordan was sprawled in an armchair with a glass of port. Jade was on the floor, surrounded by white paper and colourful chunky crayons. Casey was conspicuous by his absence.

She went over and sat next to her daughter. 'What are you drawing, honey?'

'It's for Daddy. It's Santa on his sleigh.'

'That's beautiful, he'll love it.'

'I'm going to do one for everyone. Tom wants a snowman like the Hulk.'

'A green snowman, that's novel.' She picked up a picture that Jade had obviously already finished. 'Who's this for?'

Jade lowered her voice and said in a stage whisper, 'That's for Granddad.' She sighed. 'There's a lot of people to make drawings for. I'm very busy.'

Lexi suppressed a laugh. 'Well, I better let you get on, then.' She kissed the top of her head and Jade didn't even look up, so engrossed was she in her task.

As she stood up, Riordan did too, and handed her a note he pulled out of his back pocket. 'This is from Casey. He's gone for a walk, but I'm sure you can guess where.'

Lexi took the note. Riordan was smiling and had a knowing look on his face. She raised her eyebrows in a question. The brothers were in cahoots again.

'I didn't read it, but I think I know what it contains. Us men sometimes find it hard to express our feelings verbally. I told him to write it down.'

She turned the note over, her heartbeat increasing. Was this what she'd been waiting for all this time?

Riordan's grey eyes were twinkling. 'Don't worry about Jade, she'll be fine with us.'

Lexi thanked him and went back upstairs to the bedroom. This was something she needed to read when she was alone. As she passed Tom's bedroom, she heard the murmur of voices behind the door.

There was still enough light to see by, so she left the

curtains open and clambered onto the bed, then sat cross-leg-ged in the middle and unfolded the piece of paper. It was typed and covered one side of A4. She started reading.

Chapter Thirty-Seven

My darling Lexi,

There are so many things I want to say to you, I hardly know where to begin.

Meeting you the night of the Summer Solstice Ball was the highlight of my life. I think part of me fell in love with you then – the sensible part that knows a good thing when it sees it, not the angry, hurt, resentful part of me that was to the fore that night. You changed all that. You soothed the savage beast with your beauty and downright sexiness. I felt alive in a way I hadn't for ages. Then, I woke the next morning and you were gone.

I never forgot you. I wanted to, but I couldn't.

When I returned home to Leytonsfield, a man plagued by doubts and insecurities, the last person I expected to see was you. But there you were, looking desirable in scrubs with those gorgeous blue eyes that had haunted my dreams. Not just you, also a beautiful little girl who, you told me, was my daughter. I fell in love all over again. A different kind of love. A fiercer, all-consuming, obsessive love. All I wanted was to be a good dad, but I didn't know how. I'm so sorry I keep getting it wrong. I'll try to be better, I promise. I'll listen to you from now on – in everything.

The Christmas party. I'm so sorry I didn't spend it with you. I realise now how wrong I got it. Again. I was trying to back off and give you space, as I thought that was what you wanted, but you didn't want to be unpartnered that night, did you? If it's any consolation, I spend the entire evening talking about you. Catalina Martinez is a good listener, has infinite patience and took pity on a lovesick colleague by offering me advice. I hope you get to talk to her one day – I think you'll like her.

Oh, Lexi, I wish I had the words to tell you how I feel about you. Maybe I could if I was a poet, writer or philosopher, but I'm just an ordinary man, struggling to put his feelings into words. A man who's lived a charmed life, a privileged loving childhood, surrounded by people who cared about me. Whereas you, my darling girl, have grown up in entirely different circumstances. You are the courageous one, the fighter, the strong one. I admire and respect you for that.

I want you to know how very much I love you. You have my heart. Everything I have is yours, if you want it, because you are everything I have ever wanted.

There, I've said it. If you don't feel the same way, then

please excuse this piece of self-indulgent nonsense. If you do feel the same, then you will make me the happiest man on the planet.

My future is in your hands.

Chapter Thirty-Eight

Lexi could hardly see the words by the time she'd finished reading as the room had grown dark, the sky in the distance paling to the colour of the inside of an oyster shell. She wiped the tears that had fallen as she heard the voice of the man she loved, almost as if he was in the room with her.

She had to go to him, he'd be expecting her. Riordan had intimated as much. Casey's letter had told her all she wanted to know. He loved her. He probably always had done. And the words that resonated in her heart were the same words that Walt Williamson had spoken to his beloved Maisie, "You are everything I have ever wanted."

Lexi jumped off the bed, pulled on her socks, winter coat and scarf, then made her way downstairs. She didn't open the living-room door but could hear the muffled sound of the television as the movie still played.

Riordan had said they would look after Jade, so she made her way out of the house via the back door, after pulling on her boots, into the chilly winter air and put her woollen mittens on before hurrying along the pavement, in the footsteps of pedestrians who had already made a path through the snow. She stared at the ground as she speed-walked, her arms swinging, wanting to get there as quickly as possible.

Casey's house was a few blocks from his parents, and it didn't take her long to arrive. There were few people about, and the temperature was dropping swiftly.

The house lights were on and the curtains drawn in the large bay window at the front of the house. She rang the doorbell and waited. She stamped her feet to ward off the cold. She was eager now to see him, to tell him she loved him too. He had opened his heart to her, and she yearned to hold him and kiss him. She rang the bell again and then a third time. Where was he? She was sure he was at his house and he wouldn't have left the lights on.

She walked around the side of the house to the back. Then she stopped and stared. The garden was untouched after the heavy snowfall and the lawn was a sea of white, the lights from the patio and the kitchen illuminating it, turning the surface into a mass of tiny sparkles where the light reflected off the ice crystals in the snow.

It was breathtakingly beautiful, and Lexi could have stood and stared if it hadn't been for the figure who stood in the centre of the lawn, gazing up at the twilight sky.

'Casey.' He turned and put his arms out to her. She ran to

him and they hugged. His body was warm in his winter coat, but his face was cold, his nose like a block of ice, and she kissed him on his lips, his cheeks, his eyelids. 'It's freezing out here. What are you doing?'

He hugged her closer and stared up at the sky again. 'Looking for shooting stars. I thought if I made a wish, you'd appear.'

'Did you find one?'

'No, but here you are anyway.'

'Here I am. I read your note. Thank you. But you're wrong, you know.'

He looked crestfallen. 'Which bit?'

'About not being a good dad. You're a wonderful father; Jade adores you. No parent gets it right all the time. And together, you and I will get it right most of the time. We'll work as a team, like we did today.'

He smiled, and she wanted to drag him inside and take him up to the bedroom.

'I love you so much, Lexi, and if you feel the same, then I don't feel such a twit if I do this.' He dropped to one knee in the snow and took a box out of his coat pocket. He held it out to her as if he was a knight of old offering his lady a token of his love. She knew what was in it, and her heart thumped in her chest. She'd dreamed of this moment for so long.

'Lexi Grainger, I love you more than life itself and I will be the happiest man - not just on planet earth, but in the entire universe - if you'll marry me.'

She took the box then and opened it to find an exquisite

diamond solitaire. She took it out and it sparkled as the light caught it.

'It's beautiful,' she said in wonder.

'Not as beautiful as you are, but you haven't answered my question.'

'Of course I'll marry you, Casey.'

'Thank goodness for that, my knee is getting awfully wet.'

He scrambled to his feet, picked her up and swung her around and around. 'Thank you, I don't know what I would have done if you'd said no.' Then he kissed her, long and deep, with such considered tenderness that she wanted it to go on forever. But eventually he pulled away and gazed into her eyes.

'Are you happy?' he asked.

'I couldn't be happier,' she replied, 'well, there is one other thing I'd like, but only if you agree, of course.'

'Anything – your wish is my command.'

'I'd like us to have another baby. A sibling for Jade. If you think you could stand it, that is.'

Casey's expression lit up in pure delight. His green eyes were shining, and a grin threatened to split his face in two. 'A baby? Oh my God, Lexi, are you sure? There is nothing that would make me happier. It would be a dream come true; to be there right from conception to the birth. I'd be there with you every step of the way, supporting you…'

He was thinking of all the things he'd missed out on with Jade. They'd make sure he didn't miss anything this time around.

'You sound more excited about having another baby than getting married. Maybe we should have the baby first.'

'You're going to be Lexi O'Connor when we have our next child. I can't wait to marry you, my darling.'

'So, you don't mind waiting a bit longer to be a dad again?'

'As an astute and extremely beautiful woman once said to me, "If it's worth having, it's worth waiting for". I would wait forever for you, my darling girl.'

'Good to know. Fortunately, you won't have to. Now, I think it's time you got out of those wet trousers which will give us the chance to get in some practice.'

Casey swept her up and carried her to the back door. 'And I can practice carrying you over the threshold. We'll be perfect by the time we do it for real.'

The house was warm. Casey had brought a new king-size double bed and the snow started falling again. Gently at first, then heavier, obliterating the marks Casey had made when he proposed to Lexi. Soon, the garden had been restored to a pristine condition.

In the clear night sky, a shooting star arced over the house and disappeared. Neither of them noticed it, but both had already got their wish.

THE END

ABOUT THE AUTHOR

Jax was born in Manchester where she now lives, after having lived and worked in Australia. Jax attempted various jobs before deciding on a career as a medical secretary.

She has been writing for fun all her life, but now takes it seriously, concentrating on creating sexy alpha heroes and the strong, empowered women who fall in love with them.

If you enjoyed Worth Waiting For, look out for Book 2 in the series, Riordan's story. Please also consider writing a review where you bought it, it doesn't have to be long, a sentence or two would do. The author would greatly appreciate it. Thanks.

Printed in France by Amazon
Brétigny-sur-Orge, FR

10725073R00202